BY MARGARET ATWOOD

WILDERNESS TIPS

NAN A. TALESE

DOUBLEDAY

New York London Toronto Sydney Auckland

WILDERNESS TIPS

MARGARET ATWOOD

PUBLISHED BY DOUBLEDAY

a division of
Bantam Doubleday Dell Publishing Group, Inc.
666 Fifth Avenue, New York, New York 10103

DOUBLEDAY and the portrayal of an anchor with a
dolphin are trademarks of Doubleday, a division of
Bantam Doubleday Dell Publishing Group, Inc.

Book design by Marysarah Quinn

Published simultaneously in Canada by McClelland & Stewart, Inc., Toronto,
and in the United Kingdom by Bloomsbury Publishing Ltd., London

Material in this collection has been previously published in slightly different
form as follows: "True Trash" and "Uncles" in *Saturday Night*; "Death by
Landscape" in *Saturday Night*, *Harper's*, and *New Woman* (UK); "The Bog
Man" in *Playboy*; "Hairball" (titled "Kat"), "Hack Wednesday," and
"Wilderness Tips" in *The New Yorker*; "Isis in Darkness" in *Granta* (UK);
"Weight" in *Chatelaine*, *Vogue*, and *Cosmopolitan* (UK); and "The Age of
Lead" in *Toronto Life*, *Lear's*, *The New Statesman* (UK), *Neue Rundschau*
(Germany), and *Colors of a New Day: Writing for South Africa* (Raven Press
and Pantheon, 1990).

Library of Congress Cataloging-in-Publica-
tion Data
Atwood, Margaret Eleanor.
    Wilderness tips / Margaret Atwood. —
1st ed.
        p.   cm.
    I. Title.
PR9199.3.A8W54   1991
813'.54—dc20   91-17086
                                            CIP
        ISBN 0-385-42106-0

CONTENTS

WILDERNESS TIPS

TRUE TRASH

The waitresses are basking in the sun like a herd of skinned seals, their pinky-brown bodies shining with oil. They have their bathing suits on because it's the afternoon. In the early dawn and the dusk they sometimes go skinny-dipping, which makes this itchy crouching in the mosquito-infested bushes across from their small private dock a great deal more worthwhile.

Donny has the binoculars, which are not his own but Monty's. Monty's dad gave them to him for bird-watching but Monty isn't interested in birds. He's found a better use for the binoculars: he rents them out to the other boys, five minutes maximum, a nickel a look or else a chocolate bar from the tuck shop, though he prefers the money. He doesn't eat the chocolate bars; he resells them, black market, for twice their original price; but the total supply on the island is limited, so he can get away with it.

Donny has already seen everything worth seeing, but he lingers on with the binoculars anyway, despite the hoarse whispers and the proddings from those next in line. He wants to get his money's worth.

"Would you look at that," he says, in what he hopes is a tantalizing voice. "Slobber, slobber." There's a stick poking into his stomach, right on a fresh mosquito bite, but he can't move it without taking one hand off the binoculars. He knows about flank attacks.

"Lessee," says Ritchie, tugging at his elbow.

"Piss off," says Donny. He shifts the binoculars, taking in a slippery bared haunch, a red-polka-dotted breast, a long falling strand of bleach-blond hair: Ronette the tartiest, Ronette the most forbidden. When there are lectures from the masters at St. Jude's during the winter about the dangers of consorting with the town girls, it's those like Ronette they have in mind: the ones who stand in line at the town's only movie theater, chewing gum and wearing their boyfriends' leather jackets, their ruminating mouths glistening and deep red like mushed-up raspberries. If you whistle at them or even look, they stare right through you.

Ronette has everything but the stare. Unlike the others, she has been known to smile. Every day Donny and his friends make bets over whether they will get her at their table. When she leans over to clear the plates, they try to look down the front of her sedate but V-necked uniform. They angle towards her, breathing her in: she smells of hair spray, nail polish, something artificial and too sweet. Cheap, Donny's mother would say. It's an enticing word. Most of the things in his life are expensive, and not very interesting.

Ronette changes position on the dock. Now she's lying on her stomach, chin propped on her hands, her breasts pulled down by gravity. She has a real cleavage, not like some of them. But he can see her collar-bone and some chest ribs, above the top of her suit. Despite the breasts, she's skinny, scrawny; she has little stick arms and a thin, sucked-in face. She has a missing side tooth, you can see it when she smiles, and this bothers him.

He knows he's supposed to feel lust for her, but this is not what he feels.

The waitresses know they're being looked at: they can see the bushes jiggling. The boys are only twelve or thirteen, fourteen at most, small fry. If it was counselors, the waitresses would giggle more, preen more, arch their backs. Or some of them would. As it is, they go on with their afternoon break as if no one is there. They rub oil on one another's backs, toast themselves evenly, turning lazily this way and that and causing Ritchie, who now has the binoculars, to groan in a way that is supposed to madden the other boys, and does. Small punches are dealt out, mutterings of "Jerk" and "Asshole." "Drool, drool," says Ritchie, grinning from ear to ear.

The waitresses are reading out loud. They are taking turns: their voices float across the water, punctuated by occasional snorts and barks of laughter. Donny would like to know what they're reading with such absorption, such relish, but it would be dangerous for him to admit it. It's their bodies that count. Who cares what they read?

"Time's up, shitface," he whispers to Ritchie.

"Shitface yourself," says Ritchie. The bushes thrash.

What the waitresses are reading is a *True Romance* magazine. Tricia has a whole stash of them, stowed under her mattress, and Sandy and Pat have each contributed a couple of others. Every one of these magazines has a woman on the cover, with her dress pulled down over one shoulder or a cigarette in her mouth or some other evidence of a messy life. Usually these women are in tears. Their colors are odd: sleazy, dirt-permeated, like the hand-tinted photos in the five-and-ten. Knee-between-the-legs colors. They have none of the cheerful primaries and clean, toothy smiles of the movie magazines: these are not success stories. True Trash, Hilary calls them. Joanne calls them Moan-o-dramas.

Right now it's Joanne reading. She reads in a serious, histrionic voice, like someone on the radio; she's been in a play, at school. *Our Town.* She's got her sunglasses perched on the end of her nose, like a teacher. For extra hilarity she's thrown in a fake English accent.

The story is about a girl who lives with her divorced mother in a cramped, run-down apartment above a shoe store. Her name is Marleen. She has a part-time job in the store, after school and on Saturdays, and two of the shoe clerks are chasing around after her. One is dependable and boring and wants them to get married. The other one, whose name is Dirk, rides a motorcycle and has a knowing, audacious grin that turns Marleen's knees to jelly. The mother slaves over Marleen's wardrobe, on her sewing machine—she makes a meager living doing dressmaking for rich ladies who sneer at her, so the wardrobe comes out all right—and she nags Marleen about choosing the right man and not making a terrible mistake, the way she did. The girl herself has planned to go to trade school and learn hospital management, but lack of money makes this impossible. She is in her last year of high school and her grades are slipping, because she is discouraged and also she can't decide between the two shoe clerks. Now the mother is on her case about the slipping grades as well.

"Oh God," says Hilary. She is doing her nails, with a metal file rather than an emery board. She disapproves of emery boards. "Someone please give her a double Scotch."

"Maybe she should murder the mother, collect the insurance, and get the hell out of there," says Sandy.

"Have you heard one word about any insurance?" says Joanne, peering over the tops of her glasses.

"You could put some in," says Pat.

"Maybe she should try out both of them, to see which one's the best," says Liz brazenly.

"We know which one's the best," says Tricia. "Listen, with a name like *Dirk!* How can you miss?"

"They're both creeps," says Stephanie.

"If she does that, she'll be a Fallen Woman, capital F, capital W," says Joanne. "She'd have to Repent, capital R."

The others hoot. Repentance! The girls in the stories make such fools of themselves. They are so weak. They fall helplessly in love with the wrong men, they give in, they are jilted. Then they cry.

"Wait," says Joanne. "Here comes the big night." She reads on, breathily. *"My mother had gone out to deliver a cocktail dress to one of her customers. I was all alone in our shabby apartment."*

"Pant, pant," says Liz.

"No, that comes later. *I was all alone in our shabby apartment. The evening was hot and stifling. I knew I should be studying, but I could not concentrate. I took a shower to cool off. Then, on impulse, I decided to try on the graduation formal my mother had spent so many late-night hours making for me."*

"That's right, pour on the guilt," says Hilary with satisfaction. "If it was me I'd axe the mother."

"It was a dream of pink—"

"A dream of pink what?" says Tricia.

"A dream of pink, period, and shut up. *I looked at myself in the full-length mirror in my mother's tiny bedroom. The dress was just right for me. It fitted my ripe but slender body to perfection. I looked different in it, older, beautiful, like a girl used to every luxury. Like a princess. I smiled at myself. I was transformed.*

"I had just undone the hooks at the back, meaning to take the dress off and hang it up again, when I heard footsteps on the stairs. Too late I remembered that I'd forgotten to lock the door on the inside, after my mother's departure. I rushed to the door, holding up my dress—it could be a burglar, or worse! But instead it was Dirk."

"Dirk the jerk," says Alex, from underneath her towel.

"Go back to sleep," says Liz.

Joanne drops her voice, does a drawl. *" 'Thought I'd come up and keep you company,' he said mischievously. 'I saw your mom go out.' He knew I was alone! I was blushing and shivering. I could hear the blood pounding in my veins. I couldn't speak. Every instinct warned me against him—every instinct but those of my body, and my heart."*

"So what else is there?" says Sandy. "You can't have a mental instinct."

"You want to read this?" says Joanne. "Then shush. *I held the frothy pink lace in front of me like a shield. 'Hey, you look great in that,' Dirk said. His voice was rough and tender. 'But you'd look even greater out of it.' I was frightened of him. His eyes were burning, determined. He looked like an animal stalking its prey.*"

"Pretty steamy," says Hilary.

"What kind of animal?" says Sandy.

"A weasel," says Stephanie.

"A skunk," says Tricia.

"Shh," says Liz.

"*I backed away from him,*" Joanne reads. "*I had never seen him look that way before. Now I was pressed against the wall and he was crushing me in his arms. I felt the dress slipping down . . .*"

"So much for all that sewing," says Pat.

"*. . . and his hand was on my breast, his hard mouth was seeking mine. I knew he was the wrong man for me but I could no longer resist. My whole body was crying out to his.*"

"What did it say?"

"It said, *Hey, body, over here!*"

"Shh."

"*I felt myself lifted. He was carrying me to the sofa. Then I felt the length of his hard, sinewy body pressing against mine. Feebly I tried to push his hands away, but I didn't really want to. And then*—dot dot dot—*we were One,* capital O, exclamation mark."

There is a moment of silence. Then the waitresses laugh. Their laughter is outraged, disbelieving. *One.* Just like that. There has to be more to it.

"The dress is a wreck," says Joanne in her ordinary voice. "Now the mother comes home."

"Not today, she doesn't," says Hilary briskly. "We've only got ten more minutes. I'm going for a swim, get some of this oil off me." She stands up, clips back her honey-blond hair, stretches her tanned athlete's body, and does a perfect swan-dive off the end of the dock.

"Who's got the soap?" says Stephanie.

Ronette has not said anything during the story. When the others have laughed, she has only smiled. She's smiling now. Hers is an off-center smile, puzzled, a little apologetic.

"Yeah, but," she says to Joanne, "why is it funny?"

The waitresses stand at their stations around the dining hall, hands clasped in front of them, heads bowed. Their royal-blue uniforms come down almost to the tops of their white socks, worn with white bucks or white-and-black saddle shoes or white sneakers. Over their uniforms they wear plain white aprons. The rustic log sleeping cabins at Camp Adanaqui don't have electric lights, the toilets are outhouses, the boys wash their own clothes, not even in sinks but in the lake; but there are waitresses, with uniforms and aprons. Roughing it builds a boy's character, but only certain kinds of roughing it.

Mr. B. is saying grace. He owns the camp, and is a master at St. Jude's as well, during the winters. He has a leathery, handsome face, the gray, tailored hair of a Bay Street lawyer, and the eyes of a hawk: he sees all, but pounces only sometimes. Today he's wearing a white V-necked tennis sweater. He could be drinking a gin and tonic, but is not.

Behind him on the wall, above his head, there's a weathered plank with a motto painted on it in black Gothic lettering: *As the Twig Is Bent.* A piece of bleached driftwood ornaments each end of the plank, and beneath it are two crossed paddles and a gigantic pike's head in profile, its mouth open to show its needle teeth, its one glass eye fixed in a ferocious maniac's glare.

To Mr. B.'s left is the end window, and beyond it is Georgian Bay, blue as amnesia, stretching to infinity. Rising out of it like the backs of whales, like rounded knees, like the calves and thighs of enormous floating women, are several islands of pink rock, scraped and rounded and fissured by glaciers and lapping water and endless weather, a few jack pines clinging to the larger ones, their twisted roots digging into the cracks. It was through these archipelagos that the waitresses were ferried here, twenty miles out from shore, by the same cumbersome mahogany in-board launch that brings the mail and the groceries and every-thing else to the island. Brings, and takes away. But the waitresses will not be shipped back to the mainland until the end of summer: it's too far for a day off, and they would never be allowed to stay away overnight. So here they are, for the duration. They are the only women on the island, except for Mrs. B. and Miss Fisk, the dietitian. But those two are old and don't count.

There are nine waitresses. There are always nine. Only the names and faces change, thinks Donny, who has been going to this camp ever since he was eight. When he was eight he paid no attention to the waitresses except when he felt homesick. Then he would think of excuses to go past the kitchen window when they were washing the dishes. There they would be, safely aproned, safely behind glass: nine mothers. He does not think of them as mothers anymore.

Ronette is doing his table tonight. From between his half-closed eyelids Donny watches her thin averted face. He can see one earring, a little gold hoop. It goes right through her ear. Only Italians and cheap girls have pierced ears, says his mother. It would hurt to have a hole put through your ear. It would take bravery. He wonders what the inside of Ronette's room looks like, what other cheap, intriguing things she's got in there. About someone like Hilary he doesn't have to wonder, because he already knows: the clean bedspread, the rows of shoes in their shoe-trees, the comb and brush and manicure set laid out on the dresser like implements in a surgery.

Behind Ronette's bowed head there's the skin of a rattle-snake, a big one, nailed to the wall. That's what you have to watch out for around here: rattlesnakes. Also poison ivy, thun-derstorms, and drowning. A whole war canoe full of kids drowned last year, but they were from another camp. There's been some talk of making everyone wear sissy life-jackets; the mothers want it. Donny would like a rattlesnake skin of his own, to nail up over his bed; but even if he caught the snake himself, strangled it with his bare hands, bit its head off, he'd never be allowed to keep the skin.

Mr. B. winds up the grace and sits down, and the campers begin again their three-times-daily ritual of bread-grabbing, face-stuffing, under-the-table kicking, whispered cursing. Ronette comes from the kitchen with a platter: macaroni and cheese. "There you go, boys," she says, with her good-natured, lopsided smile.

"Thank you kindly, ma'am," says Darce the counselor, with fraudulent charm. Darce has a reputation as a make-out artist; Donny knows he's after Ronette. This makes him feel sad. Sad, and too young. He would like to get out of his own body for a while; he'd like to be somebody else.

The waitresses are doing the dishes. Two to scrape, one to wash, one to rinse in the scalding-hot rinsing sink, three to dry. The other two sweep the floors and wipe off the tables. Later, the number of dryers will vary because of days off—they'll choose to take their days off in twos, so they can double-date with the counselors—but today all are here. It's early in the season, things are still fluid, the territories are not yet staked out.

While they work they sing. They're missing the ocean of music in which they float during the winter. Pat and Liz have both brought their portables, though you can't pick up much radio out here, it's too far from shore. There's a record player in the counselors' rec hall, but the records are out of date. Patti Page, The Singing Rage. "How Much Is That Doggie in the Window." "The Tennessee Waltz." Who waltzes anymore?

" 'Wake up, little Susie,' " trills Sandy. The Everly Brothers are popular this summer; or they were, on the mainland, when they left.

" 'What're we gonna tell your mama, what're we gonna tell your pa,' " sing the others. Joanne can improvise the alto harmony, which makes everything sound less screechy.

Hilary, Stephanie, and Alex don't sing this one. They go to

a private school, all girls, and are better at rounds, like "Fire's Burning" and "White Coral Bells." They are good at tennis though, and sailing, skills that have passed the others by.

It's odd that Hilary and the other two are here at all, wait-ressing at Camp Adanaqui; it's not as if they need the money. (Not like me, thinks Joanne, who haunts the mail desk every noon to see if she got her scholarship.) But it's the doing of their mothers. According to Alex, the three mothers banded together and jumped Mrs. B. at a charity function, and twisted her arm. Naturally Mrs. B. would attend the same functions as the moth-ers: they've seen her, sunglasses pushed up on her forehead, a tall drink in her hand, entertaining on the veranda of Mr. B.'s white hilltop house, which is well away from the camp proper. They've seen the guests, in their spotless, well-pressed sailing clothes. They've heard the laughter, the voices, husky and casual. *Oh God don't tell me.* Like Hilary.

"We were kidnapped," says Alex. "They thought it was time we met some boys."

Joanne can see it for Alex, who is chubby and awkward, and for Stephanie, who is built like a boy and walks like one; but Hilary? Hilary is classic. Hilary is like a shampoo ad. Hilary is perfect. She ought to be sought after. Oddly, here she is not.

Ronette is scraping, and drops a plate. "Shoot," she says. "What a stunned broad." Nobody bawls her out or even teases her as they would anyone else. She is a favorite with them, though it's hard to put your finger on why. It isn't just that she's easygoing: so is Liz, so is Pat. She has some mysterious, extra status. For instance, everyone else has a nickname: Hilary is Hil, Stephanie is Steph, Alex is Al, Joanne is Jo, Tricia is Trish, Sandy is San. Pat and Liz, who cannot be contracted any further, have become Pet and Lizard. Only Ronette has been accorded the dignity of her full, improbable name.

In some ways she is more grown-up than the rest of them. But it isn't because she knows more things. She knows fewer things; she often has trouble making her way through the vocab-ularies of the others, especially the offhand slang of the private-school trio. "I don't get that" is what she says, and the others take a delight in explaining, as if she's a foreigner, a cherished visitor from some other country. She goes to movies and watches television like the rest of them but she has few opinions about what she has seen. The most she will say is "Crap"or "He's not bad." Though friendly, she is cautious about expressing approval in words. "Fair" is her best compliment. When the others talk about what they've read or what subjects they will take next year at university, she is silent.

But she knows other things, hidden things. Secrets. And these other things are older, and on some level more important. More fundamental. Closer to the bone.

Or so thinks Joanne, who has a bad habit of novelizing.

Outside the window Darce and Perry stroll by, herding a group of campers. Joanne recognizes a few of them: Donny, Monty. It's hard to remember the campers by name. They're just a crowd of indistinguishable, usually grimy young boys who have to be fed three times a day, whose crusts and crumbs and rinds have to be cleaned up afterwards. The counselors call them Grubbies.

But some stand out. Donny is tall for his age, all elbows and spindly knees, with huge deep-blue eyes; even when he's swearing—they all swear during meals, furtively but also loudly enough so that the waitresses can hear them—it's more like a meditation, or more like a question, as if he's trying the words out, tasting them. Monty on the other hand is like a miniature forty-five-year-old: his shoulders already have a businessman's slump, his paunch is fully formed. He walks with a pompous little strut. Joanne thinks he's hilarious.

Right now he's carrying a broom with five rolls of toilet paper threaded onto the handle. All the boys are: they're on Bog Duty, sweeping out the outhouses, replacing the paper. Joanne wonders what they do with the used sanitary napkins in the brown paper bag in the waitresses' private outhouse. She can imagine the remarks.

"Company . . . halt!" shouts Darce. The group shambles to a stop in front of the window. "Present . . . arms!" The brooms are raised, the ends of the toilet-paper rolls fluttering in the breeze like flags. The girls laugh and wave.

Monty's salute is half-hearted: this is well beneath his dignity. He may rent out his binoculars—that story is all over camp, by now—but he has no interest in using them himself. He has made that known. *Not on these girls*, he says, implying higher tastes.

Darce himself gives a comic salute, then marches his bunch away. The singing in the kitchen has stopped; the topic among the waitresses is now the counselors. Darce is the best, the most admired, the most desirable. His teeth are the whitest, his hair the blondest, his grin the sexiest. In the counselors' rec hall, where they go every night after the dishes are done, after they've changed out of their blue uniforms into their jeans and pullovers, after the campers have been inserted into their beds for the night, he has flirted with each one of them in turn. So who was he really saluting?

"It was me," says Pat, joking. "Don't I wish."

"Dream on," says Liz.

"It was Hil," says Stephanie loyally. But Joanne knows it wasn't. It wasn't her, either. It was Ronette. They all suspect it. None of them says it.

"Perry likes Jo," says Sandy.

"Does not," says Joanne. She has given out that she has a boyfriend already and is therefore exempt from these contests. Half of this is true: she has a boyfriend. This summer he has a job as a salad chef on the Canadian National, running back and forth across the continent. She pictures him standing at the back of the train, on the caboose, smoking a cigarette between bouts of salad-making, watching the country slide away behind him. He writes her letters, in blue ball-point pen, on lined paper. *My first night on the Prairies*, he writes. *It's magnificent—all that land and sky. The sunsets are unbelievable.* Then there's a line across the page and a new date, and he gets to the Rockies. Joanne resents it a little that he raves on about places she's never been. It seems to her a kind of male showing-off: he's footloose. He closes with *Wish you were here* and several X's and O's. This seems too formal, like a letter to your mother. Like a peck on the cheek.

She put the first letter under her pillow, but woke up with blue smears on her face and the pillowcase both. Now she keeps the letters in her suitcase under the bed. She's having trouble remembering what he looks like. An image flits past, his face close up, at night, in the front seat of his father's car. The rustle of cloth. The smell of smoke.

Miss Fisk bumbles into the kitchen. She's short, plump, flustered; what she wears, always, is a hairnet over her gray bun, worn wool slippers—there's something wrong with her toes—and a faded blue knee-length sweater-coat, no matter how hot it is. She thinks of this summer job as her vacation. Occasionally she can be seen bobbing in the water in a droopy-chested bathing suit and a white rubber cap with the earflaps up. She never gets her head wet, so why she wears the cap is anyone's guess.

"Well, girls. Almost done?" She never calls the waitresses by name. To their faces they are *girls*, behind their backs *My girls*. They are her excuse for everything that goes wrong: *One of the girls must have done it*. She also functions as a sort of chaperon: her cabin is on the pathway that leads to theirs, and she has radar ears, like a bat.

I will never be that old, thinks Joanne. I will die before I'm thirty. She knows this absolutely. It's a tragic but satisfactory thought. If necessary, if some wasting disease refuses to carry her off, she'll do it herself, with pills. She is not at all unhappy but she intends to be, later. It seems required.

This is no country for old men, she recites to herself. One of the poems she memorized, though it wasn't on the final exam. Change that to old women.

When they're all in their pajamas, ready for bed, Joanne offers to read them the rest of the True Trash story. But everyone is too tired, so she reads it herself, with her flashlight, after the one feeble bulb has been switched off. She has a compulsion about getting to the ends of things. Sometimes she reads books backwards.

Needless to say, Marleen gets knocked up and Dirk takes off on his motorcycle when he finds out. *I'm not the settling-down type, baby. See ya round.* Vroom. The mother practically has a nervous breakdown, because she made the same mistake when young and blew her chances and now look at her. Marleen cries and regrets, and even prays. But luckily the other shoe clerk, the boring one, still wants to marry her. So that's what happens. The mother forgives her, and Marleen herself learns the true value of quiet devotion. Her life isn't exciting maybe, but it's a good life, in the trailer park, the three of them. The baby is adorable. They buy a dog. It's an Irish setter, and chases sticks in the twilight while the baby laughs. This is how the story ends, with the dog.

Joanne stuffs the magazine down between her narrow little bed and the wall. She's almost crying. She will never have a dog like that, or a baby either. She doesn't want them, and anyway how would she have time, considering everything she has to get done? She has a long, though vague, agenda. Nevertheless she feels deprived.

Between two oval hills of pink granite there's a small crescent of beach. The boys, wearing their bathing suits (as they never do on canoe trips but only around the camp where they might be seen by girls), are doing their laundry, standing up to their knees and swabbing their wet T-shirts and underpants with yellow bars of Sunlight soap. This only happens when they run out of clothes, or when the stench of dirty socks in the cabin becomes too overpowering. Darce the counselor is supervising, stretched out on a rock, taking the sun on his already tanned torso and smoking a fag. It's forbidden to smoke in front of the campers but he knows this bunch won't tell. To be on the safe side he's furtive about it, holding the cigarette down close to the rock and sneaking quick puffs.

Something hits Donny in the side of the head. It's Ritchie's wet underpants, squashed into a ball. Donny throws them back and soon there's an underpants war. Monty refuses to join in, so he becomes the common target. "Sod off!" he yells.

"Cut it out, you pinheads," Darce says. But he isn't really paying attention: he's seen something else, a flash of blue uniform, up among the trees. The waitresses aren't supposed to be over here on this side of the island. They're supposed to be on their own dock, having their afternoon break.

Darce is up among the trees now, one arm braced against a trunk. A conversation is going on; there are murmurs. Donny knows it's Ronette, he can tell by the shape, by the color of the hair. And here he is, with his wash-board ribs exposed, his hairless chest, throwing underpants around like a kid. He's disgusted with himself.

Monty, outnumbered but not wanting to admit defeat, says he needs to take a crap and disappears along the path to the outhouse. By now Darce is nowhere in sight. Donny captures Monty's laundry, which is already finished and wrung out and spread neatly on the hot rock to dry. He starts tossing it up into a jack pine, piece by piece. The others, delighted, help him. By the time Monty gets back, the tree is festooned with Monty's underpants and the other boys are innocently rinsing.

They're on one of the pink granite islands, the four of them: Joanne and Ronette, Perry and Darce. It's a double date. The two canoes have been pulled half out of the water and roped to the obligatory jack pines, the fire has done its main burning and is dying down to coals. The western sky is still peach-toned and luminous, the soft ripe juicy moon is rising, the evening air is warm and sweet, the waves wash gently against the rocks. It's the Summer Issue, thinks Joanne. *Lazy Daze. Tanning Tips. Shipboard Romance.*

Joanne is toasting a marshmallow. She has a special way of doing it: she holds it close to the coals but not so close that it catches fire, just close enough so that it swells up like a pillow and browns gently. Then she pulls off the toasted skin and eats it, and toasts the white inside part the same way, and peeling it down to the core. She licks marshmallow goo off her fingers and stares pensively into the shifting red glow of the coal bed. All of this is a way of ignoring or pretending to ignore what is really going on.

There ought to be a teardrop, painted and static, on her cheek. There ought to be a caption: *Heartbreak*. On the spread-out groundsheet right behind her, his knee touching her back, is Perry, cheesed off with her because she won't neck with him. Off behind the rocks, out of the dim circle of firelight, are Ronette and Darce. It's the third week in July and by now they're a couple, everyone knows it. In the rec hall she wears his sweatshirt with the St. Jude's crest; she smiles more these days, and even laughs when the other girls tease her about him. During this teasing Hilary does not join in. Ronette's face seems rounder, healthier, its angles smoothed out as if by a hand. She is less watchful, less diffident. She ought to have a caption too, thinks Joanne. *Was I Too Easy?*

There are rustlings from the darkness, small murmurings, breathing noises. It's like a movie theater on Saturday night. Group grope. *The young in one another's arms.* Possibly, thinks Joanne, they will disturb a rattlesnake.

Perry puts a hand, tentatively, on her shoulder. "Want me to toast you a marshmallow?" she says to him politely. The frosty freeze. Perry is no consolation prize. He merely irritates her, with his peeling sunburnt skin and begging spaniel's eyes. Her so-called real boyfriend is no help either, whizzing on his train tracks back and forth across the prairies, writing his by-now infrequent inky letters, the image of his face all but obliterated, as if it's been soaked in water.

Nor is it Darce she wants, not really. What she wants is what Ronette has: the power to give herself up, without reservation and without commentary. It's that languor, that leaning back.

Voluptuous mindlessness. Everything Joanne herself does is surrounded by quotation marks.

"Marshmallows. Geez," says Perry, in a doleful, cheated
voice. All that paddling, and what for? Why the hell did she
come along, if not to make out?

Joanne feels guilty of a lapse of manners. Would it hurt so
much to kiss him?

Yes. It would.

Donny and Monty are on a canoe trip, somewhere within the
tangled bush of the mainland. Camp Adanaqui is known for its
tripping. For five days they and the others, twelve boys in all,
have been paddling across lake after lake, hauling the gear over
wave-rounded boulders or through the suck and stench of the
moose-meadows at the portage entrances, grunting uphill with
the packs and canoes, slapping the mosquitoes off their legs.
Monty has blisters, on both his feet and his hands. Donny isn't
too sad about that. He himself has a festering sliver. Maybe he
will get blood-poisoning, become delirious, collapse and die on
a portage, among the rocks and pine needles. That will serve
someone right. Someone ought to be made to pay for the pain
he's feeling.

The counselors are Darce and Perry. During the days they
crack the whip; at night they relax, backs against a rock or tree,
smoking and supervising while the boys light the fire, carry the
water, cook the Kraft Dinners. They both have smooth large
muscles which ripple under their tans, they both—by now—have
stubbly beards. When everyone goes swimming Donny sneaks
covert, envious looks at their groins. They make him feel spindly,
and infantile in his own desires.

Right now it's night. Perry and Darce are still up, talking in
low voices, poking the embers of the dying fire. The boys are
supposed to be asleep. There are tents in case of rain, but nobody's suggested putting them up since the day before yesterday.
The smell of grime and sweaty feet and wood smoke is getting
too potent at close quarters; the sleeping bags are high as cheese.

It's better to be outside, rolled up in the bag, a groundsheet handy in case of a deluge, head under a turned-over canoe.

Monty is the only one who has voted for a tent. The bugs are getting to him; he says he's allergic. He hates canoe trips and makes no secret of it. When he's older, he says, and can finally get his hands on the family boodle, he's going to buy the place from Mr. B. and close it down. "Generations of boys unborn will thank me," he says. "They'll give me a medal." Sometimes Donny almost likes him. He's so blatant about wanting to be filthy rich. No hypocrisy about him, not like some of the other millionaire offshoots, who pretend they want to be scientists or something else that's not paid much.

Now Monty is twisting around, scratching his bites. "Hey Finley," he whispers.

"Go to sleep," says Donny.

"I bet they've got a flask."

"What?"

"I bet they're drinking. I smelled it on Perry's breath yesterday."

"So?" says Donny.

"So," says Monty. "It's against the rules. Maybe we can get something out of them."

Donny has to hand it to him. He certainly knows the angles. At the very least they might be able to share the wealth.

The two of them inch out of their sleeping bags and circle around behind the fire, keeping low. Their practice while spying on the waitresses stands them in good stead. They crouch behind a bushy spruce, watching for lifted elbows or the outlines of bottles, their ears straining.

But what they hear isn't about booze. Instead it's about Ronette. Darce is talking about her as if she's a piece of meat. From what he's implying, she lets him do anything he wants. "Summer sausage" is what he calls her. This is an expression Donny has never heard before, and ordinarily he would think it was hilarious.

Monty sniggers under his breath and pokes Donny in the ribs with his elbow. Does he know how much it hurts, is he rubbing it in? *Donny loves Ronette.* The ultimate grade six insult, to be accused of loving someone. Donny feels as if it's he himself who's been smeared with words, who's had his face rubbed in them. He knows Monty will repeat this conversation to the other boys. He will say Darce has been porking Ronette. Right now Donny detests this word, with its conjuring of two heaving pigs, or two dead but animate uncooked Sunday roasts; although just yesterday he used it himself, and found it funny enough.

He can hardly charge out of the bushes and punch Darce in the nose. Not only would he look ridiculous, he'd get flattened.

He does the only thing he can think of. Next morning, when they're breaking camp, he pinches Monty's binoculars and sinks them in the lake.

Monty guesses, and accuses him. Some sort of pride keeps Donny from denying it. Neither can he say why he did it. When they get back to the island there's an unpleasant conversation with Mr. B. in the dining hall. Or not a conversation: Mr. B. talks, Donny is silent. He does not look at Mr. B. but at the pike's head on the wall, with its goggling voyeur's eye.

The next time the mahogany inboard goes back into town, Donny is in it. His parents are not pleased.

It's the end of summer. The campers have already left, though some of the counselors and all of the waitresses are still here. Tomorrow they'll go down to the main dock, climb into the slow launch, thread their way among the pink islands, heading towards winter.

It's Joanne's half-day off so she isn't in the dining hall, washing the dishes with the others. She's in the cabin, packing up. Her duffle bag is finished, propped like an enormous canvas wiener against her bed; now she's doing her small suitcase. Her paycheck is already tucked inside: two hundred dollars, which is a lot of money.

Ronette comes into the cabin, still in her uniform, shutting the screen door quietly behind her. She sits down on Joanne's bed and lights a cigarette. Joanne is standing there with her folded-up flannelette pajamas, alert: something's going on. Lately, Ronette has returned to her previous taciturn self; her smiles have become rare. In the counselors' rec hall, Darce is again playing the field. He's been circling around Hilary, who's pretending—out of consideration for Ronette—not to notice. Maybe, now, Joanne will get to hear what caused the big split. So far Ronette has not said anything about it.

Ronette looks up at Joanne, through her long yellow bangs. Looking up like that makes her seem younger, despite the red lipstick. "I'm in trouble," she says.

"What sort of trouble?" says Joanne.

Ronette smiles sadly, blows out smoke. Now she looks old. "You know. Trouble."

"Oh," says Joanne. She sits down beside Ronette, hugging the flannelette pajamas. She feels cold. It must be Darce. *Caught in that sensual music.* Now he will have to marry her. Or something. "What're you going to do?"

"I don't know," says Ronette. "Don't tell, okay? Don't tell the others."

"Aren't you going to tell *him*?" says Joanne. She can't imagine doing that, herself. She can't imagine any of it.

"Tell who?" Ronette says.

"Darce."

Ronette blows out more smoke. "Darce," she says. "Mr. Chickenshit. It's not *his*."

Joanne is astounded, and relieved. But also annoyed with herself: what's gone past her, what has she missed? "It's not? Then whose is it?"

But Ronette has apparently changed her mind about confiding. "That's for me to know and you to find out," she says, with a small attempt at a laugh.

"Well," says Joanne. Her hands are clammy, as if it's her that's in trouble. She wants to be helpful, but has no idea how. "Maybe you could—I don't know." She doesn't know. An abortion? That is a dark and mysterious word, connected with the States. You have to go away. It costs a lot of money. A home for unwed mothers, followed by adoption? Loss washes through her.

She foresees Ronette, bloated beyond recognition, as if she's drowned—a sacrifice, captured by her own body, offered up to it. Truncated in some way, disgraced. Unfree. There is something nun-like about this condition. She is in awe. "I guess you could get rid of it, one way or another," she says; which is not at all what she feels. *Whatever is begotten, born, and dies.*

"Are you kidding?" says Ronette, with something like contempt. "Hell, not me." She throws her cigarette on the floor, grinds it out with her heel. "I'm keeping it. Don't worry, my mom will help me out."

"Yeah," says Joanne. Now she has caught her breath; now she's beginning to wonder why Ronette has dumped all this on her, especially since she isn't willing to tell the whole thing. She's beginning to feel cheated, imposed upon. So who's the guy, so which one of them? She shuffles through the faces of the counselors, trying to remember hints, traces of guilt, but finds nothing.

"Anyways," says Ronette, "I won't have to go back to school. Thank the Lord for small mercies, like they say."

Joanne hears bravado, and desolation. She reaches out a hand, gives Ronette's arm a small squeeze. "Good luck," she says. It comes out sounding like something you'd say before a race or an exam, or a war. It sounds stupid.

Ronette grins. The gap in her teeth shows, at the side. "Same to you," she says.

Eleven years later Donny is walking along Yorkville Avenue, in Toronto, in the summer heat. He's no longer Donny. At some point, which even he can't remember exactly, he has changed into Don. He's wearing sandals, and a white Indian-style shirt over his cut-off jeans. He has longish hair and a beard. The beard has come out yellow, whereas the hair is brown. He likes the effect: WASP Jesus or Hollywood Viking, depending on his mood. He has a string of wooden beads around his neck.

This is how he dresses on Saturdays, to go to Yorkville; to go there and just hang around, with the crowds of others who are doing the same. Sometimes he gets high, on the pot that circulates as freely as cigarettes did once. He thinks he should be enjoying this experience more than he actually does.

During the rest of the week he has a job in his father's law office. He can get away with the beard there, just barely, as long as he balances it with a suit. (But even the older guys are growing their sideburns and wearing colored shirts, and using words like "creative" more than they used to.) He doesn't tell the people he meets in Yorkville about this job, just as he doesn't tell the law office about his friends' acid trips. He's leading a double life. It feels precarious, and brave.

Suddenly, across the street, he sees Joanne. He hasn't even thought about her for a long time, but it's her all right. She isn't wearing the tie-dyed or flowing-shift uniform of the Yorkville girls; instead she's dressed in a brisk, businesslike white mini-skirt, with matching suit-jacket top. She's swinging a briefcase, striding along as if she has a purpose. This makes her stand out: the accepted walk here is a saunter.

Donny wonders whether he should run across the street, intercept her, reveal what he thinks of as his true but secret identity. Now all he can see is her back. In a minute she'll be gone.

"Joanne," he calls. She doesn't hear him. He dodges between cars, catches up to her, touches her elbow. "Don Finley," he says. He's conscious of himself standing there, grinning like a fool. Luckily and a little disappointingly, she recognizes him at once.

"Donny!" she says. "My God, you've grown!"

"I'm taller than you," he says, like a kid, an idiot.

"You were then," she says, smiling. "I mean you've grown *up*."

"So have you," says Donny, and they find themselves laughing, almost like equals. Three years, four years between them. It was a large difference, then. Now it's nothing.

So, thinks Joanne, Donny is no longer Donny. That must mean Ritchie is now Richard. As for Monty, he has become initials only, and a millionaire. True, he inherited some of it, but he's used it to advantage; Joanne has tuned in on his exploits now and then, in the business papers. And he got married to Hilary, three years ago. Imagine that. She saw that in the paper too.

They go for coffee and sit drinking it at one of the new, daring, outside tables, under a large, brightly painted wooden parrot. There's an intimacy between them, as if they are old friends. Donny asks Joanne what she's doing. "I live by my wits," she says. "I freelance." At the moment she's writing ad copy. Her face is thinner, she's lost that adolescent roundness; her once nondescript hair has been shaped into a stylish cap. Good enough legs too. You have to have good legs to wear a mini. So many women look stumpy in them, hams in cloth, their legs bulging out the bottom like loaves of white bread. Joanne's legs are out of sight under the table, but Donny finds himself dwelling on them as he never did when they were clearly visible, all the way up, on the waitresses' dock. He'd skimmed over those legs then, skimmed over Joanne altogether. It was Ronette who had held his attention. He is more of a connoisseur, by now.

"We used to spy on you," he says. "We used to watch you skinny-dipping." In fact they'd never managed to see much. The girls had held their towels around their bodies until the last minute, and anyway it was dusk. There would be a blur of white, some shrieking and splashing. The great thing would have been pubic hair. Several boys claimed sightings, but Donny had felt they were lying. Or was that just envy?

"Did you?" says Joanne absently. Then, "I know. We could see the bushes waving around. We thought it was so cute."

Donny feels himself blushing. He's glad he has the beard; it conceals things. "It wasn't cute," he says. "Actually we were pretty vicious." He's remembering the word *pork*. "Do you ever see the others?"

"Not anymore," says Joanne. "I used to see a few of them, at university. Hilary and Alex. Pat sometimes."

"What about Ronette?" he says, which is the only thing he really wants to ask.

"I used to see Darce," says Joanne, as if she hasn't heard him.

Used to see is an exaggeration. She saw him once.

It was in the winter, a February. He phoned her, at *The Varsity* office: that was how he knew where to find her, he'd seen her name in the campus paper. By that time Joanne scarcely remembered him. The summer she'd been a waitress was three years, light-years, away. The railroad-chef boyfriend was long gone; nobody so innocent had replaced him. She no longer wore white bucks, no longer sang songs. She wore turtlenecks and drank beer and a lot of coffee, and wrote cynical exposés of such things as the campus dining facilities. She'd given up the idea of dying young, however. By this time it seemed overly romantic.

What Darce wanted was to go out with her. Specifically, he wanted her to go to a fraternity party with him. Joanne was so taken aback that she said yes, even though fraternities were in political disfavor among the people she traveled with now. It was something she would have to do on the sly, and she did. She had to borrow a dress from her roommate, however. The thing was a semi-formal, and she had not deigned to go to a semi-formal since high school.

She had last seen Darce with sun-bleached hair and a deep glowing tan. Now, in his winter skin, he looked wan and malnourished. Also, he no longer flirted with everyone. He didn't even flirt with Joanne. Instead he introduced her to a few other couples, danced her perfunctorily around the floor, and proceeded to get very drunk on a mixture of grape juice and straight alcohol that the fraternity brothers called Purple Jesus. He told her he'd been engaged to Hilary for over six months, but she'd just ditched him. She wouldn't even say why. He said he'd asked Joanne out because she was the kind of girl you could talk to, he knew she would understand. After that he threw up a lot of Purple Jesus, first onto her dress, then—when she'd led him outside, to the veranda—onto a snowdrift. The color scheme was amazing.

Joanne got some coffee into him and hitched a lift back to the residence, where she had to climb up the icy fire escape and in at a window because it was after hours.

Joanne was hurt. All she was for him was a big flapping ear. Also she was irritated. The dress she'd borrowed was pale blue, and the Purple Jesus would not come out with just water. Darce called the next day to apologize—St. Jude's at least taught manners, of a sort—and Joanne stuck him with the cleaning bill. Even so there was a faint residual stain.

While they were dancing, before he started to slur and reel, she said, "Do you ever hear from Ronette?" She still had the narrative habit, she still wanted to know the ends of stories. But he'd looked at her in complete bewilderment.

"Who?" he said. It wasn't a put-down, he really didn't remember. She found this blank in his memory offensive. She herself might forget a name, a face even. But a body? A body that had been so close to your own, that had generated those murmurings, those rustlings in the darkness, that aching pain—it was an affront to bodies, her own included.

After the interview with Mr. B. and the stuffed pike's head, Donny walks down to the small beach where they do their laundry. The rest of his cabin is out sailing, but he's free now of camp routine, he's been discharged. A dishonorable discharge. After seven summers of being under orders here he can do what he wants. He has no idea what this might be.

He sits on a bulge of pink rock, feet on the sand. A lizard goes across the rock, near his hand, not fast. It hasn't spotted him. Its tail is blue and will come off if grabbed. Skinks, they're called. Once he would have taken joy from this knowledge. The waves wash in, wash out, the familiar heartbeat. He closes his eyes and hears only a machine. Possibly he is very angry, or sad. He hardly knows.

Ronette is there without warning. She must have come down the path behind him, through the trees. She's still in her uniform, although it isn't close to dinner. It's only late afternoon, when the waitresses usually leave their dock to go and change.

Ronette sits down beside him, takes out her cigarettes from some hidden pocket under her apron. "Want a cig?" she says.

Donny takes one and says "Thank you." Not *thanks*, not wordlessly like leather-jacketed men in movies, but "Thank you," like a good boy from St. Jude's, like a suck. He lets her light it. What else can he do? She's got the matches. Gingerly he inhales. He doesn't smoke much really, and is afraid of coughing.

"I heard they kicked you out," Ronette says. "That's really tough."

"It's okay," says Donny. "I don't care." He can't tell her why, how noble he's been. He hopes he won't cry.

"I heard you tossed Monty's binoculars," she says. "In the lake."

Donny can only nod. He glances at her. She's smiling; he can see the heartbreaking space at the side of her mouth: the missing tooth. She thinks he's funny.

"Well, I'm with you," she says. "He's a little creep."

"It wasn't because of him," says Donny, overcome by the need to confess, or to be taken seriously. "It was because of Darce." He turns, and for the first time looks her straight in the eyes. They are so green. Now his hands are shaking. He drops the cigarette into the sand. They'll find the butt tomorrow, after he's gone. After he's gone, leaving Ronette behind, at the mercy of other people's words. "It was because of you. What they were saying about you. Darce was."

Ronette isn't smiling anymore. "Such as what?" she says.

"Never mind," says Donny. "You don't want to know."

"I know anyhow," Ronette says. "That shit." She sounds resigned rather than angry. She stands up, puts both her hands behind her back. It takes Donny a moment to realize she's untying her apron. When she's got it off she takes him by the hand, pulls gently. He allows himself to be led around the hill of rock, out of sight of anything but the water. She sits down, lies down, smiles as she reaches up, arranges his hands. Her blue uniform unbuttons down the front. Donny can't believe this is happening, to him, in full daylight. It's like sleepwalking, it's like running too fast, it's like nothing else.

"Want another coffee?" Joanne says. She nods to the waitress. Donny hasn't heard her.

"She was really nice to me," he is saying. "Ronette. You know, when Mr. B. turfed me out. That meant a lot to me at the time." He's feeling guilty, because he never wrote her. He didn't know where she lived, but he didn't take any steps to find out. Also, he couldn't keep himself from thinking: *They're right. She's a slut.* Part of him had been profoundly shocked by what she'd done. He hadn't been ready for it.

Joanne is looking at him with her mouth slightly open, as if he's a talking dog, a talking stone. He fingers his beard nervously, wondering what he's said wrong, or given away.

Joanne has just seen the end of the story, or one end of one story. Or at least a missing piece. So that's why Ronette wouldn't tell: it was Donny. She'd been protecting him; or maybe she'd been protecting herself. A fourteen-year-old boy. Ludicrous.

Ludicrous then, possible now. You can do anything now and it won't cause a shock. Just a shrug. Everything is *cool.* A line has been drawn and on the other side of it is the past, both darker and more brightly intense than the present.

She looks across the line and sees the nine waitresses in their bathing suits, in the clear blazing sunlight, laughing on the dock, herself among them; and off in the shadowy rustling bushes of the shoreline, sex lurking dangerously. It had been dangerous, then. It had been sin. Forbidden, secret, sullying. *Sick with desire.* Three dots had expressed it perfectly, because there had been no ordinary words for it.

On the other hand there had been marriage, which meant wifely checked aprons, play-pens, a sugary safety.

But nothing has turned out that way. Sex has been domesticated, stripped of the promised mystery, added to the category of the merely expected. It's just what is done, mundane as hockey. It's celibacy these days that would raise eyebrows.

And what has become of Ronette, after all, left behind in the past, dappled by its chiaroscuro, stained and haloed by it, stuck with other people's adjectives? What is she doing, now that everyone else is following in her footsteps? More practically: did she have the baby, or not? Keep it or not? Donny, sitting sweetly across the table from her, is in all probability the father of a ten-year-old child, and he knows nothing about it at all.

Should she tell him? The melodrama tempts her, the idea of a revelation, a sensation, a neat ending.

But it would not be an ending, it would only be the beginning of something else. In any case, the story itself seems to her outmoded. It's an archaic story, a folk-tale, a mosaic artifact. It's a story that would never happen now.

HAIRBALL

On the thirteenth of November, day of unluck, month of the dead, Kat went into the Toronto General Hospital for an operation. It was for an ovarian cyst, a large one.

Many women had them, the doctor told her. Nobody knew why. There wasn't any way of finding out whether the thing was malignant, whether it contained, already, the spores of death. Not before they went in. He spoke of "going in" the way she'd heard old veterans in TV documentaries speak of assaults on enemy territory. There was the same tensing of the jaw, the same fierce gritting of the teeth, the same grim enjoyment. Except that what he would be going into was her body. Counting down, waiting for the anesthetic, Kat too gritted her teeth fiercely. She was terrified, but also she was curious. Curiosity has got her through a lot.

She'd made the doctor promise to save the thing for her,

whatever it was, so she could have a look. She was intensely interested in her own body, in anything it might choose to do or produce; although when flaky Dania, who did layout at the magazine, told her this growth was a message to her from her body and she ought to sleep with an amethyst under her pillow to calm her vibrations, Kat told her to stuff it.

The cyst turned out to be a benign tumor. Kat liked that use of *benign*, as if the thing had a soul and wished her well. It was big as a grapefruit, the doctor said. "Big as a coconut," said Kat. Other people had grapefruits. "Coconut" was better. It conveyed the hardness of it, and the hairiness, too.

The hair in it was red—long strands of it wound round and round inside, like a ball of wet wool gone berserk or like the guck you pulled out of a clogged bathroom-sink drain. There were little bones in it too, or fragments of bone; bird bones, the bones of a sparrow crushed by a car. There was a scattering of nails, toe or finger. There were five perfectly formed teeth.

"Is this abnormal?" Kat asked the doctor, who smiled. Now that he had gone in and come out again, unscathed, he was less clenched.

"Abnormal? No," he said carefully, as if breaking the news to a mother about a freakish accident to her newborn. "Let's just say it's fairly common." Kat was a little disappointed. She would have preferred uniqueness.

She asked for a bottle of formaldehyde, and put the cut-open tumor into it. It was hers, it was benign, it did not deserve to be thrown away. She took it back to her apartment and stuck it on the mantelpiece. She named it Hairball. It isn't that different from having a stuffed bear's head or a preserved ex-pet or anything else with fur and teeth looming over your fireplace; or she pretends it isn't. Anyway, it certainly makes an impression.

Ger doesn't like it. Despite his supposed yen for the new and outré, he is a squeamish man. The first time he comes around (sneaks around, creeps around) after the operation, he tells Kat to throw Hairball out. He calls it "disgusting." Kat refuses point-blank, and says she'd rather have Hairball in a bottle on her mantelpiece than the soppy dead flowers he's brought her, which will anyway rot a lot sooner than Hairball will. As a mantelpiece ornament, Hairball is far superior. Ger says Kat has a tendency to push things to extremes, to go over the edge, merely from a juvenile desire to shock, which is hardly a substitute for wit. One of these days, he says, she will go way too far. Too far for him, is what he means.

"That's why you hired me, isn't it?" she says. "Because I go way too far." But he's in one of his analyzing moods. He can see these tendencies of hers reflected in her work on the magazine, he says. All that leather and those grotesque and tortured-looking poses are heading down a track he and others are not at all sure they should continue to follow. Does she see what he means, does she take his point? It's a point that's been made before. She shakes her head slightly, says nothing. She knows how that translates: there have been complaints from the advertisers. *Too bizarre, too kinky*. Tough.

"Want to see my scar?" she says. "Don't make me laugh, though, you'll crack it open." Stuff like that makes him dizzy: anything with a hint of blood, anything gynecological. He almost threw up in the delivery room when his wife had a baby two years ago. He'd told her that with pride. Kat thinks about sticking a cigarette into the side of her mouth, as in a black-and-white movie of the forties. She thinks about blowing the smoke into his face.

Her insolence used to excite him, during their arguments. Then there would be a grab of her upper arms, a smoldering, violent kiss. He kisses her as if he thinks someone else is watching him, judging the image they make together. Kissing the latest thing, hard and shiny, purple-mouthed, crop-headed; kissing a girl, a woman, a girl, in a little crotch-hugger skirt and skin-tight leggings. He likes mirrors.

But he isn't excited now. And she can't decoy him into bed; she isn't ready for that yet, she isn't healed. He has a drink, which he doesn't finish, holds her hand as an afterthought, gives her a couple of avuncular pats on the off-white outsized alpaca shoulder, leaves too quickly.

"Goodbye, Gerald," she says. She pronounces the name with

mockery. It's a negation of him, an abolishment of him, like ripping a medal off his chest. It's a warning.

He'd been Gerald when they first met. It was she who transformed him, first to Gerry, then to Ger. (Rhymed with *flair*, rhymed with *dare*.) She made him get rid of those sucky pursed-mouth ties, told him what shoes to wear, got him to buy a loose-cut Italian suit, redid his hair. A lot of his current tastes—in food, in drink, in recreational drugs, in women's entertainment underwear—were once hers. In his new phase, with his new, hard, stripped-down name ending on the sharpened note of *r*, he is her creation.

As she is her own. During her childhood she was a romanticized Katherine, dressed by her misty-eyed, fussy mother in dresses that looked like ruffled pillowcases. By high school she'd shed the frills and emerged as a bouncy, round-faced Kathy, with gleaming freshly washed hair and enviable teeth, eager to please and no more interesting than a health-food ad. At university she was Kath, blunt and no-bullshit in her Take-Back-the-Night jeans and checked shirt and her bricklayer-style striped-denim peaked hat. When she ran away to England, she sliced herself down to Kat. It was economical, street-feline, and pointed as a nail. It was also unusual. In England you had to do something to get their attention, especially if you weren't English. Safe in this incarnation, she Ramboed through the eighties.

It was the name, she still thinks, that got her the interview and then the job. The job with an avant-garde magazine, the kind that was printed on matte stock in black and white, with overexposed close-ups of women with hair blowing over their eyes, one nostril prominent: *the razor's edge*, it was called. Haircuts as art, some real art, film reviews, a little stardust, wardrobes of ideas that were clothes and of clothes that were ideas—the metaphysical shoulder pad. She learned her trade well, hands-on. She learned what worked.

She made her way up the ladder, from layout to design, then to the supervision of whole spreads, and then whole issues. It wasn't easy, but it was worth it. She had become a creator; she created total looks. After a while she could walk down the street

in Soho or stand in the lobby at openings and witness her handi-
work incarnate, strolling around in outfits she'd put together,
spouting her warmed-over pronouncements. It was like being
God, only God had never got around to off-the-rack lines.

By that time her face had lost its roundness, though the teeth
of course remained: there was something to be said for North
American dentistry. She'd shaved off most of her hair, worked
on the drop-dead stare, perfected a certain turn of the neck that
conveyed an aloof inner authority. What you had to make them
believe was that you knew something they didn't know yet. What
you also had to make them believe was that they too could know
this thing, this thing that would give them eminence and power
and sexual allure, that would attract envy to them—but for a
price. The price of the magazine. What they could never get
through their heads was that it was done entirely with cameras.
Frozen light, frozen time. Given the angle, she could make any
woman look ugly. Any man as well. She could make anyone
look beautiful, or at least interesting. It was all photography, it
was all iconography. It was all in the choosing eye. This was the
thing that could never be bought, no matter how much of your
pitiful monthly wage you blew on snakeskin.

Despite the status, *the razor's edge* was fairly low-paying. Kat
herself could not afford many of the things she contextualized
so well. The grottiness and expense of London began to get to
her; she got tired of gorging on the canapés at literary launches in
order to scrimp on groceries, tired of the fuggy smell of cigarettes
ground into the red-and-maroon carpeting of pubs, tired of the
pipes bursting every time it froze in winter, and of the Clarissas
and Melissas and Penelopes at the magazine rabbiting on about
how they had been literally, absolutely, totally freezing all night,
and how it literally, absolutely, totally, usually never got that
cold. It always got that cold. The pipes always burst. Nobody
thought of putting in real pipes, ones that would not burst next
time. Burst pipes were an English tradition, like so many others.

Like, for instance, English men. Charm the knickers off you
with their mellow vowels and frivolous verbiage, and then, once
they'd got them off, panic and run. Or else stay and whinge. The

English called it *whinging* instead of whining. It was better, really. Like a creaking hinge. It was a traditional compliment to be whinged at by an Englishman. It was his way of saying he trusted you, he was conferring upon you the privilege of getting to know the real him. The inner, whinging him. That was how they thought of women, secretly: whinge receptacles. Kat could play it, but that didn't mean she liked it.

She had an advantage over the English women, though: she was of no class. She had no class. She was in a class of her own. She could roll around among the English men, all different kinds of them, secure in the knowledge that she was not being measured against the class yardsticks and accent-detectors they carried around in their back pockets, was not subject to the petty snobberies and resentments that lent such richness to their inner lives. The flip side of this freedom was that she was beyond the pale. She was a colonial—how fresh, how vital, how anonymous, how finally of no consequence. Like a hole in the wall, she could be told all secrets and then be abandoned with no guilt.

She was too smart, of course. The English men were very competitive; they liked to win. Several times it hurt. Twice she had abortions, because the men in question were not up for the alternative. She learned to say that she didn't want children anyway, that if she longed for a rug-rat she would buy a gerbil. Her life began to seem long. Her adrenalin was running out. Soon she would be thirty, and all she could see ahead was more of the same.

This was how things were when Gerald turned up. "You're terrific," he said, and she was ready to hear it, even from him, even though *terrific* was a word that had probably gone out with fifties crew-cuts. She was ready for his voice by that time too: the flat, metallic nasal tone of the Great Lakes, with its clear hard *r*'s and its absence of theatricality. Dull normal. The speech of her people. It came to her suddenly that she was an exile.

Gerald was scouting, Gerald was recruiting. He'd heard

about her, looked at her work, sought her out. One of the big companies back in Toronto was launching a new fashion-oriented magazine, he said: upmarket, international in its coverage, of course, but with some Canadian fashion in it too, and with lists of stores where the items portrayed could actually be bought. In that respect they felt they'd have it all over the competition, those American magazines that assumed you could only get Gucci in New York or Los Angeles. Heck, times had changed, you could get it in Edmonton! You could get it in Winnipeg!

Kat had been away too long. There was Canadian fashion now? The English quip would be to say that "Canadian fashion" was an oxymoron. She refrained from making it, lit a cigarette with her cyanide-green Covent Garden—boutique leather-covered lighter (as featured in the May issue of *the razor's edge*), looked Gerald in the eye. "London is a lot to give up," she said levelly. She glanced around the see-me-here Mayfair restaurant where they were finishing lunch, a restaurant she'd chosen because she'd known he was paying. She'd never spend that kind of money on food otherwise. "Where would I eat?"

Gerald assured her that Toronto was now the restaurant capital of Canada. He himself would be happy to be her guide. There was a great Chinatown, there was world-class Italian. Then he paused, took a breath. "I've been meaning to ask you," he said. "About the name. Is that Kat as in Krazy?" He thought this was suggestive. She'd heard it before.

"No," she said. "It's Kat as in KitKat. That's a chocolate bar. Melts in your mouth." She gave him her stare, quirked her mouth, just a twitch.

Gerald became flustered, but he pushed on. They wanted her, they needed her, they loved her, he said in essence. Someone with her fresh, innovative approach and her experience would be worth a lot of money to them, relatively speaking. But there were rewards other than the money. She would be in on the initial concept, she would have a formative influence, she would have a free hand. He named a sum that made her gasp, inaudibly of course. By now she knew better than to betray desire.

. . .

So she made the journey back, did her three months of culture shock, tried the world-class Italian and the great Chinese, and seduced Gerald at the first opportunity, right in his junior vice-presidential office. It was the first time Gerald had been seduced in such a location, or perhaps ever. Even though it was after hours, the danger frenzied him. It was the idea of it. The daring. The image of Kat kneeling on the broadloom, in a legendary bra that until now he'd seen only in the lingerie ads of the Sunday *New York Times*, unzipping him in full view of the silver-framed engagement portrait of his wife that complemented the impossible ball-point pen set on his desk. At that time he was so straight he felt compelled to take off his wedding ring and place it carefully in the ashtray first. The next day he brought her a box of David Wood Food Shop chocolate truffles. They were the best, he told her, anxious that she should recognize their quality. She found the gesture banal, but also sweet. The banality, the sweetness, the hunger to impress: that was Gerald.

Gerald was the kind of man she wouldn't have bothered with in London. He was not funny, he was not knowledgeable, he had little verbal charm. But he was eager, he was tractable, he was blank paper. Although he was eight years older than she was, he seemed much younger. She took pleasure from his furtive, boyish delight in his own wickedness. And he was so grateful. "I can hardly believe this is happening," he said, more frequently than was necessary and usually in bed.

His wife, whom Kat encountered (and still encounters) at many tedious company events, helped to explain his gratitude. The wife was a priss. Her name was Cheryl. Her hair looked as if she still used big rollers and embalm-your-hairdo spray; her mind was room-by-room Laura Ashley wallpaper: tiny, unopened pastel buds arranged in straight rows. She probably put on rubber gloves to make love, and checked it off on a list afterwards. One more messy household chore. She looked at Kat as if she'd like to spritz her with air deodorizer. Kat revenged herself by picturing Cheryl's bathrooms: hand towels embroidered with lilies, fuzzy covers on the toilet seats.

The magazine itself got off to a rocky start. Although Kat had lots of lovely money to play with, and although it was a challenge to be working in color, she did not have the free hand Gerald had promised her. She had to contend with the company board of directors, who were all men, who were all accountants or indistinguishable from them, who were cautious and slow as moles.

"It's simple," Kat told them. "You bombard them with images of what they ought to be, and you make them feel grotty for being the way they are. You're working with the gap between reality and perception. That's why you have to hit them with something new, something they've never seen before, something they aren't. Nothing sells like anxiety."

The board, on the other hand, felt that the readership should simply be offered more of what they already had. More fur, more sumptuous leather, more cashmere. More established names. The board had no sense of improvisation, no wish to take risks; no sporting instincts, no desire to put one over on the readers just for the hell of it. "Fashion is like hunting," Kat told them, hoping to appeal to their male hormones, if any. "It's playful, it's intense, it's predatory. It's blood and guts. It's erotic." But to them it was about good taste. They wanted Dress-for-Success. Kat wanted scattergun ambush.

Everything became a compromise. Kat had wanted to call the magazine *All the Rage*, but the board was put off by the vibrations of anger in the word "rage." They thought it was too feminist, of all things. "It's a *forties* sound," Kat said. "Forties is *back*. Don't you get it?" But they didn't. They wanted to call it *Or*. French for *gold*, and blatant enough in its values, but without any base note, as Kat told them. They sawed off at *Felice*, which had qualities each side wanted. It was vaguely French-sounding, it meant "happy" (so much less threatening than rage), and, although you couldn't expect the others to notice, for Kat it had a feline bouquet which counteracted the laciness. She had it done in hot-pink lipstick-scrawl, which helped some. She could live with it, but it had not been her first love.

This battle has been fought and refought over every innovation in design, every new angle Kat has tried to bring in, every innocuous bit of semi-kink. There was a big row over a spread that did lingerie, half pulled off and with broken glass perfume bottles strewn on the floor. There was an uproar over the two nouveau-stockinged legs, one tied to a chair with a third, different-colored stocking. They had not understood the man's three-hundred-dollar leather gloves positioned ambiguously around a neck.

And so it has gone on, for five years.

After Gerald has left, Kat paces her living room. Pace, pace. Her stitches pull. She's not looking forward to her solitary dinner of microwaved leftovers. She's not sure now why she came back here, to this flat burg beside the polluted inland sea. Was it Ger? Ludicrous thought but no longer out of the question. Is he the reason she stays, despite her growing impatience with him?

He's no longer fully rewarding. They've learned each other too well, they take short-cuts now; their time together has shrunk from whole stolen rolling and sensuous afternoons to a few hours snatched between work and dinnertime. She no longer knows what she wants from him. She tells herself she's worth more, she should branch out; but she doesn't see other men, she can't, somehow. She's tried once or twice but it didn't work. Sometimes she goes out to dinner or a flick with one of the gay designers. She likes the gossip.

Maybe she misses London. She feels caged, in this country, in this city, in this room. She could start with the room, she could open a window. It's too stuffy in here. There's an undertone of formaldehyde, from Hairball's bottle. The flowers she got for the operation are mostly wilted, all except Gerald's from today. Come to think of it, why didn't he send her any at the hospital? Did he forget, or was it a message?

"Hairball," she says, "I wish you could talk. I could have a more intelligent conversation with you than with most of the losers in this turkey farm." Hairball's baby teeth glint in the light; it looks as if it's about to speak.

Kat feels her own forehead. She wonders if she's running a temperature. Something ominous is going on, behind her back. There haven't been enough phone calls from the magazine; they've been able to muddle on without her, which is bad news. Reigning queens should never go on vacation, or have operations either. Uneasy lies the head. She has a sixth sense about these things, she's been involved in enough palace coups to know the signs, she has sensitive antennae for the footfalls of impending treachery.

The next morning she pulls herself together, downs an espresso from her mini-machine, picks out an aggressive touch-me-if-you-dare suede outfit in armor gray, and drags herself to the office, although she isn't due in till next week. Surprise, surprise. Whispering knots break up in the corridors, greet her with false welcome as she limps past. She settles herself at her minimalist desk, checks her mail. Her head is pounding, her stitches hurt. Ger gets wind of her arrival; he wants to see her a.s.a.p., and not for lunch.

He awaits her in his newly done wheat-on-white office, with the eighteenth-century desk they chose together, the Victorian inkstand, the framed blow-ups from the magazine, the hands in maroon leather, wrists manacled with pearls, the Hermès scarf twisted into a blindfold, the model's mouth blossoming lusciously beneath it. Some of her best stuff. He's beautifully done up, in a lick-my-neck silk shirt open at the throat, an eat-your-heart-out Italian silk-and-wool loose-knit sweater. Oh, cool insouciance. Oh, eyebrow language. He's a money man who lusted after art, and now he's got some, now he is some. Body art. Her art. She's done her job well; he's finally sexy.

He's smooth as lacquer. "I didn't want to break this to you until next week," he says. He breaks it to her. It's the board of directors. They think she's too bizarre, they think she goes way too far. Nothing he could do about it, although naturally he tried.

Naturally. Betrayal. The monster has turned on its own mad scientist. "I gave you life!" she wants to scream at him.

She isn't in good shape. She can hardly stand. She stands, despite his offer of a chair. She sees now what she's wanted, what she's been missing. Gerald is what she's been missing—the stable, unfashionable, previous, tight-assed Gerald. Not Ger, not the one she's made in her own image. The other one, before he got ruined. The Gerald with a house and a small child and a picture of his wife in a silver frame on his desk. She wants to be in that silver frame. She wants the child. She's been robbed.

"And who is my lucky replacement?" she says. She needs a cigarette, but does not want to reveal her shaking hands.

"Actually, it's me," he says, trying for modesty.

This is too absurd. Gerald couldn't edit a phone book. "You?" she says faintly. She has the good sense not to laugh.

"I've always wanted to get out of the money end of things here," he says, "into the creative area. I knew you'd understand, since it can't be you at any rate. I knew you'd prefer someone who could, well, sort of build on your foundations." Pompous asshole. She looks at his neck. She longs for him, hates herself for it, and is powerless.

The room wavers. He slides towards her across the wheat-colored broadloom, takes her by the gray suede upper arms. "I'll write you a good reference," he says. "Don't worry about that. Of course, we can still see one another. I'd miss our afternoons."

"Of course," she says. He kisses her, a voluptuous kiss, or it would look like one to a third party, and she lets him. *In a pig's ear.*

She makes it home in a taxi. The driver is rude to her and gets away with it; she doesn't have the energy. In her mailbox is an engraved invitation: Ger and Cheryl are having a drinks party, tomorrow evening. Postmarked five days ago. Cheryl is behind the times.

Kat undresses, runs a shallow bath. There's not much to drink around here, there's nothing to sniff or smoke. What an oversight; she's stuck with herself. There are other jobs. There are other men, or that's the theory. Still, something's been ripped out of her. How could this have happened to her? When knives were slated for backs, she'd always done the stabbing. Any headed her way she's seen coming in time, and thwarted. Maybe she's losing her edge.

She stares into the bathroom mirror, assesses her face in the misted glass. A face of the eighties, a mask face, a bottom-line face; push the weak to the wall and grab what you can. But now it's the nineties. Is she out of style, so soon? She's only thirty-five, and she's already losing track of what people ten years younger are thinking. That could be fatal. As time goes by she'll have to race faster and faster to keep up, and for what? Part of the life she should have had is just a gap, it isn't there, it's nothing. What can be salvaged from it, what can be redone, what can be done at all?

When she climbs out of the tub after her sponge bath, she almost falls. She has a fever, no doubt about it. Inside her something is leaking, or else festering; she can hear it, like a dripping tap. A running sore, a sore from running so hard. She should go to the Emergency ward at some hospital, get herself shot up with antibiotics. Instead she lurches into the living room, takes Hairball down from the mantelpiece in its bottle, places it on the coffee table. She sits cross-legged, listens. Filaments wave. She can hear a kind of buzz, like bees at work.

She'd asked the doctor if it could have started as a child, a fertilized egg that escaped somehow and got into the wrong place. No, said the doctor. Some people thought this kind of tumor was present in seedling form from birth, or before it. It might be the woman's undeveloped twin. What they really were was unknown. They had many kinds of tissue, though. Even brain tissue. Though of course all of these tissues lack structure.

Still, sitting here on the rug looking in at it, she pictures it as a child. It has come out of her, after all. It is flesh of her flesh. Her child with Gerald, her thwarted child, not allowed to grow normally. Her warped child, taking its revenge.

"Hairball," she says. "You're so ugly. Only a mother could

love you." She feels sorry for it. She feels loss. Tears run down her face. Crying is not something she does, not normally, not lately.

Hairball speaks to her, without words. It is irreducible, it has the texture of reality, it is not an image. What it tells her is everything she's never wanted to hear about herself. This is new knowledge, dark and precious and necessary. It cuts.

She shakes her head. What are you doing, sitting on the floor and talking to a hairball? You are sick, she tells herself. Take a Tylenol and go to bed.

The next day she feels a little better. Dania from layout calls her and makes dovelike, sympathetic coos at her, and wants to drop by during lunch hour to take a look at her aura. Kat tells her to come off it. Dania gets huffy, and says that Kat's losing her job is a price for immoral behavior in a previous life. Kat tells her to stuff it; anyway, she's done enough immoral behavior in this life to account for the whole thing. "Why are you so full of hate?" asks Dania. She doesn't say it like a point she's making, she sounds truly baffled.

"I don't know," says Kat. It's a straight answer.

After she hangs up she paces the floor. She's crackling inside, like hot fat under the broiler. What she's thinking about is Cheryl, bustling about her cozy house, preparing for the party. Cheryl fiddles with her freeze-framed hair, positions an over-loaded vase of flowers, fusses about the caterers. Gerald comes in, kisses her lightly on the cheek. A connubial scene. His con-science is nicely washed. The witch is dead, his foot is on the body, the trophy; he's had his dirty fling, he's ready now for the rest of his life.

Kat takes a taxi to the David Wood Food Shop and buys two dozen chocolate truffles. She has them put into an oversized box, then into an oversized bag with the store logo on it. Then she goes home and takes Hairball out of its bottle. She drains it in the kitchen strainer and pats it damp-dry, tenderly, with paper towels. She sprinkles it with powdered cocoa, which forms a brown pasty crust. It still smells like formaldehyde, so she wraps it in Saran Wrap and then in tinfoil, and then in pink tissue paper, which she ties with a mauve bow. She places it in the David Wood box in a bed of shredded tissue, with the truffles nestled around. She closes the box, tapes it, puts it into the bag, stuffs several sheets of pink paper on top. It's her gift, valuable and dangerous. It's her messenger, but the message it will deliver is its own. It will tell the truth, to whoever asks. It's right that Gerald should have it; after all, it's his child too.

She prints on the card, "Gerald, Sorry I couldn't be with you. This is all the rage. Love, K."

When evening has fallen and the party must be in full swing, she calls a delivery taxi. Cheryl will not distrust anything that arrives in such an expensive bag. She will open it in public, in front of everyone. There will be distress, there will be questions. Secrets will be unearthed. There will be pain. After that, everything will go way too far.

She is not well; her heart is pounding, space is wavering once more. But outside the window it's snowing, the soft, damp, windless flakes of her childhood. She puts on her coat and goes out, foolishly. She intends to walk just to the corner, but when she reaches the corner she goes on. The snow melts against her face like small fingers touching. She has done an outrageous thing, but she doesn't feel guilty. She feels light and peaceful and filled with charity, and temporarily without a name.

ISIS IN DARKNESS

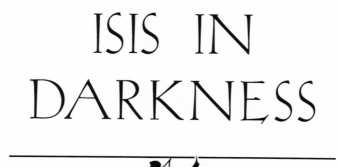

Ｈow did Selena get here? This is a question Richard is in the habit of asking himself, as he sits at his desk again, shuffling his deck of filing-cards, trying again to begin.

He has a repertoire of answers. Sometimes he pictures her drifting down towards the mundane rooftops in a giant balloon made of turquoise and emerald-green silks, or arriving on the back of a golden bird like the ones on Chinese teacups. On other days, darker ones like this Thursday—Thursday, he knows, was a sinister day in her calendar—she wends her way through a long underground tunnel encrusted with blood-red jewels and with arcane inscriptions that glitter in the light of torches. For years she walks, her garments—garments, not clothes—trailing, her eyes fixed and hypnotic, for she is one of those cursed with an unending life; walks until she reaches, one moonlit night, the iron-grilled door of the Petrowski tomb, which is real, though dug improbably into a hillside near the entrance to the also-real Mount Pleasant Cemetery.

(She would love that intersection of the banal and the numinous. She once said that the universe was a doughnut. She named the brand.)

The lock splits. The iron gate swings open. She emerges, raises her arms towards the suddenly chilled moon. The world changes.

There are other plots. It just depends which mythology he's cribbing from.

A factual account exists. She came from the same sort of area that Richard came from himself: old pre-Depression Toronto, strung out along the lake shore south of the Queen streetcar tracks, a region of small vertical houses with peeling woodwork and sagging front porches and dry, mangy lawns. Not quaint in those days, not renovated, not desirable. The sort of constipated lower-middle-class white-bread ghetto he'd fled as soon as he could, because of the dingy and limited versions of himself it had offered him. Her motivation was perhaps the same. He likes to think so.

They'd even gone to the same constricting high school, though he'd never noticed her there. But why would he? He was four years older. By the time she'd come in, a spindly, frightened grade niner, he'd been almost out the door, and none too soon for him. He couldn't imagine her there; couldn't imagine her sauntering along the same faded green hallways, banging the same scratched lockers, sticking her gum underneath the same cagelike desks.

She and the high school would have been destructive opposites, like matter and anti-matter. Every time he placed her mental image beside that of the school, one or the other of them exploded. Usually it was the school's.

Selena was not her real name. She had simply appropriated it, as she'd appropriated everything else that would help her to construct her new, preferred identity. She'd discarded the old name, which was Marjorie. Richard has learned this by mistake, in the course of his researches, and has tried in vain to forget it.

The first time he saw her is not noted on any of his filing-cards. He only makes notes of things he is not otherwise likely to remember.

It was in 1960—the end of the fifties or the beginning of the sixties, depending on how you felt about zero. Selena was later to call it *"the white-hot luminous egg/from which everything hatches,"* but for Richard, who at the time was slogging through *Being and Nothingness*, it signaled a dead end. He was in his first year of graduate school, on a meager grant eked out by the marking of woefully written undergraduate essays. He was feeling jaded, over-the-hill; senility was rapidly approaching. He was twenty-two.

He met her on a Tuesday night, at the coffee-house. *The* coffee-house, because as far as Richard knew there was not another one like it in Toronto. It was called The Bohemian Embassy, in reference to the anti-bourgeois things that were supposed to go on in there, and to a certain extent did go on. It sometimes got mail from more innocent citizens who had seen the listing in the phone book and thought it was a real embassy, and were writing about travel visas. This was a source of hilarity among the regulars, of whom Richard was not quite one.

The coffee-house was on a little cobbled side street, up on the second floor of a disused warehouse. It was reached by a treacherous flight of wooden stairs with no banister; inside, it was dimly lit, smoke-filled, and closed down at intervals by the fire department. The walls had been painted black, and there were small tables with checked cloths and dripping candles. It also had an espresso machine, the first one Richard had ever seen. This machine was practically an icon, pointing as it did to other, superior cultures, far from Toronto. But it had its drawbacks. While you were reading your poetry out loud, as Richard sometimes did, Max behind the coffee bar might turn on the machine, adding a whooshing, gurgling sound effect, as of someone being pressure-cooked and strangled.

Wednesdays and Thursdays were folk-singing, the weekends were jazz. Richard sometimes went on these nights, but he always went on Tuesdays, whether he was reading or not. He wanted to check out the competition. There wasn't a lot of it, but what there was would surely turn up at The Bohemian Embassy, sooner or later.

Poetry was the way out then, for young people who wanted some exit from the lumpen bourgeoisie and the shackles of respectable wage-earning. It was what painting had been at the turn of the century. Richard knows this now, although he did not then. He doesn't know what the equivalent is at the moment. Filmmaking, he'd guess, for those with intellectual pretensions. For those without, it's playing the drums in a group, a group with a disgusting name such as Animal Fats or The Living Snot, if his twenty-seven-year-old son is any indication. Richard can't keep close tabs though, because the son lives with Richard's ex-wife. (Still! At his age! Why doesn't he get a room, an apartment, a job, Richard finds himself thinking, sourly enough. He understands, now, his own father's irritation with the black turtlenecks he used to wear, his scruffy attempts at a beard, his declamations, over the obligatory Sunday-dinner meat and potatoes, of "The Waste Land," and, later and even more effectively, of Ginsberg's "Howl." But at least he'd been interested in *meaning*, he tells himself. Or words. At least he'd been interested in words.)

He'd been good with words, then. He'd had several of his poems published in the university literary magazine, and in two little magazines, one of them not mimeographed. Seeing these poems in print, with his name underneath—he used initials, like T. S. Eliot, to make himself sound older—had given him more satisfaction than he'd ever got out of anything before. But he'd made the mistake of showing one of these magazines to his father, who was lower-middle-management with the Post Office. This had rated nothing more than a frown and a grunt, but as he was going down the walk with his bag of freshly washed laundry, on his way back to his rented room, he'd heard his old man reading one of his free-verse anti-sonnets out loud to his mother, sputtering with mirth, punctuated by his mother's disapproving, predictable voice: "Now John! Don't be so hard on him!"

The anti-sonnet was about Mary Jo, a chunky, practical girl with an off-blond pageboy who worked at the library, and with whom Richard was almost having an affair. "*I sink into your eyes*," his father roared. "Old swamp-eyes! Cripes, what's he gonna do when he gets down as far as the tits?"

And his mother, acting her part in their ancient conspiracy: "Now John! Really! Language!"

Richard told himself severely that he didn't care. His father never read anything but the *Reader's Digest* and bad paperback novels about the war, so what did he know?

By that particular Tuesday Richard had given up free verse. It was too easy. He wanted something with more rigor, more structure; something, he admits to himself now, that not everybody else could do.

He'd read his own stuff during the first set of the evening, a group of five sestinas followed by a villanelle. His poems were elegant, intricate; he was pleased with them. The espresso machine went off during the last one—he was beginning to suspect Max of sabotage—but several people said "Shhh." When he'd finished there was polite applause. Richard sat back down in his corner, surreptitiously scratching his neck. The black turtleneck was giving him a rash. As his mother never ceased telling anyone who might be interested, he had a delicate skin.

After him there was a straw-haired older woman poet from the West Coast who read a long poem in which the wind was described as blowing up between her thighs. There were breezy disclosures in this poem, offhand four-letter words; nothing you wouldn't find in Allen Ginsberg, but Richard caught himself blushing. After her reading, this woman came over and sat down beside Richard. She squeezed his arm and whispered, "Your poems were nice." Then, staring him straight in the eye, she hitched her skirt up over her thighs. This was hidden from the rest of the room by the checked tablecloth and by the general smoky gloom. But it was a clear invitation. She was daring him to take a peek at whatever moth-eaten horror she had tucked away in there.

Richard found himself becoming coldly angry. He was supposed to salivate, jump her on the stairway like some deranged monkey. He hated those kinds of assumptions about men, about dip-stick sex and slobbery, pea-brained arousal. He felt like punching her. She must have been at least fifty.

The age he now is himself, Richard notes dejectedly. That's one thing Selena has escaped. He thinks of it as an escape.

There was a musical interlude, as there always was on Tuesdays. A girl with long, straight, dark hair parted in the middle sat on a high stool, an autoharp across her knees, and sang several mournful folk-songs in a high, clear voice. Richard was worrying about how to remove the woman poet's hand from his arm without being ruder than he wanted to be. (She was senior, she'd published books, she knew people.) He thought he might excuse himself and go to the washroom; but the washroom was just a cubicle that opened directly onto the main room. It had no lock, and Max was in the habit of opening the door when you were in there. Unless you turned out the light and pissed in the dark, you were likely to be put on exhibit, brightly lit as a Christmas crèche, hands fumbling at your crotch.

> *He held a knife against her breast,*
> *As into his arms she pressed,*

sang the girl. I could just leave, thought Richard. But he didn't want to do that.

> *Oh Willy Willy, don't you murder me,*
> *I'm not prepared for eternity.*

Sex and violence, he thinks now. A lot of the songs were about that. We didn't even notice. We thought it was art.

It was right after this that Selena came on. He hadn't seen her in the room before. It was as if she'd materialized out of nowhere, on the tiny stage, under the single spotlight.

She was slight, almost wispy. Like the singer, she had long, dark hair with a center part. Her eyes were outlined in black, as was becoming the fashion. She was wearing a long-sleeved, high-necked black dress, over which was draped a shawl embroidered with what looked like blue and green dragonflies.

Oh jeez, thought Richard, who like his father still used the laundered blasphemies of the schoolyard. Another jeezly poetess. I suppose now we'll have more pudenda, he added, from his graduate-school vocabulary.

Then the voice hit him. It was a warm, rich voice, darkly spiced, like cinnamon, and too huge to be coming from such a small person. It was a seductive voice, but not in any blunt way. What it offered was an entrée to amazement, to a shared and tingling secret; to splendors. But there was an undercurrent of amusement too, as if you were a fool for being taken in by its voluptuousness; as if there were a cosmic joke in the offing, a simple, mysterious joke, like the jokes of children.

What she read was a series of short connected lyrics, "Isis in Darkness." The Egyptian Queen of Heaven and Earth was wandering in the Underworld, gathering up the pieces of the murdered and dismembered body of her lover Osiris. At the same time, it was her own body she was putting back together; and it was also the physical universe. She was creating the universe by an act of love.

All of this was taking place, not in the ancient Middle Kingdom of the Egyptians, but in flat, dingy Toronto, on Spadina Avenue, at night, among the darkened garment factories and delicatessens and bars and pawnshops. It was a lament, and a celebration. Richard had never heard anything like it.

He sat back in his chair, fingering his patchy beard, trying as hard as he could to find this girl and her poetry trivial, overdone and pretentious. But he couldn't manage it. She was brilliant, and he was frightened. He felt his own careful talent shriveling to the size of a dried bean.

The espresso machine did not go off once. After she'd finished there was a silence, before the applause. The silence was because people didn't know what to make of it, how to take it, this thing, whatever it was, that had been done to them. For a moment she had transformed reality, and it took them a breath to get it back.

Richard stood up, pushing past the bared legs of the woman poet. He didn't care anymore who she might know. He went over to where Selena had just sat down, with a cup of coffee brought to her by Max.

"I liked your poems," he managed to get out.

"Liked? Liked?" He thought she was making fun of him, although she wasn't smiling. "*Liked* is so margarine. How about *adored*?"

"Adored, then," he said, feeling like an idiot twice over—for having said *liked* in the first place, and for jumping through her hoop in the second. But he got his reward. She asked him to sit down.

Up close her eyes were turquoise, the irises dark-ringed like a cat's. In her ears were blue-green earrings in the form of scarabs. Her face was heart-shaped, her skin pale; to Richard, who had been dabbling in the French Symbolists, it evoked the word *lilac*. The shawl, the darkly outlined eyes, the earrings—few would have been able to pull it off. But she acted as if this was just her ordinary get-up. What you'd wear any day on a journey down the Nile, five thousand years ago.

It was of a piece with her performance—bizarre, but assured. Fully achieved. The worst of it was that she was only eighteen.

"That's a lovely shawl," Richard attempted. His tongue felt like a beef sandwich.

"It's not a shawl, it's a tablecloth," she said. She looked down at it, stroked it. Then she laughed a little. "It's a shawl *now*."

Richard wondered if he should dare to ask—what? If he

could walk her home? Did she have anything so mundane as a home? But what if she said no? While he was deliberating, Max the bullet-headed coffee hack walked over and put a possessive hand on her shoulder, and she smiled up at him. Richard didn't wait to see if it meant anything. He excused himself, and left.

He went back to his rented room and composed a sestina to her. It was a dismal effort; it captured nothing about her. He did what he had never before done to one of his poems. He burnt it.

Over the next few weeks Richard got to know her better. Or he thought he did. When he came into the coffee-house on Tuesday nights, she would greet him with a nod, a smile. He would go over and sit down, and they would talk. She never spoke about herself, her life. Instead she treated him as if he were a fellow professional, an initiate, like herself. Her talk was about the magazines which had accepted her poems, about projects she'd begun. She was writing a verse play for radio; she would be paid for it. She seemed to think it was only a matter of time before she'd be earning enough money to live on, though she had very little conception of how much *enough* would be. She didn't say what she was living on at the moment.

Richard found her naïve. He himself had taken the sensible course: with a graduate degree he could always make an income of some sort in the academic salt-mines. But who would pay a living wage for poetry, especially the kind she wrote? It wasn't in the style of anyone, it didn't sound like anything else. It was too eccentric.

She was like a child sleepwalking along a roof-ledge ten stories up. He was afraid to call out in warning, in case she should wake, and fall.

Mary Jo the librarian had phoned him several times. He'd put her off with vague mumbles about overwork. On the rare Sunday when he still turned up at his parents' house to do his laundry and eat what his father called a decent meal for once, he had to endure the pained scrutiny of his mother. Her theory was that he was straining his brain, which could lead to anemia. In fact he was hardly working at all. His room was silting up with unmarked, overdue student papers; he hadn't written another poem, another line. Instead he went out for gummy egg sandwiches or glasses of draft beer at the local beverage room, or to afternoon movies, sleazy double features about women with two heads or men who got changed into flies. Evenings he spent at the coffee-house. He was no longer feeling jaded. He was feeling desperate.

It was Selena who was causing this desperation, but he had no name for why. Partly he wanted to get inside her, find that innermost cave where she hid her talent. But she kept him at a distance. Him, and in some way everyone else.

She read several times. The poems were astonishing again, again unique. Nothing about her grandmother, or about snow, or about childhood; nothing about dying dogs, or family members of any kind. Instead there were regal, tricky women, magical, shape-shifting men; in whom, however, he thought he could recognize the transposed outlines of some of the regulars from The Bohemian Embassy. Was that Max's white-blond bullet head, his lidded ice-blue eyes? There was another man, a thin intense one with a mustache and a smoldering Spanish look that set Richard's teeth on edge. One night he'd announced to the whole table that he'd caught a bad case of crabs, that he'd had to shave himself and paint his groin blue. Could that be his torso, equipped with burning wings? Richard couldn't tell, and it was driving him crazy.

(It was never Richard himself though. Never his own stubby features, his own brownish hair and hazel eyes. Never even a line, about him.)

He pulled himself together, got the papers marked, finished off an essay on the imagery of mechanism in Herrick which he needed in order to haul himself safely from this academic year into the next one. He took Mary Jo to one of the Tuesday poetry evenings. He thought it might neutralize Selena, like an acid neutralizing an alkali; get her out of his head. Mary Jo was not impressed.

"Where does she *get* those tatty old clothes?" she said.

"She's a brilliant poet," said Richard.

"I don't care. That thing looks like a tablecloth. And why does she do her eyes in that phony way?"

Richard felt this like a cut, like a personal wound.

He didn't want to marry Selena. He couldn't imagine marriage with her. He could not place her within the tedious, comforting scenery of domesticity: a wife doing his laundry, a wife cooking his meals, a wife pouring his tea. All he wanted was a month, a week, a night even. Not in a motel room, not in the back of a car; these squalid venues left over from his fumbling youth would not do. It would have to be somewhere else, somewhere darker and infinitely more strange. He imagined a crypt, with hieroglyphics; like the last act of *Aida*. The same despair, the same exultation, the same annihilation. From such an experience you would emerge reborn, or not at all.

It was not lust. Lust was what you felt for Marilyn Monroe, or sometimes for the strippers at the Victory Burlesque. (Selena had a poem about the Victory Burlesque. The strippers, for her, were not a bunch of fat sluts with jiggling, dimpled flesh. They were diaphanous; they were surreal butterflies, emerging from cocoons of light; they were splendid.)

What he craved was not her body as such. He wanted to be transformed by her, into someone he was not.

By now it was summer, and the university and the coffee-house were both closed. On rainy days Richard lay on the lumpy bed in his humid, stifling room, listening to the thunder; on sunny ones, which were just as humid, he made his way from tree to tree, staying in the shade. He avoided the library. One more session of sticky near-sex with Mary Jo, with her damp kisses and her nurselike manipulations of his body, and especially the way she sensibly stopped short of anything final, would leave him with a permanent limp.

"You wouldn't want to get me knocked up," she would say, and she was right, he wouldn't. For a girl who worked among books, she was breathtakingly prosaic. But then, her forte was cataloguing.

Richard knew she was a healthy girl with a normal outlook. She would be good for him. This was his mother's opinion, delivered after he'd made the mistake—just once—of taking her home with him to Sunday dinner. She was like corned beef, cottage cheese, cod-liver oil. She was like milk.

One day he bought a bottle of Italian red wine and took the ferry over to Wards Island. He knew Selena lived over there. That at least had been in the poems.

He didn't know what he intended to do. He wanted to see her, take hold of her, go to bed with her. He didn't know how he was going to get from the first step to the last. He didn't care what came of it. He wanted.

He got off the ferry and walked up and down the small streets of the island, where he had never been. These were summer homes, cheap and insubstantial, white clapboard or pastel, or sided with insulbrick. Cars were not permitted. There were kids on bicycles, dumpy women in swimsuits taking sunbaths on their lawns. Portable radios played. It was not what he'd had in mind as Selena's milieu. He thought of asking someone where she lived—they would know, she'd stand out here—but he didn't want to advertise his presence. He considered turning around, taking the next ferry back.

Then, off at the end of one of the streets, he saw a minute one-story cottage, in the shade of two large willows. There had been willows in the poems. He could at least try.

The door was open. It was her house, because she was in it. She was not at all surprised to see him.

"I was just making some peanut-butter sandwiches," she

said, "so we could have a picnic." She was wearing loose black cotton slacks, Oriental in tone, and a sleeveless black top. Her arms were white and thin. Her feet were in sandals; he looked at her long toes, with the toenails painted a light peach-pink. He noted with a wrench of the heart that the nail polish was chipped.

"Peanut butter?" he said stupidly. She was talking as if she'd been expecting him.

"And strawberry jam," she said. "Unless you don't like jam." Still that courteous distance.

He proffered his bottle of wine. "Thanks," she said, "but you'll have to drink it all by yourself."

"Why?" he said. He'd intended this to go differently. A recognition. A wordless embrace.

"If I ever started I'd never stop. My father was an alcoholic," she told him gravely. "He's somewhere else, because of it."

"In the Underworld?" he said, in what he hoped was a graceful allusion to her poetry.

She shrugged. "Or wherever." He felt like a dunce. She went back to spreading the peanut butter, at her diminutive kitchen table. Richard, wrung dry of conversation, looked around him. There was only the one room, sparsely furnished. It was almost like a religious cell, or his idea of one. In one corner was a desk with an old black typewriter, and a bookshelf made of boards and bricks. The bed was narrow and covered with a swath of bright purple Indian cotton, to double as a sofa. There was a tiny sink, a tiny stove. One easy chair, Sally-Ann issue. A braided, faded rug. On the walls there were no pictures at all.

"I don't need them," she said. She'd put the sandwiches into a crumpled paper bag and was motioning him out the door.

She led him to a stone breakwater overlooking the lake, and they sat on it and ate the sandwiches. She had some lemonade in a milk bottle; they passed it back and forth. It was like a ritual, like a communion; she was letting him partake. She sat cross-legged, with sunglasses on. Two people went by in a canoe. The lake rippled, threw off glints of light. Richard felt absurd, and happy.

"We can't be lovers," she said to him after a time. She was

licking jam off her fingers. Richard jolted awake. He had never been so abruptly understood. It was like a trick; it made him uncomfortable.

He could have pretended he didn't know what she was talking about. Instead he said, "Why not?"

"You would get used up," she said. "Then you wouldn't be there, later."

This was what he wanted: to be used up. To burn in divine conflagration. At the same time, he realized that he could not summon up any actual, carnal desire for this woman; this *girl*, sitting beside him on the breakwater with her skinny arms and minimal breasts, dangling her legs now like a nine-year-old.

"Later?" he said. Was she telling him he was too good to be wasted? Was this a compliment, or not?

"When I'll need you," she said. She was stuffing the waxed-paper sandwich wrapping into the paper bag. "I'll walk you to the ferry."

He had been circumvented, outmaneuvered; also spied on. Maybe he was an open book and a dolt as well, but she didn't have to rub it in. As they walked, he found himself getting angry. He still clutched the wine bottle in its liquor-store bag.

At the ferry dock she took his hand, shook it formally. "Thank you for coming," she said. Then she pushed the sunglasses up onto her hair, giving him her turquoise eyes full force. "The light only shines for some," she said, kindly and sadly. "And even for them it's not all the time. The rest of the time you're alone."

But he'd had enough of gnomic utterances for one day. Theatrical bitch, he told himself on the ferry.

He went back to his room and drank most of the bottle of wine. Then he phoned Mary Jo. When she'd negotiated her way as usual past the snoopy landlady on the ground floor and arrived on tiptoe at his door, he pulled her inside roughly and bent her backwards in a tipsy, mocking embrace. She started to giggle, but he kissed her seriously and pushed her onto the bed. If he couldn't have what he wanted he would at least have something. The bristles of her shaved legs rasped against him; her breath smelled like grape bubble gum. When she began to protest, warning him again of the danger of pregnancy, he said it didn't matter. She took this as a marriage proposal. In the event, it was one.

With the arrival of the baby his academic work ceased to be a thing he did disdainfully, on sufferance, and became a necessity of life. He needed the money, and then he needed more money. He labored over his Ph.D. thesis, on cartographic imagery in John Donne, interrupted by infant squalling and the dentist's-drill whine of the vacuum cleaner, and by the cups of tea brought to him by Mary Jo at inappropriate moments. She told him he was a grouch, but since that was more or less the behavior she expected from husbands she didn't seem to mind. She typed his thesis for him and did the footnotes, and showed him off to her relatives, him and his new degree. He got a job teaching composition and grammar to veterinary students at the agricultural college in Guelph.

He did not write poetry anymore. Some days he hardly even thought about it. It was like a third arm, or a third eye, that had atrophied. He'd been a freak when he'd had it.

Once in a while, though, he went on binges. He would sneak into bookstores or libraries, lurk around the racks where the little magazines were kept; sometimes he'd buy one. Dead poets were his business, living ones his vice. Much of the stuff he read was crap and he knew it; still, it gave him an odd lift. Then there would be the occasional real poem, and he would catch his breath. Nothing else could drop him through space like that, then catch him; nothing else could peel him open.

Sometimes these poems were Selena's. He would read them, and part of him—a small, constricted part—would hope for some lapse, some decline; but she just got better. Those nights, when he was lying in bed on the threshold of sleep, he would remember her or she would appear to him, he was never sure which; a dark-haired woman with her arms upstretched, in a long cloak of blue and dull gold or of feathers or of white linen. The costumes were variable, but she herself remained a constant. She was something of his own that he had lost.

He didn't see her again until 1970, another zero year. By that time he'd managed to get himself hired back to Toronto, to teach graduate-level Puritan literary theory and freshman English at a new campus in the suburbs. He did not yet have tenure: in the age of publish-or-perish, he'd published only two papers, one on witchcraft as sexual metaphor, the other on *The Pilgrim's Progress* and architecture. Now that their son was in school Mary Jo had gone back to cataloguing, and with their savings they'd made a down payment on a Victorian semi-detached in the Annex. It had a small back lawn, which Richard mowed. They kept talking about a garden, but there was never the energy.

At this time Richard was at a low point, though it was Mary Jo's contention that he was always at a low point. She fed him vitamin pills and nagged him to see a shrink so he could become more assertive, though when he was assertive with her she would accuse him of throwing his patriarchal weight around. He'd realized by now that he could always depend on her to do the socially correct thing. At the moment she was attending a women's consciousness-raising group and was (possibly) having an affair with a sandy-haired, pasty-faced linguist at the university whose name was Johanson. Whether it existed or not, this affair suited Richard, in a way: it allowed him to think badly of her.

It was April. Mary Jo was at her women's group or screwing Johanson, or both; she was efficient, she could get a lot done in one evening. His son was staying overnight with a friend. Richard was supposed to be working on his book, the book that was going to do it for him, make his name, get him tenure: *Spiritual Carnality: Marvell and Vaughan and the Seventeenth Century.* He'd hesitated between *carnal spirituality and spiritual carnality,* but the latter had more zing. The book was not going all that well. There was a problem of focus. Instead of rewriting the second chapter again, he'd come downstairs to rummage in the refrigerator for a beer.

"And tear our pleasures with rough strife / Thorough the iron gates of life, Olé!" he sang, to the tune of "Hernando's Hideaway." He got out two beers and filled a cereal bowl with potato chips. Then he went into the living room and settled into the easy chair to slurp and munch, flipping through the channels on the television set, looking for the crassest, most idiotic thing he could find. He badly needed something to sneer at.

This was when the doorbell rang. When he saw who it was he was very glad he'd had the sense to click off the item he'd been watching, a tits-and-bums extravaganza posing as a detective show.

It was Selena, wearing a wide-brimmed black hat and a long, black knitted coat, and carrying a battered suitcase. "May I come in?" she said.

Richard, amazed and a little frightened, and then suddenly delighted, stood back to let her in. He'd forgotten what delight felt like. In the last few years he'd given up even on the little magazines, preferring numbness.

He didn't ask her what she was doing at his house, or how she'd found him. Instead he said, "Would you like a drink?"

"No," she said. "I don't drink, remember?" He did remember then; he remembered her tiny house on the island, in every clear detail: the pattern of small gold lions on the purple bedspread, the shells and round stones on the window-sill, the daisies in a jam jar. He remembered her long toes. He'd made a fool of himself that day, but now she was here it no longer mattered. He wanted to wrap his arms around her, hold her closely; rescue her, be rescued.

"Some coffee would be nice though," she said, and he led her to the kitchen and made her some. She didn't take off her coat. The sleeves were threadbare; he could see the places where she'd stitched over the raveled edges with mending wool. She smiled at him with the same acceptance of him she'd always shown, taking for granted that he was a friend and equal, and he was ashamed of the way he'd spent the last ten years. He must be absurd to her; he was absurd to himself. He had a paunch and a mortgage, a bedraggled marriage; he mowed the lawn, he owned sports jackets, grudgingly he raked the autumn leaves and shoveled the winter snow. He indulged his own sloth. He should have been living in an attic, eating bread and maggoty cheese, washing his one shirt out at night, his head incandescent with words.

She was not noticeably older. If anything she was thinner. He saw what he thought was the fading shadow of a bruise over her right cheekbone, but it could have been the light. She sipped at her coffee, fiddled with the spoon. She seemed to have drifted off somewhere. "Are you writing much?" he said, seizing on something he knew would interest her.

"Oh yes," she said brightly, returning to her body. "I have another book coming out." How had he missed the first one? "How about you?"

He shrugged. "Not for a long time."

"That's a shame," she said. "That's terrible." She meant it. It was as if he'd told her someone she'd known had died, and he was touched. It wasn't his actual poems she was regretting, unless she had no taste at all. They hadn't been any good, he knew that now and certainly she did too. It was the poems, the ones he might have written, if. If what?

"Could I stay here?" she said, putting down her cup.

Richard was taken aback. She'd meant business with that suitcase. Nothing would have pleased him more, he told himself, but there was Mary Jo to be considered. "Of course," he said, hoping his hesitation hadn't shown.

"Thank you," said Selena. "I don't have anywhere else right now. Anywhere safe."

He didn't ask her to explain this. Her voice was the same, rich and tantalizing, on the edge of ruin; it was having its old devastating effect on him. "You can sleep in the rec room," he said. "There's a sofa that folds out."

"Oh good." She sighed. "It's Thursday." Thursday, he recalled, was a significant day in her poetry, but at the time he couldn't remember whether it was good or bad. Now he knows. Now he has three filing-cards with nothing but Thursdays on them.

When Mary Jo got home, brisk and defensive as he'd decided she always was after furtive sex, they were still sitting in the kitchen. Selena was having another cup of coffee, Richard another beer. Selena's hat and mended coat were on top of her suitcase. Mary Jo saw them and scowled.

"Mary Jo, you remember Selena," Richard said. "From the Embassy?"

"Right," said Mary Jo. "Did you put out the trash?"

"I will," said Richard. "She's staying overnight."

"I'll put it out myself then," said Mary Jo, stomping off towards the glassed-in back porch where they kept the garbage cans. Richard followed her and they fought, at first in whispers.

"What the hell is she doing in my house?" Mary Jo hissed.

"It's not just your house, it's my house too. She's got nowhere else to go."

"That's what they all say. What happened, some boyfriend beat her up?"

"I didn't ask. She's an old friend."

"Look, if you want to sleep with that weird flake you can do it somewhere else."

"As you do?" said Richard, with what he hoped was bitter dignity.

"What the hell are you talking about? Are you accusing me of something?" said Mary Jo. Her eyes were bulging out, as they did when she was really angry and not just acting. "Oh. You'd love that, wouldn't you. Give you a voyeuristic thrill."

"Anyway I'm not sleeping with her," said Richard, reminding Mary Jo that the first false accusation had been hers.

"Why not?" said Mary Jo. "You've been leching after her for ten years. I've seen you mooning over those stupid poetry magazines. *On Thursdays you are a banana*," she intoned, in savage mimicry of Selena's deeper voice. "Why don't you just screw her and get it over with?"

"I would if I could," Richard said. This truth saddened him.

"Oh. Holding out on you? Tough shit. Do me a favor, just rape her in the rec room and get it out of your system."

"My, my," said Richard. "Sisterhood *is* powerful." As soon as he said it he knew he'd gone too far.

"How dare you use my feminism against me like that?" said Mary Jo, her voice up an octave. "That is so cheap! You always were a cheap little prick!"

Selena was standing in the doorway watching them. "Richard," she said, "I think I'd better go."

"Oh no," said Mary Jo, with a chirpy parody of hospitality. "Stay! It's no trouble! Stay a week! Stay a month! Consider us your hotel!"

Richard walked Selena to the front door. "Where will you go?" he said.

"Oh," she said, "there's always somewhere." She stood under the porch light, looking up the street. It *was* a bruise. "But right now I don't have any money."

Richard dug out his wallet, emptied it. He wished it was more.

"I'll pay you back," she said.

If he has to date it, Richard pinpoints this Thursday as the day his marriage was finally over. Even though he and Mary Jo went through the form of apologizing, even though they had more than a few drinks and smoked a joint and had dislocated, impersonal sex, nothing got fixed. Mary Jo left him soon after, in quest of the self she claimed she needed to find. She took their son with her. Richard, who hadn't paid that much attention to the boy, was now reduced to nostalgic, interminable weekends with him. He tried out several other women, but couldn't concentrate on them.

He looked for Selena but she'd disappeared. One magazine editor told him she'd gone out west. Richard felt he'd let her down. He had failed to be a place of refuge.

. . .

Ten years later he saw her again. It was 1980, another year of the nothing, or of the white-hot egg. He notes this coincidence only now, laying out the filing-cards like a fortuneteller across the surface of his particle-board desk.

He'd just got out of his car, having returned through thickening traffic from the university, where he was still clinging on by his fingernails. It was mid-March, during the spring melt, an irritating and scruffy time of year. Mud and rain and scraps of garbage left over from the winter. His mood was similar. He'd recently had the manuscript of *Spiritual Carnality* returned to him by a publisher, the fourth rejection. The covering letter informed him that he'd failed sufficiently to problematize the texts. On the title page someone had written, in faint, semi-erased pencil, *fatuously romantic.* He suspected that shrike Johanson, who was one of their readers, and who'd had it in for him ever since Mary Jo had left. After a brief interval of firm-chinned single coping she'd moved in on Johanson and they'd lived together for six months of blitzkrieg. Then she'd tried to hit him up for half the value of his house. Johanson had been blaming this on Richard ever since.

He was thinking about this, and about the batch of student papers in his briefcase: James Joyce from a Marxist perspective, or garbled structuralism seeping in from France to dilute the student brain yet further. The papers had to be marked by tomorrow. He had a satisfying fantasy of laying them all out in the muddy street and running over them with his car. He would say he'd been in an accident.

Coming towards him was a short, thickish woman in a black trench coat. She was carrying a large, brown tapestry bag; she seemed to be looking at the numbers on the houses, or possibly the snowdrops and crocuses on the lawns. Richard did not understand that it was Selena until she'd almost passed him.

"Selena," he said, touching her arm.

She turned up to him a blank face, the turquoise eyes dull.

"No," she said. "That's not my name." Then she peered more closely. "Richard. Is that you?" Either she was feigning pleasure, or she really felt it. Again, for him, there was a stab of unaccustomed joy.

He stood awkwardly. No wonder she'd had trouble recognizing him. He was prematurely gray, overweight; Mary Jo had told him, on the last, unpleasant occasion on which he'd seen her, that he was slug-colored. "I didn't know you were still here," he said. "I thought you'd moved out west."

"Traveled," she said. "I'm through with that." There was an edge to her voice he'd never heard before.

"And your work?" he said. It was always the thing to ask her.

"What work?" she said, and laughed.

"Your poetry." He was beginning to be alarmed. She was more matter-of-fact than he'd ever known her to be, but somehow this struck him as crazy.

"Poetry," she said with scorn. "I hate poetry. It's just this. This is all there is. This stupid city."

He went cold with dread. What was she saying, what had she done? It was like a blasphemy, it was like an act of desecration. Though how could he expect her to maintain faith in something he himself had so blatantly failed?

She'd been frowning, but now her face wrinkled in anxiety. She put a hand on his arm, stood on tiptoe. "Richard," she whispered. "What happened to us? Where did everyone go?" A mist came up with her, an odor. He recognized sweetish wine, a whiff of cat.

He wanted to shake her, enfold her, lead her to safety, wherever that might be. "We just changed, that's all," he said gently. "We got older."

"Change and decay in all around I see," she said, smiling in a way he did not like at all. "I'm not prepared for eternity."

It wasn't until she'd walked away—refusing tea, hurrying off as if she couldn't wait to see the last of him—that he realized she'd been quoting from a folk-song. It was the same one he'd heard sung to the autoharp in the coffee-house, the night he'd first seen her, standing under the single spotlight in her dragonfly shawl.

That, and a hymn. He wondered whether she'd become what his students called "religious."

Months later he heard she was dead. Then there was a piece in the paper. The details were vague. It was the picture that caught his eye: an earlier picture of her, from the jacket of one of her books. Probably there was nothing more recent, because she hadn't published anything for years. Even her death belonged to an earlier time; even the people in the small, closed world of poetry had largely forgotten about her.

Now that she's dead, however, she's become newly respectable. In several quarterly reviews the country has been lambasted for its indifference towards her, its withholding of recognition during her lifetime. There's a move afoot to name a parkette after her, or else a scholarship, and the academics are swarming like bot-flies. A thin volume has appeared, of essays on her work, shoddy stuff in Richard's opinion, flimsy and superficial; another one is rumored to be in the offing.

This is not the reason Richard is writing about her, however. Nor is it to cover his professional ass: he's going to be axed from the university anyway, there are new cut-backs, he lacks tenure, his head is on the block. It's merely because she's the one thing left he still values, or wants to write about. She is his last hope.

Isis in Darkness, he writes. *The Genesis*. It exalts him simply to form the words. He will exist for her at last, he will be created by her, he will have a place in her mythology after all. It will not be what he once wanted: not Osiris, not a blue-eyed god with burning wings. His are humbler metaphors. He will only be the archeologist; not part of the main story, but the one who stumbles upon it afterwards, making his way for his own obscure and battered reasons through the jungle, over the mountains, across the desert, until he discovers at last the pillaged and abandoned temple. In the ruined sanctuary, in the moonlight, he will find the Queen of Heaven and Earth and the Underworld lying in shattered white marble on the floor. He is the one who will sift through the rubble, groping for the shape of the past. He is the one who will say it has meaning. That too is a calling, that also can be a fate.

He picks up a filing-card, jots a small footnote on it in his careful writing, and replaces it neatly in the mosaic of paper he is making across his desk. His eyes hurt. He closes them and rests his forehead on his two fisted hands, summoning up whatever is left of his knowledge and skill, kneeling beside her in the darkness, fitting her broken pieces back together.

THE BOG MAN

Julie broke up with Connor in the middle of a swamp.

Julie silently revises: not exactly in the middle, not knee-deep in rotting leaves and dubious brown water. More or less on the edge; sort of within striking distance. Well, in an inn, to be precise. Or not even an inn. A room in a pub. What was available.

And not in a swamp anyway. In a bog. *Swamp* is when the water goes in one end and out the other, *bog* is when it goes in and stays in. How many times did Connor have to explain the difference? Quite a few. But Julie prefers the sound of *swamp*. It is mistier, more haunted. *Bog* is a slang word for toilet, and when you hear *bog* you know the toilet will be a battered and smelly one, and that there will be no toilet paper.

So Julie always says: *I broke up with Connor in the middle of a swamp.*

. . .

There are other things she revises as well. She revises Connor. She revises herself. Connor's wife stays approximately the same, but she was an invention of Julie's in the first place, since Julie never met her. Sometimes she used to wonder whether the wife really existed at all, or was just a fiction of Connor's, useful for keeping Julie at arm's length. But no, the wife existed all right. She was solid, and she became more solid as time went on.

Connor mentioned the wife, and the three children and the dog, fairly soon after he and Julie met. Well, not met. Slept together. It was almost the same thing.

Julie supposes, now, that he didn't want to scare her off by bringing up the subject too soon. She herself was only twenty, and too naïve to even think of looking for clues, such as the white circle on the ring finger. By the time he did get around to making a sheepish avowal or confession, Julie was in no position to be scared off. She was already lying in a motel room, wound loosely in a sheet. She was too tired to be scared off and also too amazed, and also too grateful. Connor was not her first lover but he was her first grown-up one, he was the first who did not treat sex as some kind of panty-raid. He took her body seriously, which impressed her no end.

At the time—what was the time? It was twenty years ago, or twenty-five. More like thirty. It was the early sixties; the precise year had to do with bubble-cut hairdos, with white lipstick, with dark rings penciled around the eyes. Also, purple was big as a color, although Julie herself favored the more rebellious black. She thought of herself as a sort of pirate. A dark-eyed, hawk-faced, shaggy-haired raider, making daring inroads on the borders of smug domestic settlements. Setting fire to the roofs, getting away with the loot, suiting herself. She studied modern philosophy, read Sartre on the side, smoked Gitanes, and cultivated a look of bored contempt. But inwardly, she was seething with unfocused excitement, and looking for someone to worship.

Connor was it. Julie was in her last year of university, in

Toronto, and Connor was her professor for Archeology—a one-hour-a-week course you could take instead of Religious Knowledge. Julie fell in love with his voice, rich and rough-edged, persuasive and abraded, rising and falling in the darkness like a stroking, insistent hand while he showed slides of Celtic tombs. Then she got tangled up with him in his office, where she'd gone intentionally late in the day to discuss her final term paper. Then they'd ended up in the motel. In that era such things happened more easily between students and their professors, without any fear on the part of the professors that they would be accused of sexual harassment and lose their jobs. There was no such phrase as "sexual harassment," even. There was no such thought.

At the time, Julie did not think the wife and the three kids and the dog had anything to do with her and Connor. She was too young to make such connections: the wife was as old as her own mother, almost, and women like that did not really have lives. She could not picture Connor in any context other than the motel rooms they would sneak into, or the apartments of Julie's friends, shambling, cheap apartments furnished with mattresses and decorated with egg cartons painted black nailed to the ceiling and with Chianti-bottle candle-holders. She did not think of him as having an existence apart from her: the wife and kids were just boring subsistence details, like brushing your teeth. Instead she saw him in glorious and noble isolation, a man singled out, like an astronaut, like a diver in a bell-jar, like a saint in a medieval painting, surrounded by a golden atmosphere of his own, a total-body halo. She wanted to be in there with him, participating in his radiance, basking in his light.

Because of her original awe of Connor—he was very smart, he knew a lot about ancient bones, about foreign travel, about how to mix drinks—she did not drive nearly as hard a bargain with him as she could have. But then, she had not been conscious of driving a bargain at all. She had been possessed by some notion of self-sacrifice; she had asked nothing for herself, except that Connor should continue to be superhuman.

. . .

The first motel was two months ago. Julie feels she has aged a great deal since then. She sits in the uncomfortable maroon plush armchair in her room in the Scottish pub in the small town near the bog, beside the window with its grubby white curtains and the clear northern light coming in, smoking Gitanes and drinking from a cold cup of tea she's brought up from her spectacularly awful breakfast with its limp, underdone bacon and its burnt grilled tomatoes. She sits and she smokes, and she knits.

Knitting is something she has just taken up again, having learned it as a child from a mother who believed in the female domestic virtues. She was also taught to crochet, to set in zippers, to polish silverware, to produce a gleaming toilet. This was baggage she'd discarded as soon as she hit Spinoza; two years, a year ago, she would have despised knitting. But there is not a lot to do in this town when Connor is not here. Julie has been up and down the main street several times; she has been drizzled on by the weather, she has been scowled at by the tweed-covered inhabitants. She has sat in the one café and drunk vile coffee and eaten bland and lard-flavored scones. She has inspected the ancient church: not a lot to see there. The stained-glass windows must have gone when the Presbyterians took over. Dead soldiers' names on the wall, as if God were interested.

The knitting is a last resort. Whatever else tiny Scottish towns like this one may lack, they all have wool stores. Julie had gone into the wool store, fended off inquiries as to her marital status and general mode of existence, and bought a pattern for a sweater—jumper, they call it here—and some big needles, and a number of skeins of dark gray wool. She'd wound the skeins into balls, and then she'd gone back to the store and bought an ugly tapestry bag with wooden handles to put them in.

What she's knitting is a sweater for Connor. She's doing the first sleeve. After a while she realizes that she's knitted the sleeve eight inches longer than it should be. It will make Connor look like an orangutan. Let him complain, she thinks. She leaves it that way and begins on the other sleeve. She intends to make it equally long.

While Julie knits, Connor is off inspecting the bog man. The bog man is why they are here.

When the bog-man find was announced, they were on the island of Orkney. Connor was looking at standing-stone ring sites and Julie was pretending to be his assistant. This was Connor's bright idea. It has allowed him to write off Julie as part of the expense of this particular expedition, but it has fooled nobody for long; at least not the barmen, at least not the maids in the various inns where they've been staying, who sneer at Julie in a dour, self-righteous way, despite the fact that Julie and Connor have taken care to book separate rooms. Maybe Julie should look more industrious; maybe she should carry notebooks and bustle around more.

Despite the sneers of the maids and the innuendoes of the barmen, Julie enjoyed herself quite a lot in Orkney. Not even the breakfasts dismayed her, not even the congealed oatmeal and the dry toast. Not even the dinners. It would have taken a good many rock-hard lamb chops, a great deal of over-fried fish, to dampen her spirits. It was her first trip across the Atlantic Ocean; she wanted things to be old and picturesque. More important, it was the first time she and Connor had been alone together for any length of time. She felt almost marooned with him. He felt it too; he was more uninhibited, less nervous about footsteps outside the door; and although he still had to get up and sneak out in the middle of the night, it was comforting to know that he only snuck next door.

The fields were green, the sun shone, the stone circles were suitably mysterious. If Julie stood in the centers of them and closed her eyes and kept still, she thought she could hear a sort of hum. Connor's theory was that these rings were not merely large harmless primitive calendars, erected for the purpose of determining the solstices. He thought they were the sites of ritual human sacrifices. This should have made them more sinister for Julie, but it did not. Instead she felt a connection with her ancestors. Her mother's family had come from this part of the world, more or less; from somewhere in the north of Scotland. She liked to sit among the standing stones and picture her ancestors running around naked and covered with blue tattoos, offering cups of blood to the gods, or whatever they did. Some bloodthirsty, indecipherable Pictish thing. The blood made them authentic, as authentic as the Mayans; or at least more authentic than all that clan and tartan and bagpipe stuff, which Julie found tedious and sentimental. There had been enough of it at her university, enough to last her for a while.

But then the bog man had been discovered and they'd had to pack and take the ferry to the mainland, where it was rainier. Julie would have liked to stay on Orkney but Connor was hot on the trail. He wanted to get there before the bog man had been completely, as he said, ruined. He wanted to get there before everyone else.

This particular bog man had been unearthed by a peat-digger, who'd cut into him accidentally with the sharp blade of his shovel, severing the feet. He'd thought he was a recent murder victim. It was hard for him to believe the bog man was two thousand years old: he was so perfectly preserved.

Some of the previously uncovered bog people aren't much to look at, judging by the pictures of them Connor has shown her. The bog water has tanned their skins and preserved their hair, but often their bones have dissolved and the weight of the peat has squashed them flat, so that they resemble extremely sick items of leather gear. Julie does not feel the same connection with them that she felt with the standing stones. The idea of human sacrifice is one thing, but the leftovers are something else again.

Before this trip, Julie didn't know very much about bog people, but now she does. For instance, this bog man died by being strangled with a twisted leather noose and sunk in the bog, probably as a sacrifice to the Great Goddess Nerthus, or someone like her, to insure the fertility of the crops. "After a sexual orgy of some kind," said Connor hopefully. "Those nature goddesses were voracious."

He proceeded to give examples of the things that had been sacrificed to the nature goddesses. Necklaces were a feature, and pots. Many pots and caldrons had been dug up out of the bogs, here and there around northern Europe. Connor has a map, with the sites marked and a list of what has been found at each one. He seems to think Julie ought to have memorized this list, that she ought to have its details at her fingertips, and acts surprised when it turns out she doesn't. Among his other virtues, or defects—Julie is just beginning to find it hard to tell the difference—Connor is very pedagogical. Julie has started to suspect him of trying to mold her mind. Into what, is the question.

As she knits, she makes a mental list of other things that get molded. Steamed Christmas puddings, poured-concrete lawn dwarfs, gelatin desserts, wobbly and bright pink and dotted with baby marshmallows. Thinking of these reminds Julie of her own mother, and then of Connor's wife.

It's astounding to her, the way this invisible wife has put on flesh, has gradually acquired solidity and presence. At the beginning of her two months with Connor the wife was a negligible shadow. Julie wasn't even that interested in going through Connor's wallet to look for family photos while he was out of the way in the shower.

She didn't bother then, but she's bothered since. Tucked behind the driver's license there's the whole family group, in color, taken on the lawn in summer: the wife, huge in a flowered dress and squinting; the three boys, with Connor's red hair, squinting also; the dog, a black Labrador that knew better than to look at the sun, its tongue out and drooling. The ordinariness, the plainness of this picture, offends Julie deeply. It interferes with her idea of Connor, with his status as romantic isolate; it diminishes him, and it has made Julie feel, for the first time, cheap and furtive. Extraneous, auxiliary. If they were all on a troika and the wolves were gaining, she has no doubt—looking at the dog, the red-headed kids, the suburban lawn—that she herself would be the first to be hurled off. Compared to those upper arms emerging from the short sleeves of the wife's florid dress—those laundry-toting, child-whacking arms—Julie, with her long dark pirate's hair and her twenty-four-inch waist, is a frill.

It's all very well for Connor to say that his wife doesn't understand him. This hefty, squinting woman looks as if she already understands a great deal too much. If she and Julie were to meet, she would not take Julie seriously. She would glance at Julie, merely glance, and then she would chuckle, and Julie would shrivel away to nothing.

Homely, is the word. That is the wife's ace up the sleeve, her insurance policy. Even though she looks like a truck tire, she has the territory staked out. She has the home. She has the house, she has the garage, she has the doghouse and the dog to put into it. She has Connor's children, forming together with them a single invincible monster with four heads and sixteen arms and legs. She has the cupboard where Connor hangs his clothes and the washing machine where his socks whirl on washdays, ridding themselves of the lint they've picked up from the bathmats in the rooms he's shared with Julie. Motels are a no man's land: they are not a territory, they cannot be defended. Julie has Connor's sexual attention, but the wife has Connor.

Julie has knitted enough for one day; she rolls the newly begun second sleeve around the needles and tucks it into her tapestry bag. She decides to walk out to the bog, to find Connor. She has not seen the bog before; she has not seen the bog man. She has picked up the impression from Connor that she would be in the way. Even he has dropped the pretense that she is an assistant in any real sense. She runs the risk of being treated as an interruption, but it's a risk she is now willing to take. Boredom is the mother of invention.

She picks up her shoulder bag from the chipped dressing table, peers at herself in the decaying mirror, pushing her hair back off her face. She is getting that sunless look. She ferrets in the closet for her raincoat, stuffs her Gitanes into her pocket, closes and locks the door and descends the stairs, skirting the cleaning woman, who gives her a baleful glare, and heads out into the mist.

She knows where the bog is; everyone knows. It takes her half an hour to walk there, along the road that is so old it has cut itself into the land like a rut. Connor goes there in a car that has been rented in Edinburgh by one of the other archeologists. No hope of renting a car in this town.

The bog does not look much like a bog. It looks more like a damp field; tall grasses grow on it, small shrubs. The chocolate-brown scars of the peat-cuttings open into it here and there. It would have been more watery in the days of the bog man; more like a lake. More convenient for drowning.

Connor is over by a roughly constructed tarpaulin shelter. There's another man with him, and several others out on the bog surface, fooling around in the peat-cutting, Julie supposes, to see what other buried treasures may come to light. Julie says hello but does not otherwise account for her presence. Let Connor explain it. Connor gives her a quick, annoyed glance.

"How did you get here?" he says, as if she's dropped from the sky.

"Walked," says Julie.

"Ah, the vigor of youth," says the other man, with a smile. He's fairly young himself, or anyway younger than Connor, a tall blond Norwegian. Another archeologist. He looks like something out of a Viking movie. The metallic scent of rivalry is in the air.

"Julie is my assistant," Connor says. The Norwegian knows better.

"Ah yes," he says mockingly. He gives Julie a bone-crushing handshake, gazing into her eyes while she flinches. "Did I hurt you?" he asks tenderly.

"Can I see the bog man?" Julie says. The Norwegian expresses mock surprise that she has not done so already, an assistant like her. With a proprietary air—he was in the area, he got there right after the Scots, he beat Connor to it—he ushers Julie into the tent.

The bog man is lying on a piece of canvas, curled on his side. His hands have deft, slender fingers, each fingerprint intact. His face is a little sunken-in but perfectly preserved; you can see every pore. His skin is dark brown, the bristles of his beard and the wisps of hair that escape from under his leather helmet are an alarming bright red. The colors are the effects of the tannic acid in the bog, Julie knows that. But still it is hard to picture him as any other color. His eyes are closed. He does not look dead or even asleep, however. Instead he seems to be meditating, concentrating: his lips are slightly pursed, a furrow of deep thought runs between his eyes. Around his neck is the twisted double cord used to strangle him. His two cut-off feet have been placed neatly beside him, like bedroom slippers waiting to be put on.

For a moment, Julie feels this digging-up, this unearthing of him, as a desecration. Surely there should be boundaries set upon the wish to know, on knowledge merely for its own sake. This man is being invaded. But the moment passes, and Julie goes out of the tent. Maybe she looks a little green in the face: after all, she's just seen a dead body. When she lights a cigarette her hands are shaky. The Norwegian gives her a solicitous look and places a hand beneath her elbow. Connor does not like this.

The three men who have been out at the peat-cutting return: one Scottish physical anthropologist and two workmen with peat-cutting spades. Lunch is proposed. The workmen have brought their own, and stay to guard the tent. The archeologists and Julie get into the Norwegian's rented car. There's no place to eat except the pub, so that is where they go.

For lunch Julie has bread and cheese, which is the safest thing, a lot safer than the flabby Scotch eggs and the barely warmed, fat-saturated meat pasties. The three men talk about the bog man. That he was a sacrifice is beyond a doubt. The question is, to which goddess? And at which solstice? Was he bumped off at the winter solstice, to make the sun return, or at the summer solstice, to make the crops prosper? Or perhaps in spring or fall?

An examination of the stomach—which they intend to remove, not here and now but later and in Edinburgh—will reveal clues. Seeds, grains, and the like. This has been done with all the other bog people that have been found, those who still had stomachs. Julie is just as glad she has stuck to the bread and cheese.

"Some have said the dead cannot talk," says the Norwegian, twinkling at Julie. Many of his remarks have been addressed to Connor, but aimed at her. Under the table he lays a hand, briefly, upon her knee. "But these bog men have many wonderful secrets to tell us. However, they are shy, like other men. They don't know how to convey their message. They must have a little help. Some encouragement. Don't you agree?"

Julie doesn't answer. There's no way she can answer without participating, beneath Connor's very nose, in what amounts to a flagrant proposition. It's a possibility; or would be, if she weren't in love with Connor.

"Perhaps such things as stomachs disgust you?" says the Norwegian. "Things of the flesh. My wife does not like them either." He gives her a hyena grin.

Julie smiles, and lights a Gitane. "Oh, do you have a wife?" she says brightly. "So does Connor. Maybe the two of you can discuss your wives."

She doesn't know why she has just said this. She doesn't look at Connor, but she can feel his anger coming at her like heat from a stove. She gathers up her purse and coat, still smiling, and walks out. What's running through her head is one of the first axioms from Logic: *A thing cannot be both self and non-self at the same time.* She has never been entirely convinced by this, and now she is even less so.

Connor does not follow her to her room. He doesn't reappear all afternoon. Julie knits and reads, knits and smokes. She's waiting. Something has changed, she has changed something, but she doesn't yet know what.

When Connor does show up, after sundown, he's morose. He says nothing about her piece of rudeness. He says nothing much at all. They have dinner with the Norwegian and the Scot, and the three of them talk about the bog man's feet. In some of these cases the feet have been tied together, to keep the dead from walking, returning to the land of the living, for revenge or some other reason. But not in this instance; or they think not. The cutting off of the feet may have interfered with something, of course. Ropes, thongs.

The Norwegian is no longer flirting; the looks he gives her are speculative, as if there is more to her than he'd thought and he'd like to know what. Julie doesn't care. She eats her ossified lamb chop and says nothing. She thinks of the bog man out there under his tarpaulin. Of all of them at this moment, she would rather be with him. He is of more interest.

She excuses herself before dessert. Connor, she thinks, will stay down there, drinking beer in the pub, and he does.

Around ten-thirty he knocks on Julie's door as usual, then comes in. Julie is already in bed, propped up on the pillows, knitting. She has been sure he will come, but also not sure. She shoves the wool and needles into her tapestry bag and waits to see what he will do.

Connor does not say anything. He takes off his sweater, drapes it over the back of the chair, undoes deliberately the buttons of his shirt. He is not looking at Julie, but into the wavering, patchy glass of the dressing-table mirror. His reflection there has a watery look, as if a lake bottom with decaying leaves on it is visible in glimpses beneath him, beneath his face and the whiter skin of his torso. In this light his red hair has faded. "I'm getting love-handles," he says, slapping his belly. This room flattens his beautiful voice, muffles it. "The curse of the middle-aged." It's a signal: if he's angry with her he's not going to mention it. They will go on as if nothing has happened. Maybe nothing has.

That's fine with her. She smiles. "No you aren't," she says. She doesn't like him doing this. He's not supposed to examine himself in mirrors or think about his appearance. Men are not supposed to.

Connor gives her a reproachful glance. "One of these days," he says, "you're going to run off with some young stud."

He has said such things before, about Julie's future lovers. Julie has not paid much attention. Now she does. Is this about the Norwegian; is he looking for reassurance? Does he want to hear from her that he is still young? Or is he telling her something real? Julie has never before thought of him as middle-aged, but now she can see that there might be a difference between her idea of him and his own idea of himself.

He climbs into the sagging bed with something like a sigh of resignation. He smells of beer and pub smoke. "You're wearing me out," he says. He has said this before also, and Julie has taken it as a sexual compliment. But he means it.

Julie turns out the bedside lamp. Once she wouldn't have bothered; once she wouldn't have had time. Once Connor would have turned it back on. Now he does not. He does not need to see her, she has been seen enough.

Meditatively and without ardor, he begins to run his hand along her: knee to thigh to hip, hip to knee. Julie lies stiffly, eyes wide open. The wind gusts through the cracks around the window, handfuls of rain are thrown against the glass. Light seeps in from under the door, and from the few streetlamps outside: in it the dressing-table mirror gleams like dark oil. Connor is a bulk beside her. His stroking does not excite her. It irritates her, like sandpaper, like the kneading paws of a cat. She feels that she's been demoted, against her will. What to her has been self-abandonment, to him has been merely sin. Grubby sin, sin of a small order. Cheating. Now he feels trapped by it. She is no longer a desire for him, she is a duty.

"I think we should get married," says Julie. She has no idea where these words have come from. But yes, this is what she thinks.

Connor's hand stops. Then it's withdrawn suddenly, as if Julie's body is hot, hot as coals, or else cold; as if Connor has found himself in bed with a mermaid, all scales and fishy slime from the waist down.

"What?" he says, in a shocked voice. An offended voice, as if she's insulted him.

"Forget it," says Julie. But Connor will not be able to forget it. She has said the unforgettable thing, and from now on it will be hopeless. But it has been hopeless anyway. Connor's unseen wife is in the bed with them, where she's been all along. Now she is materializing, taking on flesh. The springs creak with her added weight.

"Let's talk about it tomorrow," says Connor. He has recovered himself, he's plotting. "I love you," he adds. He kisses her. His mouth feels separate from him; soft, moist, coolish. It feels like uncooked bacon.

"I could use a drink," Julie says. Connor keeps a flask of Scotch in his room. Grateful that she has given him something to do, some small thing he can offer her instead of what she really wants, he clambers out of bed, pulls on his sweater and cords, and goes in search of it.

As soon as he's out of the room, Julie locks the door. Connor comes back. He shakes the doorknob; he whispers and taps, but she does not answer. She lies in her bed, shivering with grief and anger, waiting to see whether Connor loves her enough to kick at the door, to shout. Whether she's important enough. He does not. She is not. After a while he goes away.

Julie hunches up under the mound of damp coverings and tries without success to go to sleep. When at last she manages it, she dreams of the bog man, climbing in through her window, a dark tender shape, a shape of baffled longing, slippery with rain.

In the morning Connor makes another attempt. "If you don't answer me," he says through the keyhole, "I'll get them to break down the door. I'll tell them you've committed suicide."

"Don't flatter yourself," says Julie. This morning she's no longer sad. She's furious, and determined.

"Julie, what did I do?" says Connor. "I thought we were getting along so well." He sounds truly perplexed.

"We were," says Julie. "Go away."

She knows he will try to ambush her in the breakfast room. She waits him out, her stomach growling. Instead of eating she packs her bag, glancing from time to time out the window. At last she sees him leaving for the bog, in the Norwegian's car. There's a noon bus that will get her to another bus that will get her to a train for Edinburgh. She leaves behind the tapestry bag and the unfinished sweater. It's as good as a note.

Back in Toronto, Julie pins her hair into a brisk but demure French roll. She buys herself a beige cotton-twill suit and a white blouse, and deludes the Bell Telephone Company into hiring her as a personnel trainee. She's supposed to learn how to train other women in the job of complaint management. She doesn't intend to stay with this for long, but it's good money. She rents herself a large, empty apartment on the top floor of a house. She has no long-term plans. Although she was the one who left Connor, she feels deserted by him. At night she listens to the radio and cooks subsistence meals, and cries onto her plate.

After a while she resumes her black clothes, at night, and goes to folk clubs. She no longer smokes Gitanes, because they frighten men. She picks up with a boy she knew slightly from her Spinoza course. He makes a crack about windowless monads and buys her a beer, and tells her he used to be terrified of her. They end up in bed.

For Julie, this is like a romp with a litter of puppies. There's the same effect of gangly enthusiasm, of wriggling, of uncontrolled tongues. It's not passionate or even sensuous, but it's invigorating. Julie tells herself she's enjoying it, and she is. Or she would be, except for Connor. She wants him to know about it. Then she would really enjoy it. Even better would be the Norwegian. She should have taken advantage of that while she had the chance.

· · ·

Connor returns at the end of August. It doesn't take long for him to track her down.

"I've missed you," he says. "I think we should talk."

"What about?" says Julie warily. She thought she was over him, but it isn't true.

"Why can't we go back the way we were?" he says.

"Where were we?" says Julie.

Connor sighs. "Maybe we should get married, after all. I'll divorce her." He says this as if it's being torn out of him.

Julie starts to cry. She's crying because she no longer wants to marry Connor. She no longer wants him. The divinity is going out of him, like air. He is no longer a glorious blimp, larger than life and free in the heavens. Soon he will be just a damp piece of flabby rubber. She is mourning his collapse.

"I'll come right over," says Connor, in a pleased, consoling voice. Tears mean he's made headway.

"No," says Julie, and hangs up.

She puts on her black clothes, eats quickly, finds her cigarettes. She phones her boyish lover. She wants to pull him over her like a blanket, hug him to her like a stuffed animal. She wants comfort.

She goes out the door of her building and there is Connor, waiting for her. She has imagined him so much that she's forgotten what he looks like. He's shorter than she thought, he's saggier. His eyes look sunken and also too bright, a little wild. Is this what she's changed him into, or was he always like that?

"Julie," he says.

"No," says Julie. The knees of his brown cords are baggy. This is the only detail Julie finds actually repulsive. The rest just leaves her cold.

He reaches out a hand towards her. "I need you," he says. It's a trite line, a line from a mushy song, but he does need her. It's in his eyes. This is the worst thing yet. It was always supposed to be her who needed him; he was supposed to be well above such a weak thing as need.

"I can't help it," says Julie. She means she can't help it that things are the way they are, that she herself is without feeling for him; but it comes out more flippant, more pitiless, than she intended.

"Jesus Christ," says Connor. He moves as if to grab her. She dodges around him and begins to run down the street. She's got her black pants on, and her flat black shoes. Now that she's cut down on her smoking she's a decent runner.

What does she expect, now that she's in full flight? That he will go away finally, that he'll never be able to catch up? But he hasn't gone away, he is catching up. She can hear the thudding of his feet, the gasping of his breath. Her own breath is rasping in her throat; she's losing speed.

She's come to a cross-street, there's a phone booth. She ducks into it, slams the folding glass door shut, pushes against it with both of her feet, leaning her back against the phone-book shelf for leverage. The smell of ancient pee surrounds her. Then Connor is right there, outside, pushing at the door, pounding at it.

"Let me in!" he says.

Her heart thuds in panic. "No! No!" she yells. Her voice is tiny, as if she's in a soundproof booth. He presses his whole body against the glass door, wraps his arms as far around the phone booth as they will go.

"I love you!" he shouts. "God damn it, can't you hear me? I said I love you!" Julie covers her ears. She is truly frightened of him now, she's whimpering with fright. He's no longer anyone she knows; he's the universal child's nightmare, the evil violent thing, fanged and monstrous, trying to get in at the door. He mashes his face frontways into the glass, in a gesture of desperation or a parody of a kiss. She can see the squashed tip of his nose, his mouth deformed, the lips shoved back from the teeth.

Julie remembers that she's in a phone booth. Without taking her eyes off him, she fumbles in her purse for change. "I'll call the police," she screams at him. And she does.

. . .

It took them some time to come. By the time they did, Connor was gone. Whatever else he wanted, he did not want to be caught in the act of sexually attacking a phone booth. Or this is how Julie puts it, when she tells the story these days.

At first she did not tell it at all. It was too painful for her, in too complicated a way. Also she did not know what it was about. Was it about the way she had been taken advantage of, by some-one older and more experienced and superior to her in power? Or was it about how she had saved herself from an ogre in the nick of time? But Connor was not an ogre. She had loved him, uselessly. This was the painful thing: that she had been so wrong about him. That she was capable, once, of such abject self-deception. Or still is, because in some way she still misses him; him, or her own mistaken adoration.

Then, after she was married, after she was divorced, she began to tell the story of Connor once in a while. She told it late at night, after the kids were in bed and after a few drinks, always to women. It became part of an exchange, the price she was willing to pay for hearing other, similar stories. These were mystery stories. The mysterious objects in them were the men; men and their obscure behavior. Clues were discovered and examined, points of view exchanged. No definite solutions were found.

Now that she has married again, she tells it more frequently. By this time she concentrates on the atmosphere—the Scottish rain, the awful food in the pub, the scowling inhabitants of the town, the bog itself. She puts in the more comic elements: her own obsessive knitting, the long dangling sleeves, the lumpiness of the bed.

As for Connor, how can she explain him, him and his once-golden aura? She no longer tries. She skims over the worshipping love she once felt for him, which would be mawkish out loud. She skims over the wife, who is no longer the menacing rival of the piece: Julie has now been a wife herself, and feels a sneaking sympathy.

She skims over the grief.

She leaves out entirely any damage she may have caused to Connor. She knows the damage was done, was severe, at least at the time; but how can it be acknowledged without sounding like a form of gloating? It was unintentional on her part; more or less. At any rate, it does not really fit into the story.

Julie eases forward in her chair, leans her arms on the table, lights a cigarette. She still smokes, though not as much. Over the years she has put on weight around the face, and her waist has solidified. Also she's cut her hair; it's no longer a mane, it's fashionably short at the back and sides, with a wispy, puckish mop on the top. She wears silver earrings in the shape of starfish, an eccentric touch, the last vestige of her days of piracy. Except for these earrings, she looks like any woman of that age you might see, walking a dog or shopping, in one of the newly renovated neighborhoods.

"God knows," she says, "what I thought I was doing." She laughs, a rueful, puzzled laugh that is also indulgent.

The story has now become a story about her own stupidity, or call it innocence, which shines at this distance with a soft and mellowing light. The story is now like an artifact from a vanished civilization, the customs of which have become obscure. And yet every one of its physical details is clear to her: she can see the ruined mirror in the room, the slabs of dry toast at breakfast, the grasses moving on the surface of the bog. For all of this, she has total recall. With each retelling, she feels herself more present in it.

Connor, however, loses in substance every time she forms him in words. He become flatter and more leathery, more life goes out of him, he becomes more dead. By this time he is almost an anecdote, and Julie is almost old.

DEATH BY LANDSCAPE

Now that the boys are grown up and Rob is dead, Lois has moved to a condominium apartment in one of the newer waterfront developments. She is relieved not to have to worry about the lawn, or about the ivy pushing its muscular little suckers into the brickwork, or the squirrels gnawing their way into the attic and eating the insulation off the wiring, or about strange noises. This building has a security system, and the only plant life is in pots in the solarium.

Lois is glad she's been able to find an apartment big enough for her pictures. They are more crowded together than they were in the house, but this arrangement gives the walls a European look: blocks of pictures, above and beside one another, rather than one over the chesterfield, one over the fireplace, one in the front hall, in the old acceptable manner of sprinkling art around so it does not get too intrusive. This way has more of an impact. You know it's not supposed to be furniture.

None of the pictures is very large, which doesn't mean they aren't valuable. They are paintings, or sketches and drawings, by artists who were not nearly as well known when Lois began to buy them as they are now. Their work later turned up on stamps, or as silk-screen reproductions hung in the principals' offices of high schools, or as jigsaw puzzles, or on beautifully printed calendars sent out by corporations as Christmas gifts, to their less important clients. These artists painted mostly in the twenties and thirties and forties; they painted landscapes. Lois has two Tom Thomsons, three A. Y. Jacksons, a Lawren Harris. She has an Arthur Lismer, she has a J. E. H. MacDonald. She has a David Milne. They are pictures of convoluted tree trunks on an island of pink wave-smoothed stone, with more islands behind; of a lake with rough, bright, sparsely wooded cliffs; of a vivid river shore with a tangle of bush and two beached canoes, one red, one gray; of a yellow autumn woods with the ice-blue gleam of a pond half-seen through the interlaced branches.

It was Lois who'd chosen them. Rob had no interest in art, although he could see the necessity of having something on the walls. He left all the decorating decisions to her, while providing the money, of course. Because of this collection of hers, Lois's friends—especially the men—have given her the reputation of having a good nose for art investments.

But this is not why she bought the pictures, way back then. She bought them because she wanted them. She wanted something that was in them, although she could not have said at the time what it was. It was not peace: she does not find them peaceful in the least. Looking at them fills her with a wordless unease. Despite the fact that there are no people in them or even animals, it's as if there is something, or someone, looking back out.

When she was thirteen, Lois went on a canoe trip. She'd only been on overnights before. This was to be a long one, into the trackless wilderness, as Cappie put it. It was Lois's first canoe trip, and her last.

Cappie was the head of the summer camp to which Lois had been sent ever since she was nine. Camp Manitou, it was called; it was one of the better ones, for girls, though not the best. Girls of her age whose parents could afford it were routinely packed off to such camps, which bore a generic resemblance to one another. They favored Indian names and had hearty, energetic leaders, who were called Cappie or Skip or Scottie. At these camps you learned to swim well and sail, and paddle a canoe, and perhaps ride a horse or play tennis. When you weren't doing these things you could do Arts and Crafts and turn out dingy, lumpish clay ashtrays for your mother—mothers smoked more, then—or bracelets made of colored braided string.

Cheerfulness was required at all times, even at breakfast. Loud shouting and the banging of spoons on the tables were allowed, and even encouraged, at ritual intervals. Chocolate bars were rationed, to control tooth decay and pimples. At night, after supper, in the dining hall or outside around a mosquito-infested campfire ring for special treats, there were singsongs. Lois can still remember all the words to "My Darling Clementine," and to "My Bonnie Lies over the Ocean," with acting-out gestures: a rippling of the hands for "the ocean," two hands together under the cheek for "lies." She will never be able to forget them, which is a sad thought.

Lois thinks she can recognize women who went to these camps, and were good at it. They have a hardness to their handshakes, even now; a way of standing, legs planted firmly and farther apart than usual; a way of sizing you up, to see if you'd be any good in a canoe—the front, not the back. They themselves would be in the back. They would call it the stern.

She knows that such camps still exist, although Camp Manitou does not. They are one of the few things that haven't changed much. They now offer copper enameling, and functionless pieces of stained glass baked in electric ovens, though judging from the productions of her friends' grandchildren the artistic standards have not improved.

To Lois, encountering it in the first year after the war, Camp Manitou seemed ancient. Its log-sided buildings with the white cement in between the half-logs, its flagpole ringed with white-washed stones, its weathered gray dock jutting out into Lake Prospect, with its woven rope bumpers and its rusty rings for tying up, its prim round flowerbed of petunias near the office door, must surely have been there always. In truth it dated only from the first decade of the century; it had been founded by Cappie's parents, who'd thought of camping as bracing to the character, like cold showers, and had been passed along to her as an inheritance, and an obligation.

Lois realized, later, that it must have been a struggle for Cappie to keep Camp Manitou going, during the Depression and then the war, when money did not flow freely. If it had been a camp for the very rich, instead of the merely well off, there would have been fewer problems. But there must have been enough Old Girls, ones with daughters, to keep the thing in operation, though not entirely shipshape: furniture was battered, painted trim was peeling, roofs leaked. There were dim photographs of these Old Girls dotted around the dining hall, wearing ample woolen bathing suits and showing their fat, dimpled legs, or standing, arms twined, in odd tennis outfits with baggy skirts.

In the dining hall, over the stone fireplace that was never used, there was a huge molting stuffed moose head, which looked somehow carnivorous. It was a sort of mascot; its name was Monty Manitou. The older campers spread the story that it was haunted, and came to life in the dark, when the feeble and undependable lights had been turned off or, due to yet another generator failure, had gone out. Lois was afraid of it at first, but not after she got used to it.

Cappie was the same: you had to get used to her. Possibly she was forty, or thirty-five, or fifty. She had fawn-colored hair that looked as if it was cut with a bowl. Her head jutted forward, jigging like a chicken's as she strode around the camp, clutching notebooks and checking things off in them. She was like their minister in church: both of them smiled a lot and were anxious because they wanted things to go well; they both had the same overwashed skins and stringy necks. But all this disappeared when Cappie was leading a singsong, or otherwise leading. Then she was happy, sure of herself, her plain face almost luminous. She wanted to cause joy. At these times she was loved, at others merely trusted.

There were many things Lois didn't like about Camp Manitou, at first. She hated the noisy chaos and spoon-banging of the dining hall, the rowdy singsongs at which you were expected to yell in order to show that you were enjoying yourself. Hers was not a household that encouraged yelling. She hated the necessity of having to write dutiful letters to her parents claiming she was having fun. She could not complain, because camp cost so much money.

She didn't much like having to undress in a roomful of other girls, even in the dim light, although nobody paid any attention, or sleeping in a cabin with seven other girls, some of whom snored because they had adenoids or colds, some of whom had nightmares, or wet their beds and cried about it. Bottom bunks made her feel closed in, and she was afraid of falling out of top ones; she was afraid of heights. She got homesick, and suspected her parents of having a better time when she wasn't there than when she was, although her mother wrote to her every week saying how much they missed her. All this was when she was nine. By the time she was thirteen she liked it. She was an old hand by then.

Lucy was her best friend at camp. Lois had other friends in winter, when there was school and itchy woolen clothing and darkness in the afternoons, but Lucy was her summer friend.

She turned up the second year, when Lois was ten, and a Bluejay. (Chickadees, Bluejays, Ravens, and Kingfishers—these were the names Camp Manitou assigned to the different age groups, a sort of totemic clan system. In those days, thinks Lois, it was birds for girls, animals for boys: wolves, and so forth. Though some animals and birds were suitable and some were not. Never vultures, for instance; never skunks, or rats.)

Lois helped Lucy to unpack her tin trunk and place the folded clothes on the wooden shelves, and to make up her bed. She put her in the top bunk right above her, where she could keep an eye on her. Already she knew that Lucy was an exception, to a good many rules; already she felt proprietorial.

Lucy was from the United States, where the comic books came from, and the movies. She wasn't from New York or Hollywood or Buffalo, the only American cities Lois knew the names of, but from Chicago. Her house was on the lake shore and had gates to it, and grounds. They had a maid, all of the time. Lois's family only had a cleaning lady twice a week.

The only reason Lucy was being sent to *this* camp (she cast a look of minor scorn around the cabin, diminishing it and also offending Lois, while at the same time daunting her) was that her mother had been a camper here. Her mother had been a Canadian once, but had married her father, who had a patch over one eye, like a pirate. She showed Lois the picture of him in her wallet. He got the patch in the war. "Shrapnel," said Lucy. Lois, who was unsure about shrapnel, was so impressed she could only grunt. Her own two-eyed, unwounded father was tame by comparison.

"My father plays golf," she ventured at last.

"*Everyone* plays golf," said Lucy. "My *mother* plays golf."

Lois's mother did not. Lois took Lucy to see the outhouses and the swimming dock and the dining hall with Monty Manitou's baleful head, knowing in advance they would not measure up.

This was a bad beginning; but Lucy was good-natured, and accepted Camp Manitou with the same casual shrug with which she seemed to accept everything. She would make the best of it, without letting Lois forget that this was what she was doing.

However, there were things Lois knew that Lucy did not. Lucy scratched the tops off all her mosquito bites and had to be taken to the infirmary to be daubed with Ozonol. She took her T-shirt off while sailing, and although the counselor spotted her after a while and made her put it back on, she burnt spectacularly, bright red, with the X of her bathing-suit straps standing out in alarming white; she let Lois peel the sheets of whispery-thin burned skin off her shoulders. When they sang "Alouette" around the campfire, she did not know any of the French words. The difference was that Lucy did not care about the things she didn't know, whereas Lois did.

During the next winter, and subsequent winters, Lucy and Lois wrote to each other. They were both only children, at a time when this was thought to be a disadvantage, so in their letters they pretended to be sisters, or even twins. Lois had to strain a little over this, because Lucy was so blond, with translucent skin and large blue eyes like a doll's, and Lois was nothing out of the ordinary—just a tallish, thinnish, brownish person with freckles. They signed their letters LL, with the L's entwined together like the monograms on a towel. (Lois and Lucy, thinks Lois. How our names date us. Lois Lane, Superman's girlfriend, enterprising female reporter; "I Love Lucy." Now we are obsolete, and it's little Jennifers, little Emilys, little Alexandras and Carolines and Tiffanys.)

They were more effusive in their letters than they ever were in person. They bordered their pages with X's and O's, but when they met again in the summers it was always a shock. They had changed so much, or Lucy had. It was like watching someone grow up in jolts. At first it would be hard to think up things to say.

But Lucy always had a surprise or two, something to show, some marvel to reveal. The first year she had a picture of herself in a tutu, her hair in a ballerina's knot on the top of her head; she pirouetted around the swimming dock, to show Lois how it was done, and almost fell off. The next year she had given that up and was taking horseback riding. (Camp Manitou did not have horses.) The next year her mother and father had been divorced, and she had a new stepfather, one with both eyes, and a new house, although the maid was the same. The next year, when they had graduated from Bluejays and entered Ravens, she got her period, right in the first week of camp. The two of them snitched some matches from their counselor, who smoked illegally, and made a small fire out behind the farthest outhouse, at dusk, using their flashlights. They could set all kinds of fires by now; they had learned how in Campcraft. On this fire they burned one of Lucy's used sanitary napkins. Lois is not sure why they did this, or whose idea it was. But she can remember the feeling of deep satisfaction it gave her as the white fluff singed and the blood sizzled, as if some wordless ritual had been fulfilled.

They did not get caught, but then they rarely got caught at any of their camp transgressions. Lucy had such large eyes, and was such an accomplished liar.

This year Lucy is different again: slower, more languorous. She is no longer interested in sneaking around after dark, purloining cigarettes from the counselor, dealing in black-market candy bars. She is pensive, and hard to wake in the mornings. She doesn't like her stepfather, but she doesn't want to live with her real father either, who has a new wife. She thinks her mother may be having a love affair with a doctor; she doesn't know for sure, but she's seen them smooching in his car, out on the driveway, when her stepfather wasn't there. It serves him right. She hates her private school. She has a boyfriend, who is sixteen and works as a gardener's assistant. This is how she met him: in the garden. She describes to Lois what it is like when he kisses her—rubbery at first, but then your knees go limp. She has been forbidden to see him, and threatened with boarding school. She wants to run away from home.

Lois has little to offer in return. Her own life is placid and satisfactory, but there is nothing much that can be said about happiness. "You're so lucky," Lucy tells her, a little smugly. She might as well say *boring* because this is how it makes Lois feel.

Lucy is apathetic about the canoe trip, so Lois has to disguise her own excitement. The evening before they are to leave, she slouches into the campfire ring as if coerced, and sits down with a sigh of endurance, just as Lucy does.

Every canoe trip that went out of camp was given a special send-off by Cappie and the section leader and counselors, with the whole section in attendance. Cappie painted three streaks of red across each of her cheeks with a lipstick. They looked like three-fingered claw marks. She put a blue circle on her forehead with fountain-pen ink, and tied a twisted bandanna around her head and stuck a row of frazzle-ended feathers around it, and wrapped herself in a red-and-black Hudson's Bay blanket. The counselors, also in blankets but with only two streaks of red, beat on tom-toms made of round wooden cheese boxes with leather stretched over the top and nailed in place. Cappie was Chief Cappeosota. They all had to say "How!" when she walked into the circle and stood there with one hand raised.

Looking back on this, Lois finds it disquieting. She knows too much about Indians: this is why. She knows, for instance, that they should not even be called Indians, and that they have enough worries without other people taking their names and dressing up as them. It has all been a form of stealing.

But she remembers, too, that she was once ignorant of this. Once she loved the campfire, the flickering of light on the ring of faces, the sound of the fake tom-toms, heavy and fast like a scared heartbeat; she loved Cappie in a red blanket and feathers, solemn, as a chief should be, raising her hand and saying, "Greetings, my Ravens." It was not funny, it was not making fun. She wanted to be an Indian. She wanted to be adventurous and pure, and aboriginal.

"You go on big water," says Cappie. This is her idea—all their ideas—of how Indians talk. "You go where no man has ever trod. You go many moons." This is not true. They are only going for a week, not many moons. The canoe route is clearly marked, they have gone over it on a map, and there are prepared camp-sites with names which are used year after year. But when Cappie says this—and despite the way Lucy rolls up her eyes—Lois can feel the water stretching out, with the shores twisting away on either side, immense and a little frightening.

"You bring back much wampum," says Cappie. "Do good in war, my braves, and capture many scalps." This is another of her pretenses: that they are boys, and bloodthirsty. But such a game cannot be played by substituting the word "squaw." It would not work at all.

Each of them has to stand up and step forward and have a red line drawn across her cheeks by Cappie. She tells them they must follow in the paths of their ancestors (who most certainly, thinks Lois, looking out the window of her apartment and remembering the family stash of daguerreotypes and sepia-colored portraits on her mother's dressing table, the stiff-shirted, black-coated, grim-faced men and the beflounced women with their severe hair and their corseted respectability, would never have considered heading off onto an open lake, in a canoe, just for fun).

At the end of the ceremony they all stood and held hands around the circle, and sang taps. This did not sound very Indian, thinks Lois. It sounded like a bugle call at a military post, in a movie. But Cappie was never one to be much concerned with consistency, or with archeology.

After breakfast the next morning they set out from the main dock, in four canoes, three in each. The lipstick stripes have not come off completely, and still show faintly pink, like healing burns. They wear their white denim sailing hats, because of the sun, and thin-striped T-shirts, and pale baggy shorts with the cuffs rolled up. The middle one kneels, propping her rear end against the rolled sleeping bags. The counselors going with them are Pat and Kip. Kip is no-nonsense; Pat is easier to wheedle, or fool.

There are white puffy clouds and a small breeze. Glints come from the little waves. Lois is in the bow of Kip's canoe. She still can't do a J-stroke very well, and she will have to be in the bow or the middle for the whole trip. Lucy is behind her; her own J-stroke is even worse. She splashes Lois with her paddle, quite a big splash.

"I'll get you back," says Lois.

"There was a stable fly on your shoulder," Lucy says.

Lois turns to look at her, to see if she's grinning. They're in the habit of splashing each other. Back there, the camp has vanished behind the first long point of rock and rough trees. Lois feels as if an invisible rope has broken. They're floating free, on their own, cut loose. Beneath the canoe the lake goes down, deeper and colder than it was a minute before.

"No horsing around in the canoe," says Kip. She's rolled her T-shirt sleeves up to the shoulder; her arms are brown and sinewy, her jaw determined, her stroke perfect. She looks as if she knows exactly what she is doing.

The four canoes keep close together. They sing, raucously and with defiance; they sing "The Quartermaster's Store," and "Clementine," and "Alouette." It is more like bellowing than singing.

After that the wind grows stronger, blowing slantwise against the bows, and they have to put all their energy into shoving themselves through the water.

Was there anything important, anything that would provide some sort of reason or clue to what happened next? Lois can remember everything, every detail; but it does her no good.

They stopped at noon for a swim and lunch, and went on in the afternoon. At last they reached Little Birch, which was the first campsite for overnight. Lois and Lucy made the fire, while the others pitched the heavy canvas tents. The fireplace was already there, flat stones piled into a U. A burned tin can and a beer bottle had been left in it. Their fire went out, and they had to restart it. "Hustle your bustle," said Kip. "We're starving."

The sun went down, and in the pink sunset light they brushed their teeth and spat the toothpaste froth into the lake. Kip and Pat put all the food that wasn't in cans into a packsack and slung it into a tree, in case of bears.

Lois and Lucy weren't sleeping in a tent. They'd begged to be allowed to sleep out; that way they could talk without the others hearing. If it rained, they told Kip, they promised not to crawl dripping into the tent over everyone's legs: they would get under the canoes. So they were out on the point.

Lois tried to get comfortable inside her sleeping bag, which smelled of musty storage and of earlier campers, a stale salty sweetness. She curled herself up, with her sweater rolled up under her head for a pillow and her flashlight inside her sleeping bag so it wouldn't roll away. The muscles of her sore arms were making small pings, like rubber bands breaking.

Beside her Lucy was rustling around. Lois could see the glimmering oval of her white face.

"I've got a rock poking into my back," said Lucy.

"So do I," said Lois. "You want to go into the tent?" She herself didn't, but it was right to ask.

"No," said Lucy. She subsided into her sleeping bag. After a moment she said, "It would be nice not to go back."

"To camp?" said Lois.

"To Chicago," said Lucy. "I hate it there."

"What about your boyfriend?" said Lois. Lucy didn't answer. She was either asleep or pretending to be.

There was a moon, and a movement of the trees. In the sky there were stars, layers of stars that went down and down. Kip said that when the stars were bright like that instead of hazy it meant bad weather later on. Out on the lake there were two loons, calling to each other in their insane, mournful voices. At the time it did not sound like grief. It was just background.

The lake in the morning was flat calm. They skimmed along over the glassy surface, leaving V-shaped trails behind them; it felt like flying. As the sun rose higher it got hot, almost too hot. There were stable flies in the canoes, landing on a bare arm or leg for a quick sting. Lois hoped for wind.

They stopped for lunch at the next of the named campsites, Lookout Point. It was called this because, although the site itself was down near the water on a flat shelf of rock, there was a sheer cliff nearby and a trail that led up to the top. The top was the lookout, although what you were supposed to see from there was not clear. Kip said it was just a view.

Lois and Lucy decided to make the climb anyway. They didn't want to hang around waiting for lunch. It wasn't their turn to cook, though they hadn't avoided much by not doing it, because cooking lunch was no big deal, it was just unwrapping the cheese and getting out the bread and peanut butter, but Pat and Kip always had to do their woodsy act and boil up a billy tin for their own tea.

They told Kip where they were going. You had to tell Kip where you were going, even if it was only a little way into the woods to get dry twigs for kindling. You could never go anywhere without a buddy.

"Sure," said Kip, who was crouching over the fire, feeding driftwood into it. "Fifteen minutes to lunch."

"Where are they off to?" said Pat. She was bringing their billy tin of water from the lake.

"Lookout," said Kip.

"Be careful," said Pat. She said it as an afterthought, because it was what she always said.

"They're old hands," Kip said.

Lois looks at her watch: it's ten to twelve. She is the watch-minder; Lucy is careless of time. They walk up the path, which is dry earth and rocks, big rounded pinky-gray boulders or split-open ones with jagged edges. Spindly balsam and spruce trees grow to either side, the lake is blue fragments to the left. The sun is right overhead; there are no shadows anywhere. The heat comes up at them as well as down. The forest is dry and crackly.

It isn't far, but it's a steep climb and they're sweating when they reach the top. They wipe their faces with their bare arms, sit gingerly down on a scorching-hot rock, five feet from the edge but too close for Lois. It's a lookout all right, a sheer drop to the lake and a long view over the water, back the way they've come. It's amazing to Lois that they've traveled so far, over all that water, with nothing to propel them but their own arms. It makes her feel strong. There are all kinds of things she is capable of doing.

"It would be quite a dive off here," says Lucy.

"You'd have to be nuts," says Lois.

"Why?" says Lucy. "It's really deep. It goes straight down." She stands up and takes a step nearer the edge. Lois gets a stab in her midriff, the kind she gets when a car goes too fast over a bump. "Don't," she says.

"Don't what?" says Lucy, glancing around at her mischievously. She knows how Lois feels about heights. But she turns back. "I really have to pee," she says.

"You have toilet paper?" says Lois, who is never without it. She digs in her shorts pocket.

"Thanks," says Lucy.

They are both adept at peeing in the woods: doing it fast so the mosquitoes don't get you, the underwear pulled up between the knees, the squat with the feet apart so you don't wet your legs, facing downhill. The exposed feeling of your bum, as if someone is looking at you from behind. The etiquette when you're with someone else is not to look. Lois stands up and starts to walk back down the path, to be out of sight.

"Wait for me?" says Lucy.

Lois climbed down, over and around the boulders, until she could not see Lucy; she waited. She could hear the voices of the others, talking and laughing, down near the shore. One voice was yelling, "Ants! Ants!" Someone must have sat on an ant hill. Off to the side, in the woods, a raven was croaking, a hoarse single note.

She looked at her watch: it was noon. This is when she heard the shout.

She has gone over and over it in her mind since, so many times that the first, real shout has been obliterated, like a footprint trampled by other footprints. But she is sure (she is almost positive, she is nearly certain) that it was not a shout of fear. Not a scream. More like a cry of surprise, cut off too soon. Short, like a dog's bark.

"Lucy?" Lois said. Then she called "Lucy!" By now she was clambering back up, over the stones of the path. Lucy was not up there. Or she was not in sight.

"Stop fooling around," Lois said. "It's lunchtime." But Lucy did not rise from behind a rock or step out, smiling, from behind a tree. The sunlight was all around; the rocks looked white. "This isn't funny!" Lois said, and it wasn't, panic was rising in her, the panic of a small child who does not know where the bigger ones are hidden. She could hear her own heart. She looked quickly around; she lay down on the ground and looked over the edge of the cliff. It made her feel cold. There was nothing.

She went back down the path, stumbling; she was breathing too quickly; she was too frightened to cry. She felt terrible—guilty and dismayed, as if she had done something very bad, by mistake. Something that could never be repaired. "Lucy's gone," she told Kip.

Kip looked up from her fire, annoyed. The water in the billy can was boiling. "What do you mean, gone?" she said. "Where did she go?"

"I don't know," said Lois. "She's just gone."

No one had heard the shout, but then no one had heard Lois calling, either. They had been talking among themselves, by the water.

Kip and Pat went up to the lookout and searched and called, and blew their whistles. Nothing answered.

Then they came back down, and Lois had to tell exactly what had happened. The other girls all sat in a circle and listened to her. Nobody said anything. They all looked frightened, especially Pat and Kip. They were the leaders. You did not just lose a camper like this, for no reason at all.

"Why did you leave her alone?" said Kip.

"I was just down the path," said Lois. "I told you. She had to go to the bathroom." She did not say *pee* in front of people older than herself.

Kip looked disgusted.

"Maybe she just walked off into the woods and got turned around," said one of the girls.

"Maybe she's doing it on purpose," said another.

Nobody believed either of these theories.

They took the canoes and searched around the base of the cliff, and peered down into the water. But there had been no sound of falling rock; there had been no splash. There was no clue, nothing at all. Lucy had simply vanished.

That was the end of the canoe trip. It took them the same two days to go back that it had taken coming in, even though they were short a paddler. They did not sing.

After that, the police went in a motorboat, with dogs; they were the Mounties and the dogs were German shepherds, trained to follow trails in the woods. But it had rained since, and they could find nothing.

Lois is sitting in Cappie's office. Her face is bloated with crying, she's seen that in the mirror. By now she feels numbed; she feels as if she has drowned. She can't stay here. It has been too much of a shock. Tomorrow her parents are coming to take her away. Several of the other girls who were on the canoe trip are also being collected. The others will have to stay, because their parents are in Europe, or cannot be reached.

Cappie is grim. They've tried to hush it up, but of course everyone in camp knows. Soon the papers will know too. You can't keep it quiet, but what can be said? What can be said that makes any sense? "Girl vanishes in broad daylight, without a trace." It can't be believed. Other things, worse things, will be suspected. Negligence, at the very least. But they have always taken such care. Bad luck will gather around Camp Manitou like a fog; parents will avoid it, in favor of other, luckier places. Lois can see Cappie thinking all this, even through her numbness. It's what anyone would think.

Lois sits on the hard wooden chair in Cappie's office, beside the old wooden desk, over which hangs the thumbtacked bulletin board of normal camp routine, and gazes at Cappie through her puffy eyelids. Cappie is now smiling what is supposed to be a reassuring smile. Her manner is too casual: she's after something. Lois has seen this look on Cappie's face when she's been sniffing out contraband chocolate bars, hunting down those rumored to have snuck out of their cabins at night.

"Tell me again," says Cappie, "from the beginning."

Lois has told her story so many times by now, to Pat and Kip, to Cappie, to the police, that she knows it word for word. She knows it, but she no longer believes it. It has become a story. "I told you," she said. "She wanted to go to the bathroom. I gave her my toilet paper. I went down the path, I waited for her. I heard this kind of shout . . ."

"Yes," says Cappie, smiling confidingly, "but before that. What did you say to one another?"

Lois thinks. Nobody has asked her this before. "She said you could dive off there. She said it went straight down."

"And what did you say?"

"I said you'd have to be nuts."

"Were you mad at Lucy?" says Cappie, in an encouraging voice.

"No," says Lois. "Why would I be mad at Lucy? I wasn't ever mad at Lucy." She feels like crying again. The times when she has in fact been mad at Lucy have been erased already. Lucy was always perfect.

"Sometimes we're angry when we don't know we're angry," says Cappie, as if to herself. "Sometimes we get really mad and we don't even know it. Sometimes we might do a thing without meaning to, or without knowing what will happen. We lose our tempers."

Lois is only thirteen, but it doesn't take her long to figure out that Cappie is not including herself in any of this. By we she means Lois. She is accusing Lois of pushing Lucy off the cliff. The unfairness of this hits her like a slap. "I didn't!" she says.

"Didn't what?" says Cappie softly. "Didn't what, Lois?"

Lois does the worst thing, she begins to cry. Cappie gives her a look like a pounce. She's got what she wanted.

• • •

Later, when she was grown up, Lois was able to understand what this interview had been about. She could see Cappie's desperation, her need for a story, a real story with a reason in it; anything but the senseless vacancy Lucy had left for her to deal with. Cappie wanted Lois to supply the reason, to be the reason. It wasn't even for the newspapers or the parents, because she could never make such an accusation without proof. It was for herself: something to explain the loss of Camp Manitou and of all she had worked for, the years of entertaining spoiled children and buttering up parents and making a fool of herself with feathers stuck in her hair. Camp Manitou was in fact lost. It did not survive.

Lois worked all this out, twenty years later. But it was far too late. It was too late even ten minutes afterwards, when she'd left Cappie's office and was walking slowly back to her cabin to pack. Lucy's clothes were still there, folded on the shelves, as if waiting. She felt the other girls in the cabin watching her with speculation in their eyes. *Could she have done it? She must have done it.* For the rest of her life, she has caught people watching her in this way.

Maybe they weren't thinking this. Maybe they were merely sorry for her. But she felt she had been tried and sentenced, and this is what has stayed with her: the knowledge that she had been singled out, condemned for something that was not her fault.

Lois sits in the living room of her apartment, drinking a cup of tea. Through the knee-to-ceiling window she has a wide view of Lake Ontario, with its skin of wrinkled blue-gray light, and of the willows of Centre Island shaken by a wind, which is silent at this distance, and on this side of the glass. When there isn't too much pollution she can see the far shore, the foreign shore; though today it is obscured.

Possibly she could go out, go downstairs, do some shopping;

there isn't much in the refrigerator. The boys say she doesn't get out enough. But she isn't hungry, and moving, stirring from this space, is increasingly an effort.

She can hardly remember, now, having her two boys in the hospital, nursing them as babies; she can hardly remember getting married, or what Rob looked like. Even at the time she never felt she was paying full attention. She was tired a lot, as if she was living not one life but two: her own, and another, shadowy life that hovered around her and would not let itself be realized—the life of what would have happened if Lucy had not stepped sideways, and disappeared from time.

She would never go up north, to Rob's family cottage or to any place with wild lakes and wild trees and the calls of loons. She would never go anywhere near. Still, it was as if she was always listening for another voice, the voice of a person who should have been there but was not. An echo.

While Rob was alive, while the boys were growing up, she could pretend she didn't hear it, this empty space in sound. But now there is nothing much left to distract her.

She turns away from the window and looks at her pictures. There is the pinkish island, in the lake, with the intertwisted trees. It's the same landscape they paddled through, that distant summer. She's seen travelogues of this country, aerial photographs; it looks different from above, bigger, more hopeless: lake after lake, random blue puddles in dark green bush, the trees like bristles.

How could you ever find anything there, once it was lost? Maybe if they cut it all down, drained it all away, they might find Lucy's bones, some time, wherever they are hidden. A few bones, some buttons, the buckle from her shorts.

But a dead person is a body; a body occupies space, it exists somewhere. You can see it; you put it in a box and bury it in the ground, and then it's in a box in the ground. But Lucy is not in a box, or in the ground. Because she is nowhere definite, she could be anywhere.

And these paintings are not landscape paintings. Because there aren't any landscapes up there, not in the old, tidy European sense, with a gentle hill, a curving river, a cottage, a mountain in the background, a golden evening sky. Instead there's a tangle, a receding maze, in which you can become lost almost as soon as you step off the path. There are no backgrounds in any of these paintings, no vistas; only a great deal of foreground that goes back and back, endlessly, involving you in its twists and turns of tree and branch and rock. No matter how far back in you go, there will be more. And the trees themselves are hardly trees; they are currents of energy, charged with violent color.

Who knows how many trees there were on the cliff just before Lucy disappeared? Who counted? Maybe there was one more, afterwards.

Lois sits in her chair and does not move. Her hand with the cup is raised halfway to her mouth. She hears something, almost hears it: a shout of recognition, or of joy.

She looks at the paintings, she looks into them. Every one of them is a picture of Lucy. You can't see her exactly, but she's there, in behind the pink stone island or the one behind that. In the picture of the cliff she is hidden by the clutch of fallen rocks towards the bottom, in the one of the river shore she is crouching beneath the overturned canoe. In the yellow autumn woods she's behind the tree that cannot be seen because of the other trees, over beside the blue sliver of pond; but if you walked into the picture and found the tree, it would be the wrong one, because the right one would be further on.

Everyone has to be somewhere, and this is where Lucy is. She is in Lois's apartment, in the holes that open inwards on the wall, not like windows but like doors. She is here. She is entirely alive.

UNCLES

When she was nearly five, Su-
sanna did a tap dance on a cheese box. The cheese box was
cylindrical and made of wood, and decorated with white crêpe
paper and criss-crossed red ribbons to look like a drum. There
were two other cheese boxes with girls on them, but their decorations were blue. Susanna's was the only red one. She was in the
center, and she was also the youngest and the smallest. She had
to be lifted up. In the back, behind, there were three rows of
other girls who were not good enough to be up on cheese boxes.

It was for a recital. Susanna wore white socks and shoes
and a red hair-ribbon, and a white sailor dress with red braid
painstakingly stitched around the square collar by her mother,
who could pull herself up out of her daily lethargy for special
occasions and clothes. Before the recital Susanna became over-
excited backstage and had to go to the bathroom three times;

but once she was out on the stage, under the lights, she was fine and did not miss a beat.

The tune was "Anchors Aweigh." Everything for girls was military that year, because it was still the war. In the magazines there were pictures of women in white navy-cut shorts and middy blouses tied so that their tummies showed, and sailor hats cocked on their heads, looking sideways out with pert, impudent expressions, or with surprised pouts. These women, and these outfits, were said to be cute as a button, which was what was said about Susanna also. Susanna didn't see what was so cute about buttons. She found them hard to do up. But she knew when something good was being said about her.

It was the aunts who said it. They came with their husbands, the uncles, and sat in the front row, and hugged and kissed Susanna insincerely with their stiff arms and powdery faces. The uncles said little and did not hug or kiss. But Susanna wriggled away from the aunts and ran to be taken out of the auditorium in glory, swinging like a monkey between two of the uncles. It was the uncles that counted.

Susanna's mother came too, of course. Her father didn't come because he had been lost in the war. No one said *killed*, so Susanna got the idea that he was wandering around somewhere—she pictured a vacant lot, like the one at the end of her street, where she was forbidden to play—trying to find his way home.

Susanna repeated the tap dance on Sunday afternoons, for the benefit of the uncles. It was summer, and they would sit on the front porch after dinner. It was when people still sat on their front porches, in rocking chairs or on porch swings. Susanna's front porch had both; the uncles used the chairs. They would be sitting in the sun, blinking like bears, drinking a glass of beer each. They only drank one or two glasses, and never anything stronger; still, the aunts didn't think they should do it on the porch, where people could see. The uncles paid no attention. They blinked, and kept on drinking.

There were three of them, all fair-haired, balding, and red-faced. They were big men. You did not say "fat" about men.

They were strong, too; when they came over to mow Susanna's mother's lawn—they took turns doing it—they would use only one hand to push the lawn mower. They could hold one arm out straight and Susanna could sit on it, steadying herself against their massive beet-colored necks. They were not rich, but they were comfortable. That was what her mother called it, and Susanna thought this was right: they were like easy chairs. One of them had the hardware store, another was the bank manager, the third was in insurance. This was why the aunts worried about the beer.

Their conversation on the porch was minimal, so there was lots of room for Susanna, in her ruffled yellow cotton sun-dress, to hum the tune, stamp her feet, hop up and down, tap her heels and toes, do the salutes. The uncles would beam and clap, and afterwards she would get to sit on one of their enormous laps and smell their beery, soapy, shaving-lotion smells and go through their pockets, looking for the Chiclets that would be hidden there, or cajole them into doing tricks. They each had a different trick. One could blow smoke rings. Another could make his handkerchief into a mouse that would hop up his arm. The third would sing "Oh Susanna" in a funny woman's voice, squeaky and mournful, making lugubrious faces while he did it. It was about the only time his face ever changed expression.

"Oh Susanna, oh don't you cry for me. . . ." He would pretend to cry, and Susanna would pretend to console him. This, and these afternoons, set a high standard for delight which in later years she found hard to match.

Once in a while Susanna's mother would make an appearance on the porch. "Susanna, don't show off," she would say, or, "Susanna, don't pester your uncles." Then an uncle would say, "She's no trouble, Mae." Mostly Susanna's mother stayed in the kitchen, doing the dishes along with the aunts, which in Susanna's opinion was where they all belonged.

It was the aunts who brought most of the food for the Sunday dinners. They would arrive with roasts, lemon meringue pies, cookies, jars of their own pickles. Her mother might cook some potatoes, or make a jellied salad. Not a great deal was expected of her, because she was a war widow; she was still getting over the loss, and she had a child to bring up single-handed. On the outside it didn't seem to bother her. She was cheerful and rounded, and slow-moving by nature. The uncles had clubbed together to buy her the house, because she was their little sister, they had all grown up on a farm together, they were close.

The aunts had a hard time forgiving this. It would come up at the dinner table, in oblique references to how you had to scrimp to meet two sets of mortgage payments. The uncles would look at their wives with baffled reproach, and pass their plates down to Susanna's mother for another helping of mashed potatoes. You could not turn your own flesh and blood out on the streets to starve. Susanna knew this because she heard an uncle saying it as he lumbered down the front walk to his car.

"You didn't have to get such a big house," the aunt said. "It's almost as big as ours." Her high heels clipped on the cement as she hurried to keep up. All of the aunts were small, brisk women, with short legs.

Susanna was rocking in the giant white wicker rocker on the porch. She stopped rocking and scrunched down so her head was out of sight, to listen in.

"Come on, Adele," said the uncle. "You wouldn't want them living in a hut."

"She could get a job." This was an insult and the aunt knew it. It would mean that the uncle could not provide.

"Who would look after Susanna?" said the uncle, coming to a stop while he hunted for his keys. "Not you, that's for sure."

There was a note of bitterness in the uncle's voice that was new to Susanna. She felt sorry for him. For the aunt she felt no pity.

The uncles had children, but they were all boys, and older. They ran in a pack. They were told to sit up straight, to take their fingers out of their ears. They were told they had dirty fingernails. They were forbidden to talk back. "Don't be a smart aleck," they were told. They took it out on the local cats, in the vacant lot, with stones and slingshots. When they were over for Sunday dinner they ignored Susanna, or stared at her across the table with impersonal disdain. Susanna stayed out of their way, and within reach of the protective shadows cast by the uncles on the porch floor. The uncles would take care of her; she knew she was valuable to them. Yet in another way she was unimportant. It didn't really matter whether she sat up straight or not. She could put her finger into her ear, she could be a smart aleck. She could do whatever she liked, and still be cute as a button.

When she was old enough to go to school, the more sentimental of her teachers would attempt to coddle her, because she had no father. "But I have three uncles," she would say, and they would shake their heads and sigh. But three were better than one.

She did have a father, in a way. He was in two pictures: one of him alone, on the mantelpiece over the fireplace with its glass coals that lit up when you turned the switch, one on her mother's dressing table, of the two of them. In both he was in uniform. In the mantelpiece picture he was solemn and unsmiling, his dark eyes looking straight out from his thin face with an expression that made Susanna uneasy. Sometimes it was like longing, at others like determination; or fear, or anger.

The summer she was ten, Susanna decided to lay a flower in front of this picture every day. The flowers were always marigolds, because that was the only kind Susanna's mother ever got around to planting, in a straggly, unweeded row along the two sides of the front walk. Susanna kept the flowers up for almost a month. Her mother thought it was because she loved her father, or this is what Susanna overheard her telling the aunts in the kitchen. But it was not. How could she love someone she'd never known? The flowers were because she didn't love him, but was terrified he would find out. She didn't want him reading her thoughts, as it was well known God did; so why not dead people, who were in the same place? During this time his expression seemed to be one of pure and intense resentment. He hated it that he was dead, and Susanna herself was still alive.

At times she indulged in the old fantasy that he was only lost, that he would come back. But what if he did? She had several nightmares about it, this return: a long shadow coming in through her bedroom door, a pair of baleful eyes. He might not like her.

In the dressing-table picture he was different. For one thing, he was handsomer. He was looking down at the ground, smiling as if embarrassed. Her mother, apple-cheeked and only eighteen, too young, as she never tired of saying, was holding on to his arm, gazing at the camera with a soulful, pensive smirk Susanna had never seen on her in daily life. This picture was a disappointment, because it was a wedding picture but Susanna's mother was only wearing an ordinary hat and dress, not a long white gown. Susanna's mother explained that this was because of the war. People got married in a hurry then, they didn't have time for all the trimmings.

Susanna put it down to laziness: really it was because her mother couldn't be bothered. She cut corners in the housekeeping too. Susanna had seen the aunts tut-tutting over the part of the kitchen floor that was under the kitchen table, or taking the jumble of tea towels out of the drawer where they'd been stuffed and refolding them neatly, or twitching weeds out from among the ratty marigolds as they went down the walk. In some ways the aunts regarded Susanna's house as their own. They pointedly gave Susanna's mother fancy aprons for Christmas, but it did no good. The aprons too were stuffed into drawers, and Susanna's mother spent hours in the bath, or lying on her unmade bed in her slip reading women's magazines, or doing her nails in front of her dressing-table mirror even though she wasn't going out, and the dirty laundry accumulated in stale, fragrant little piles in the corners of her room. Even her sewing projects went as often as not unfinished; there were cut-out dresses pinned into bundles and crammed behind the magazine rack; there were stray threads on the chesterfield that clung to you when you stood up.

The good part was that she didn't expect Susanna to help that much. When she hit the age of twelve and began to take home economics in school, Susanna would sometimes clean up in self-defense, or nag her mother. This too had no effect.

Susanna herself was not lazy, though she didn't put much effort into the tea towels. That was aunts' work. She was thin and wiry, more like her father's side of the family, and she had the energy to go with it. In grade nine she did high jumping, and after that volleyball. She was in the Drama Club, which put on one-act plays with no dubious language in them, and also Gilbert and Sullivan operettas, varied occasionally by *Oklahoma!* and *Brigadoon*. The uncles came and sat in the front row, and beamed and clapped. They were older now and redder, and almost completely bald. They still came to do the lawn, though by this time they had a power mower. Susanna put her head to one side and smiled roguishly at them and sang and danced; though she knew that singing and dancing was no longer quite enough to please them.

One of the uncles, the one with the hardware store, took her aside one Sunday and told her she had a head on her shoulders and ought to use it. Another, the banker, said that a knowledge of double-entry bookkeeping never hurt you in any line of work, and showed her how to do it. The third said she should not throw herself away by getting married too soon, and that a woman who knew how to earn a living would never have to be dependent. Susanna knew they were talking about her mother. She paid attention.

In the last years of high school, Susanna studied hard and performed well—"performed well" was what the uncles said—and won a small scholarship to university. The uncles paid for the rest. Their own sons had not turned out as well as expected. One of them had become a ballet dancer.

Soon after Susanna graduated, in a black gown, with the uncles applauding and the aunts beside them smiling their tight little smiles because they knew how much it had cost, the uncles died, one after the other. They had remained big eaters, lovers of roast beef and fried chicken, of whipped cream and thick slabs of pie. They had never grown any thinner, only softer. They all died suddenly, of heart attacks, and for a time Susanna felt the world had gone deaf.

Each of the uncles had left some money to Susanna's mother, and some to Susanna as well. Not a lot, but it was too much for the aunts, who felt that enough had been spent on Susanna already. When, soon afterwards, her mother married again, a man she'd met through the uncles—a widower, once in the roofing business, now retired—and went to live in California, they were even more outraged. Her mother's worst crime was to sell the house and keep the money for herself. They felt it should have gone to them, because of everything the uncles had invested. That the widower was well off made it worse. They took his wealth as a personal affront.

This was a relief for Susanna: she no longer had to pretend to like them. She found a job in Toronto, a minor job with one of the big daily papers, compiling obituaries and birth notices and accounts of weddings and doing dogsbody research. She was marking time. The money from the uncles was stowed safely away in the bank. She could have used it to go on in school, in graduate school or one of the professions; her marks were high enough. But although she was good at a lot of things, there was nothing in particular she especially wanted to do.

It was the same with men. She'd had boyfriends over the years, by this time even a couple of lovers, but they were her own age and she had trouble taking them seriously. She told them jokes when the conversation got too personal, when they wanted to know what she really felt about them; she teased, asked impudent questions, pushed herself into their privacy. She had the knack of appearing warmly interested, although she was not. Curious was more like it. She assumed that flirtation was harmless, and that men would always indulge her. There had been some bad scenes. Angry boys had cornered her in the kitchen at parties, or in the room where the coats were piled, and accused her of leading them on. She'd had a couple of narrow escapes from parked cars. She'd laughed during a marriage proposal; she hadn't meant to be nasty, but the idea had struck her as funny. The man threw a plate at her, but he was drunk. It was at another party, and that was what men did at parties, then.

Susanna's reaction on these occasions was never anger, only surprise. The surprise was that she had somehow failed to please.

At the newspaper there was one man she truly admired. His name was Percy Marrow. He did most of the cultural things: not that there were many of them in Toronto, in those days. But if a play came to town it was Percy who reviewed it; or a dance company from England, or a visiting string quartet. Percy was known to take trips to New York, although the paper didn't pay for them. This gave him a cosmopolitan outlook: he was fond of decrying the provincial tastes and boorishness of the locals. He did jazz too, and film reviews, and sometimes a book. He did these things because nobody else at the paper wanted to do them.

"Percy does all the fairy stuff," was how it was explained to Susanna in the newsroom, which she had to walk through in order to get to her own cramped desk with its stacks of the newly married and the freshly dead. The newsroom prided itself on being rough on people. Percy Marrow was known there, behind his back, as Vedge, which was short for vegetable marrow. This was cruel, because it did describe his shape. From a distance, which was the only vantage point from which Susanna had yet seen him, he looked like Humpty Dumpty, or like Mr. Weatherbee, the bald egg-shaped high-school principal in the *Archie* comic books. The photo of his head that appeared above his weekly "Doings Around Town" column resembled a peeled potato, with small features glued on, old-fashioned rimless half-glasses, and a little tuft of fuzz on top.

"Don't be so mean," Susanna said when she first heard his nickname. "He's not fat. He's just *big*."

"Susie-Q's sticking up for Vedge," said Marty, the sports editor. "Vedge is a busy bee. He looks after himself."

"Vedge is a pompous twit," said Bill, who was an imported Cockney and did hard news such as murders. He was the paper's pet left-winger, excused because he was foreign. "All those artsy-fartsies are."

"Artsy-*fatsies*," said Cam, who covered politicians and was the most cynical of them all.

Susanna, who usually joked back with them, found herself getting angry. She thought they were jealous because Percy Marrow knew a lot more than they did, about more interesting things. But she knew better than to say this. She walked past them to her desk, through the smoke-filled, raucous, clattering air, followed by the yum-yum noises and lip-smackings that were their habit.

Susanna did not see a big future for herself in obituaries. She began to stalk Percy Marrow. She noted his comings and goings, and finally managed to introduce herself to him at the water cooler. She was impressed by him, but she was not intimidated. She told him she very much appreciated his work, that she thought of him as a sort of model. She suggested they have lunch: maybe he could give her some pointers? She was prepared for him to brush her off—after all, who was she?—but after a moment, during which his round face registered something like horror, he accepted. He was diffident, almost shy. Susanna got the impression he was not used to compliments.

Out on the street, he walked slowly, deliberately, with his toes out like a penguin. They went to a restaurant where no one from the newsroom was likely to go. Susanna thought he might order an exotic wine—she counted on him to know something about that, too—but he didn't. He explained that he never drank while he was working, and called for two glasses of water. Susanna was pleased: this was a reversal of newsroom values. The boys there came in from lunch reeking like a brewery; or they kept pocket flasks in their desks.

Susanna launched right in. What she wanted was a chance, a foot in the door. No one else at the paper was likely to give her one. She knew she was worth more than births and deaths. If she was no good, he could just dump her back, and no hard feelings.

Percy Marrow regarded her over the tops of his half-moon glasses. He was thinking. He took off the glasses and polished them on his tie. His hands were small; like many large men, he had delicate hands and feet. Up close, he was a lot younger than he looked in the paper. Not fifty at all. Probably no more than ten years older than she was; or maybe five. It was hard to tell, because of his shape.

Maybe she could try some art reviews, he said at last. That was something he didn't care for much himself. She would be doing him a favor. She could do them at night, and keep on with her regular job as well. That way she wouldn't be risking a lot.

"But I don't know anything about art," said Susanna, a little dismayed. She'd been picturing something more like a column, with her photo above it.

"You don't need to," Percy said. "I'll give you some samples." He paused to examine his green beans. "Overcooked," he pronounced. He was a picky eater. "Just remember, this place is still a small town. All the artists know and loathe one another. You'll find out how easy it is to get yourself hated."

"By writing bad reviews?" said Susanna.

"No. By writing good ones." For the first time, Percy smiled at her. It was an odd smile. It didn't quite go with his shyness. There was a hint of malice in it, as if he knew she was heading for trouble, and enjoyed the idea.

But that was only a flash, and she quickly decided she'd been wrong. The next instant his face was back to its usual repose; like a Buddha, she thought, or a benign walrus, without the tusks and mustache.

Over the next few months Percy took her on as a sort of protégée. They were both from small towns, maybe that was it. Maybe that was why she felt so comfortable with him. He helped her with her first reviews, commenting on the shape, the style; he suggested approaches, and praised her when in his estimation she'd done well. Susanna herself thought her reviews were fraudulent, but that nobody would be able to tell, considering what the other art reviews were like. She learned to use a lot of adjectives. They came in pairs, good and bad. The same painting could be energetic or chaotic, static or imbued with classical values, depending on whim. She got her first hate letter, and read it out to Percy at lunch.

Their lunches did not go unnoticed in the newsroom. "You got warm drawers for old Vedge, then?" said Bill.

"Don't be stupid," said Susanna, more defensively than she should have. "He's married." This was true. She'd met Percy's wife, bumped into the two of them in the elevator. Percy had stumbled over the introduction. The wife was a short, sharp-eyed woman, who had made it clear to Susanna that she did not care for her one bit.

"Married! Oh dew tell! Getting some on the side then is he? Shocking!"

"I would too if I had a wife like that. The Human Wen, we call her."

"Vedge is wen-pecked."

"If I gained two hundred pounds, would you screw me too, darling?"

"Susie-Q is sleeping her way up the ladder. We've seen those artsy-fartsy reviews of yours. By-line and all, very nice."

"Listen to this: 'Lyrical, uncluttered line, and good placing of spatial mass.' "

"What's that from, a girdle ad? Sounds like a nice bum to me."

"She's got old Vedge by the balls."

"If he has any."

"If he has any *left*."

"Bugger off," said Susanna, resorting to their own language. The newsroom hooted.

They were wrong, of course. There was nothing like that going on. True, Susanna felt protective about Percy, but he was like family. Right now she was seeing somebody new, an ad-agency man who wore ascots and whose hobby was sports cars. She regarded him with what she considered sexual passion, but underneath she thought he was lightweight. Percy was still the most intelligent man she'd ever met. This was how she accounted for him to her friends, of whom she now had many. Also he was kind.

He had begun giving her advice on how to dress. He had views on that subject, as on most others; now that he was used to her, she was hearing more of them. She looked forward to their meetings: she never knew what piece of advice or gossip, what hint or treasure he might have in store for her. He doled them out sparingly, one at a time, like candies.

An opening came up for a column. It was in the women's pages, but it was a column nevertheless. Anyway, there were some stirrings just then about women. It was an area that was heating up. "Women" were no longer only recipes and clothes and advice about dry underarms. Women were beginning to make a fuss.

The column was offered to Susanna, who took it. "Did you do that?" she asked Percy. But he smiled and was inscrutable, and polished his glasses.

Susanna invested some of the uncles' money in clothes, good ones, and some in an unlisted telephone number. Now that her picture was in the paper, above her column, she'd begun to attract heavy breathers. She made the mistake of mentioning this to Bill, and for a week the entire newsroom took turns calling her up on the office phone and breathing at her. She was getting sick of them.

Her column was fresh and breezy. These were the adjectives Percy applied to it. Informal and witty, but with punch. He thought she dealt with the issues, but in a questioning, balanced way. Not fanatical. He congratulated her, and after several months he mentioned that there was an opening at one of the bigger radio stations. The show was called "In Depth." They wanted someone who could do interviews on current topics; they were looking for a woman. It could be just the thing for her.

"I've never done anything like that before," said Susanna, waiting for encouragement.

"That doesn't matter," said Percy. "What they need is some-one who can improvise, and sound warm and friendly. You can do that, can't you? Because it's genuine." He had his glasses off and was polishing them. He raised his head; his eyes looked unprotected. There was something watery and pleading about them that alarmed her.

She laughed. "I can fake anything," she said. "I'll give it a try."

She got the job. The paper threw a farewell party for her, in the newsroom. It was June; they served gin and tonic in paper cups.

"A toast to Susie, who never blew her cool!"

"Or me either, worse luck!"

"Hey honeysuckle, where's your pal Vedge?"

"He couldn't come."

"His wife wouldn't let him. Get it? Haha."

"Shut up, you foul-mouthed twit. Susie's high society now."

In their own way they were sorry to see her go. Susanna was touched.

When the party was over and Susanna was heading for the door, Bill overtook her. "So old Vedge got you off the paper, eh?"

"What do you mean?" Susanna said. "This is a great job!"

"Not the point," said Bill. "You were getting too good. You were cramping his style."

"That's ungenerous," said Susanna.

"Maybe I'm a jaded old hack," said Bill. "But watch your back. You're getting too big."

"For my britches?" said Susanna lightly.

"Nope," said Bill. "For his *idea* of your britches." He kissed her on the cheek. "Give 'em hell," he said.

. . .

On the radio show Susanna was a natural. Everybody said so. Some called her brash, others unaffected, but all agreed that her prime asset was that she was not awed by power. She wasn't afraid to ask anybody anything, even if they were royalty, which they sometimes were. The interview would go along in a friendly, familiar groove while the visiting dignitary, the politician or scientist or expert or movie star, would settle down, and then would come Susanna's whammy—some backhanded question, such as who did their laundry or whether they thought rapists should be castrated—and the thing would break wide open. There were a couple of near-catastrophes and one walk-out, until Susanna learned to modify her impetuous delivery.

She quickly gathered a wide audience. People listened to her because she asked the questions they would never have the nerve or innocence to ask themselves. Also there was the shock value: anything at all might come out of her mouth. Some people found her too nosy, inconsiderate even, but they listened anyway. And the more successful her program became, the more the really important people wanted to be on it. There was a line-up.

Percy Mallow did a column on her, entitled "Oh Susanna." He said she was democracy in action.

She saw less of him now, naturally. There were few occasions for lunch, although she still kept in touch with him by phone. He was helpful with leads for the program. "Hi, what's the gossip?" she would say. He always had some little thing for her.

She would listen, jotting notes; but also she just liked the sound of his voice. It was reassuring; it made her feel valuable. Behind it she could sense the unseen chorus of her dead uncles, watching her from the darkness, presiding over her, approving of everything she did.

After a decade, when people were already calling her a national institution, Susanna made the transition to television. She liked it even better.

The radio show had been casual. The technicians had made faces at her through the glass or put plastic dog turds into her coffee: they'd liked trying to crack her up on air. There was none of that in television, and no old sweatshirts either. It was make-up and dress-up, and no funny business. Her face was good. Luckily she was not too beautiful; extreme beauty put people off. Instead she looked healthy, vitaminized. Trustworthy.

The television show was an early prime-time round-up; it was called "Moving Along." She found the glaring lights and the tension exhilarating, and though she paced nervously before every take, once the countdown started she was in full control. She attempted to keep the offhand tone of the radio show, and by and large she succeeded. There was less room for each subject, of course: people would spend more time listening than they would looking. Her friends said her nose twitched just before she went in for the killer question. She watched the tapes: they were right. But there wasn't a lot to be done about that, and it didn't seem to matter.

Meanwhile she had finally married. She invited her mother to the wedding, but got a vague answer. Soon after that her mother was no longer there. Susanna did not think of it as a death, but as a fading away, like a pattern on washed cloth. It was the continuation of something that had been happening all her life anyway.

Susanna's new husband was a corporation president with the improbable name of Emmett. Susanna was not sure what his company did; it seemed mostly to buy other companies. He was fifteen years older than she was and had three children already, so she did not feel under pressure to have any more. She was a good stepmother to the children; Emmett said she was like an older sister to them. Her artier friends found Emmett hard going, a boring old stuffed shirt in fact, and wondered why she had done a thing like that when she could have had her pick. But it was no secret to Susanna. Emmett was solid. He was reliable, he was always there, he knew things she didn't know, and he adored her.

Susanna and Emmett bought a large house in Rosedale and

Susanna had it done; the walls were painted to complement Emmett's extensive collection of Impressionist paintings. Some days, having coffee with Emmett on the terrace overlooking the beautifully kept garden, Susanna could hardly believe she'd grown up in that other house, the white frame oblong box with the porch swing and the tattered marigolds and her mother's lingerie in scented piles on the floor. Between the two houses was an enormous gap, almost like a memory lapse. The white frame house was on the other side, fading; like a mirage, like her mother. The uncles, however, were still vivid and clear.

Susanna and Emmett threw dinner parties, at which Emmett said little. They invited all kinds of people. Emmett enjoyed displaying the artistic bright lights to his business friends, and Susanna liked to get an overview for the show.

Percy Marrow and his wife were asked to some of the larger parties, at first; but this was not a success. The wife acted aggrieved, and although Susanna took him by the arm and steered him around as if he were a celebrity, Percy sulked.

"I miss our lunches," she said to him. But he ducked his head and did not answer. As she left him to greet a different guest, she caught him looking at her sideways: a curious, assessing look; or perhaps fearful, or annoyed. Unfathomable. Susanna was hurt. What had happened to their old mutual helpfulness and ease?

Once he called her. She hadn't seen him or talked to him for a while, although she still occasionally read his pieces in the paper. He was beginning to repeat himself. Getting older, she thought. It was bound to happen.

"Susanna. I thought maybe we might entice you back to the paper, to do a special piece. A sort of guest feature. We'd pay well, of course."

Susanna had no intention of writing anything for a newspaper, ever again. She remembered it as drudgery. But she thought it would be courteous to show some interest. "Oh Percy, how nice of you to think of me. What about?"

"Well, I thought it could be about the women's movement."

"Oh, not the dreaded women's movement! I mean, I know it's worthy, but hasn't it been done to death? We did a whole series two years ago."

"This would be a different angle." There was a pause; she imagined him polishing his glasses. "It would be—now that the women's movement has accomplished its goals, isn't it time to talk about men, and the ways they've been hurt by it?"

"Percy," she said carefully, "where do you get the idea that the women's movement has accomplished its goals?"

Another pause. "Well, there are a lot of successful women around."

"Such as for instance?"

"Such as you."

"Oh Vedge—oh Percy, I couldn't." Now I've torn it, she thought. I've called him *Vedge*. "I've done the cross-country surveys, I've done the personal-interest interviews. How about the wage differential? How about the rape statistics? How about all those single mothers on welfare? They're the fastest-growing group below the poverty line! I don't think *that* was a goal, do you? If I did a piece like that I'd get stoned to death!" She was babbling a little, covering up, afraid she'd hurt his feelings.

"It wasn't my idea," he said coldly. "I was told to ask you." She suspected he was lying.

The next time she saw him was years later. It was his own farewell party at the paper.

Bill called her about it. "Old Vedge is leaving," he said. "We thought you'd like to come."

"Really? He can't be retiring. He isn't old enough. What happened?"

"Let's just say it was mutual," said Bill, who was now the managing editor.

"I think that's sad," said Susanna.

"Don't worry about old Vedge," said Bill. "He's pretty chipper. He's already got other plans."

· · ·

Susanna took a taxi to the party. Emmett was out of town, so she went alone. She wore her fur coat, because it was December; it was a dark ranch mink, a present from Emmett. When she was standing on the sidewalk paying the taxi, somebody spat on the coat. She made a note not to wear it in public, only to private parties, where there were driveways.

The newspaper was still in the same building, but inside everything was different. Smooth veneer was in. The newsroom had been entirely redone. There was no more mess and boisterousness, no noisy clatter of typewriters. It was all computers now, with their green luminous underwater screens, silent as sharks. If there were dirty jokes, they were going on in whispers. Nobody smoked anymore; or not visibly.

Bill, entirely gray-haired now, was the only person she knew. It turned out she did know others, but they had been so transformed by age, and by the addition and subtraction of facial hair, that she failed to recognize them.

Percy himself was cheerful. He was better-looking as an older man than he'd been as a younger one. It was as if his shape had been a loose garment he'd had to grow into, and now it fitted. He was wearing a waistcoat and a watch chain; his glasses were perched on the end of his nose; he looked like Ben Franklin. Susanna felt a rush of affection for him.

"Ah," he said, "the star," and took her hands and showed her off. When that was over Susanna spoke with him privately.

"Aren't you sorry to be leaving?" she said. "After all those years?"

"Not at all," he said. "It was time. There are other things I want to do." He had a little secretive smile.

"What will you do first?" she asked him gently. She was worried for him. How would he make any money?

"I'm writing my memoirs," he said. "I've already got a publisher. They're giving me a nice-sized advance."

"Oh," she said dubiously, "that sounds fascinating."

"Actually it is," he said. "It's not so much about me; it's

about the people I've met. Quite a few interesting people, in my day." A pause. "You're in it."

"I am? Why?"

"Don't be coy," he said. "You're an important lady. You've cut quite a swath." Another pause. "I think you'll like it." He gave her a sunny but watchful smile, a plump middle-aged schoolboy with a surprise tucked away in his pocket.

"How sweet of you to include me," she said. It would be like the "Oh Susanna" piece he'd done about the radio show, no doubt. About her verve and her nerve. She squeezed his arm, and kissed him goodbye on the cheek.

When Percy's book came out half a year later, it was Bill who phoned her about it. "It's called *Stellar Heights*," he said. "All about the famous creeps he has known and whether their knickers smell. You're not going to like it."

"Why?" she said, not believing him. He'd always disliked Percy.

"Hatchet job, I'd say," said Bill. "Not just a mention. Twenty pages of you. Didn't know the old man had so much bad blood in him."

"Oh well," she said, catching her breath, trying to laugh it off. "Who's going to read it?"

"The paper's done an excerpt," he said. "The stuff about you. Almost the whole bit."

"Why me?" she said. The decision must have been his.

"Stands to reason," he said. "You're the most prominent person in there, at least for the locals, and he knocks the stuffing out of you."

"You shit!"

"Grow up, Susanna. You know the business. It sells copies. But I thought I should warn you."

"Thanks a heap," she said. She slammed down the phone and went out for a paper. There was a large picture of her, a smaller one of Percy, and a big black header: DRAGON LADY

REVEALED. She took it back to her office and closed the door, and told the switchboard she was in a meeting.

It was all there—their first encounter, their friendship, almost every conversation they'd ever had. Percy had total recall, of a kind. But it was all skewed. How she'd jumped him at the water cooler as a raw girl from the sticks, practically drooling with ambition. How he'd discovered her single-handed, and nursed her along through the initial fumblings and stumblings. How greener pastures had beckoned; how she never called her old newspaper buddies anymore. How her path was strewn with the bodies she'd stepped on, going up. A small-town girl with a heart of nails. As for her effortless friendliness, her enthusiastic, puppyish charm, her face of a healthy kindergarten teacher that photographed so well, it was all done with lights and mirrors, and calculation. There was even a hint—though he didn't come right out and say it—that she'd married Emmett for the money.

There was nothing about how she'd defended him, in the newsroom, behind his back; how she'd stuck up for him and trusted him. That was the worst: she'd trusted him. He was supposed to be older, benign, receptive, appreciative of her. Instead he was spiteful. Petty and malicious. She couldn't understand how she'd been so wrong about him, for so many years.

She went home and got into the bathtub, where she cried for half an hour with the soapsuds running down her. Then she called the studio. "I have to cancel tomorrow's show. Get a substitute, or something. I'm running a temperature."

"What is it? Nothing serious, I hope?" Already she could hear the speculation, the unasked questions.

"Who cares?" she said. "Tell them leukemia."

Then she called Bill at the newspaper. "Why did he do that to me?" she said. "I was always so nice to him."

"Tell a skunk about nice," said Bill. "I warned you, if you'll recall. Come on, buck up, you've had bad press before."

"Not that bad," she said. "Not from a *friend*."

"Some friend," said Bill. "Face it, Susie. He's jealous of you."

"Why is he jealous?" said Susanna. "Men shouldn't be jealous of women."

"Why not?" said Bill.

"Because they're *men*!" Because I'm the smallest, because I'm the youngest, she was thinking. Because they're bigger.

"Everyone in the universe is jealous of you, Susie-Q," said Bill in a tired voice. "You've got it all. *I'm* jealous of you. I just have different ways of showing it, like being the first to tell you about Vedge's nasty little book. It would help if you broke your leg or got a pimple. People don't think of you as human, you know."

"It isn't fair," said Susanna. She was crying again.

"Never mind, it's already coming back on him. I've seen two interviews already. He keeps trying to talk about himself, but all they want to ask him about is you. It's like watching an ant trying to get out of a teacup."

"*What* about me?"

"Whether you wear rubber underwear. Whether your claws light up in the dark. Whether you're really Superbitch. He hems and haws, and says you can be nice on occasion."

"Oh great. I'm going to have to *live* with this."

"Don't take it so hard, Susie," said Bill. "It's only old Vedge. Nobody cares what he says, really. You're all right, you know. A bit snobby of late, but all right."

"Thank you, Bill," said Susanna. She felt unusually grateful.

She climbed into bed in her dressing gown with a box of Kleenex, and tried to watch a cop show on television. She thought it would help to see people murdering one another. But she couldn't concentrate, so she turned it off. She was shivering. She felt betrayed, bereft. Loss of face, the Japanese called it. They knew. She felt as though her face, so carefully prepared and nourished, had been ripped off.

When Emmett came home he found her in the darkened bedroom. She held on to him, and cried and cried.

"Honey, what's wrong?" he said. "I've never seen you like this."

"Do you think I'm a nice person?" she said, while he cradled her and stroked her hair. She no longer trusted herself to know how he felt about her.

After a while she stopped crying and blew her nose. She asked him not to turn on the light; she knew her face was all puffy. "Maybe I've remembered my whole life wrong," she told him. "Maybe I've been wrong about everyone."

"I'll get you a drink," Emmett said, as if to a sick child. "We'll talk about it." He patted her hand and left the room.

Susanna lay propped up, gazing through the twilight at the opposite wall. She was back in the auditorium, at the recital, in her sailor suit and her flapping red hair-ribbon, on top of the cheese box in the glare of the lights, hopping up and down and grinning like a trained monkey, making a fool of herself. Sassy and obsolete; a show-off, an obnoxious brat. Was that how the uncles had really seen her, all along?

But the uncles were not there, in the front row where they should have been, beaming at her, applauding. Instead there was only her mother, in the wedding-picture dress, looking sideways off into the wings, bored by her dance. Beside her sat Susanna's lost father, come home at last from the war, from the vacant lot. He was in his uniform. His face was thin and resentful. He was staring at her with hate.

THE AGE
OF LEAD

The man has been buried for a hundred and fifty years. They dug a hole in the frozen gravel, deep into the permafrost, and put him down there so the wolves couldn't get to him. Or that is the speculation.

When they dug the hole the permafrost was exposed to the air, which was warmer. This made the permafrost melt. But it froze again after the man was covered up, so that when he was brought to the surface he was completely enclosed in ice. They took the lid off the coffin and it was like those maraschino cherries you used to freeze in ice-cube trays for fancy tropical drinks: a vague shape, looming through a solid cloud.

Then they melted the ice and he came to light. He is almost the same as when he was buried. The freezing water has pushed his lips away from his teeth into an astonished snarl, and he's a beige color, like a gravy stain on linen, instead of pink, but everything is still there. He even has eyeballs, except that they aren't white but the light brown of milky tea. With these tea-stained eyes he regards Jane: an indecipherable gaze, innocent, ferocious, amazed, but contemplative, like a werewolf meditating, caught in a flash of lightning at the exact split second of his tumultuous change.

Jane doesn't watch very much television. She used to watch it more. She used to watch comedy series, in the evenings, and when she was a student at university she would watch afternoon soaps about hospitals and rich people, as a way of procrastinating. For a while, not so long ago, she would watch the evening news, taking in the disasters with her feet tucked up on the chesterfield, a throw rug over her legs, drinking a hot milk and rum to relax before bed. It was all a form of escape.

But what you can see on the television, at whatever time of day, is edging too close to her own life; though in her life, nothing stays put in those tidy compartments, comedy here, seedy romance and sentimental tears there, accidents and violent deaths in thirty-second clips they call *bites*, as if they were chocolate bars. In her life, everything is mixed together. *Laugh, I thought I'd die*, Vincent used to say, a very long time ago, in a voice imitating the banality of mothers; and that's how it's getting to be. So when she flicks on the television these days, she flicks it off again soon enough. Even the commercials, with their surreal dailiness, are beginning to look sinister, to suggest meanings behind themselves, behind their façade of cleanliness, lusciousness, health, power, and speed.

Tonight she leaves the television on, because what she is seeing is so unlike what she usually sees. There is nothing sinister behind this image of the frozen man. It is entirely itself. *What you sees is what you gets*, as Vincent also used to say, crossing his eyes, baring his teeth at one side, pushing his nose into a horror-movie snout. Although it never was, with him.

. . .

The man they've dug up and melted was a young man. Or still is: it's difficult to know what tense should be applied to him, he is so insistently present. Despite the distortions caused by the ice and the emaciation of his illness, you can see his youthfulness, the absence of toughening, of wear. According to the dates painted carefully onto his nameplate, he was only twenty years old. His name was John Torrington. He was, or is, a sailor, a seaman. He wasn't an able-bodied seaman though; he was a petty officer, one of those marginally in command. Being in command has little to do with the ableness of the body.

He was one of the first to die. This is why he got a coffin and a metal nameplate, and a deep hole in the permafrost—because they still had the energy, and the piety, for such things, that early. There would have been a burial service read over him, and prayers. As time went on and became nebulous and things did not get better, they must have kept the energy for themselves; and also the prayers. The prayers would have ceased to be routine and become desperate, and then hopeless. The later dead ones got cairns of piled stones, and the much later ones not even that. They ended up as bones, and as the soles of boots and the occasional button, sprinkled over the frozen stony treeless relentless ground in a trail heading south. It was like the trails in fairy tales, of bread crumbs or seeds or white stones. But in this case nothing had sprouted or lit up in the moonlight, forming a miraculous pathway to life; no rescuers had followed. It took ten years before anyone knew even the barest beginnings of what had been happening to them.

All of them together were the Franklin Expedition. Jane has seldom paid much attention to history except when it has overlapped with her knowledge of antique furniture and real estate—"19th C. pine harvest table," or "Prime location Georgian center hall, impeccable reno"—but she knows what the Franklin Expedition was. The two ships with their bad-luck names have been on stamps—the *Terror*, the *Erebus*. Also she took it in school, along with a lot of other doomed expeditions. Not many of those explorers seemed to have come out of it very well. They were always getting scurvy, or lost.

What the Franklin Expedition was looking for was the Northwest Passage, an open seaway across the top of the Arctic, so people, merchants, could get to India from England without going all the way around South America. They wanted to go that way because it would cost less and increase their profits. This was much less exotic than Marco Polo or the headwaters of the Nile; nevertheless, the idea of exploration appealed to her then: to get onto a boat and just go somewhere, somewhere mapless, off into the unknown. To launch yourself into fright; to find things out. There was something daring and noble about it, despite all of the losses and failures, or perhaps because of them. It was like having sex, in high school, in those days before the Pill, even if you took precautions. If you were a girl, that is. If you were a boy, for whom such a risk was fairly minimal, you had to do other things: things with weapons or large amounts of alcohol, or high-speed vehicles, which at her suburban Toronto high school, back then at the beginning of the sixties, meant switchblades, beer, and drag races down the main streets on Saturday nights.

Now, gazing at the television as the lozenge of ice gradually melts and the outline of the young sailor's body clears and sharpens, Jane remembers Vincent, sixteen and with more hair then, quirking one eyebrow and lifting his lip in a mock sneer and saying, "Franklin, my dear, I don't give a damn." He said it loud enough to be heard, but the history teacher ignored him, not knowing what else to do. It was hard for the teachers to keep Vincent in line, because he never seemed to be afraid of anything that might happen to him.

He was hollow-eyed even then; he frequently looked as if he'd been up all night. Even then he resembled a very young old man, or else a dissipated child. The dark circles under his eyes were the ancient part, but when he smiled he had lovely small white teeth, like the magazine ads for baby foods. He made fun of everything, and was adored. He wasn't adored the way other boys were adored, those boys with surly lower lips and greased hair and a studied air of smoldering menace. He was adored like a pet. Not a dog, but a cat. He went where he liked, and nobody owned him. Nobody called him Vince.

Strangely enough, Jane's mother approved of him. She didn't usually approve of the boys Jane went out with. Maybe she approved of him because it was obvious to her that no bad results would follow from Jane's going out with him: no heartaches, no heaviness, nothing burdensome. None of what she called *consequences*. Consequences: the weightiness of the body, the growing flesh hauled around like a bundle, the tiny frill-framed goblin head in the carriage. Babies and marriage, in that order. This was how she understood men and their furtive, fumbling, threatening desires, because Jane herself had been a consequence. She had been a mistake, she had been a war baby. She had been a crime that had needed to be paid for, over and over.

By the time she was sixteen, Jane had heard enough about this to last her several lifetimes. In her mother's account of the way things were, you were young briefly and then you fell. You plummeted downwards like an overripe apple and hit the ground with a squash; you fell, and everything about you fell too. You got fallen arches and a fallen womb, and your hair and teeth fell out. That's what having a baby did to you. It subjected you to the force of gravity.

This is how she remembers her mother, still: in terms of a pendulous, drooping, wilting motion. Her sagging breasts, the downturned lines around her mouth. Jane conjures her up: there she is, as usual, sitting at the kitchen table with a cup of cooling tea, exhausted after her job clerking at Eaton's department store, standing all day behind the jewelry counter with her bum stuffed into a girdle and her swelling feet crammed into the mandatory medium-heeled shoes, smiling her envious, disapproving smile at the spoiled customers who turned up their noses at pieces of glittering junk she herself could never afford to buy. Jane's mother sighs, picks at the canned spaghetti Jane has heated up for her. Silent words waft out of her like stale talcum powder: *What can you expect*, always a statement, never a question. Jane tries at this distance for pity, but comes up with none.

As for Jane's father, he'd run away from home when Jane was five, leaving her mother in the lurch. That's what her mother called it—"running away from home"—as if he'd been an irresponsible child. Money arrived from time to time, but that was the sum total of his contribution to family life. Jane resented him for it, but she didn't blame him. Her mother inspired in almost everyone who encountered her a vicious desire for escape.

Jane and Vincent would sit out in the cramped backyard of Jane's house, which was one of the squinty-windowed little stuccoed wartime bungalows at the bottom of the hill. At the top of the hill were the richer houses, and the richer people: the girls who owned cashmere sweaters, at least one of them, instead of the Orlon and lambswool so familiar to Jane. Vincent lived about halfway up the hill. He still had a father, in theory.

They would sit against the back fence, near the spindly cosmos flowers that passed for a garden, as far away from the house itself as they could get. They would drink gin, decanted by Vincent from his father's liquor hoard and smuggled in an old military pocket flask he'd picked up somewhere. They would imitate their mothers.

"I pinch and I scrape and I work my fingers to the bone, and what thanks do I get?" Vincent would say peevishly. "No help from you, Sonny Boy. You're just like your father. Free as the birds, out all night, do as you like and you don't care one pin about anyone else's feelings. Now take out that garbage."

"It's love that does it to you," Jane would reply, in the resigned, ponderous voice of her mother. "You wait and see, my girl. One of these days you'll come down off your devil-may-care high horse." As Jane said this, and even though she was making fun, she could picture love, with a capital L, descending out of the sky towards her like a huge foot. Her mother's life had been a disaster, but in her own view an inevitable disaster, as in songs and movies. It was Love that was responsible, and in the face of Love, what could be done? Love was like a steamroller. There was no avoiding it, it went over you and you came out flat.

Jane's mother waited, fearfully and uttering warnings, but with a sort of gloating relish, for the same thing to happen to Jane. Every time Jane went out with a new boy her mother inspected him as a potential agent of downfall. She distrusted most of these boys; she distrusted their sulky, pulpy mouths, their eyes half-closed in the up-drifting smoke of their cigarettes, their slow, sauntering manner of walking, their clothing that was too tight, too full: too full of their bodies. They looked this way even when they weren't putting on the sulks and swaggers, when they were trying to appear bright-eyed and industrious and polite for Jane's mother's benefit, saying goodbye at the front door, dressed in their shirts and ties and their pressed heavy-date suits. They couldn't help the way they looked, the way they were. They were helpless; one kiss in a dark corner would reduce them to speechlessness; they were sleepwalkers in their own liquid bodies. Jane, on the other hand, was wide awake.

Jane and Vincent did not exactly go out together. Instead they made fun of going out. When the coast was clear and Jane's mother wasn't home, Vincent would appear at the door with his face painted bright yellow, and Jane would put her bathrobe on back to front and they would order Chinese food and alarm the delivery boy and eat sitting cross-legged on the floor, clumsily, with chopsticks. Or Vincent would turn up in a threadbare thirty-year-old suit and a bowler hat and a cane, and Jane would rummage around in the cupboard for a discarded church-going hat of her mother's, with smashed cloth violets and a veil, and they would go downtown and walk around, making loud remarks about the passers-by, pretending to be old, or poor, or crazy. It was thoughtless and in bad taste, which was what they both liked about it.

Vincent took Jane to the graduation formal, and they picked out her dress together at one of the second-hand clothing shops Vincent frequented, giggling at the shock and admiration they hoped to cause. They hesitated between a flame-red with falling-off sequins and a backless hip-hugging black with a plunge front, and chose the black, to go with Jane's hair. Vincent sent a poisonous-looking lime-green orchid, the color of her eyes, he said, and Jane painted her eyelids and fingernails to match. Vincent wore white tie and tails, and a top hat, all frayed Sally-Ann issue and ludicrously too large for him. They tangoed around the gymnasium, even though the music was not a tango, under the tissue-paper flowers, cutting a black swath through the sea of pastel tulle, unsmiling, projecting a corny sexual menace, Vincent with Jane's long pearl necklace clenched between his teeth.

The applause was mostly for him, because of the way he was adored. Though mostly by the girls, thinks Jane. But he seemed to be popular enough among the boys as well. Probably he told them dirty jokes, in the proverbial locker room. He knew enough of them.

As he dipped Jane backwards, he dropped the pearls and whispered into her ear, "No belts, no pins, no pads, no chafing." It was from an ad for tampons, but it was also their leitmotif. It was what they both wanted: freedom from the world of mothers, the world of precautions, the world of burdens and fate and heavy female constraints upon the flesh. They wanted a life without consequences. Until recently, they'd managed it.

The scientists have melted the entire length of the young sailor now, at least the upper layer of him. They've been pouring warm water over him, gently and patiently; they don't want to thaw him too abruptly. It's as if John Torrington is asleep and they don't want to startle him.

Now his feet have been revealed. They're bare, and white rather than beige; they look like the feet of someone who's been walking on a cold floor, on a winter day. That is the quality of the light that they reflect: winter sunlight, in early morning. There is something intensely painful to Jane about the absence of socks. They could have left him his socks. But maybe the others needed them. His big toes are tied together with a strip of cloth; the man talking says this was to keep the body tidily packaged for burial, but Jane is not convinced. His arms are tied to his body, his ankles are tied together. You do that when you don't want a person walking around.

This part is almost too much for Jane; it is too reminiscent. She reaches for the channel switcher, but luckily the show (it is only a show, it's only another show) changes to two of the historical experts, analyzing the clothing. There's a close-up of John Torrington's shirt, a simple, high-collared, pin-striped white-and-blue cotton, with mother-of-pearl buttons. The stripes are a printed pattern, rather than a woven one; woven would have been more expensive. The trousers are gray linen. Ah, thinks Jane. Wardrobe. She feels better: this is something she knows about. She loves the solemnity, the reverence, with which the stripes and buttons are discussed. An interest in the clothing of the present is frivolity, an interest in the clothing of the past is archeology; a point Vincent would have appreciated.

After high school, Jane and Vincent both got scholarships to university, although Vincent had appeared to study less, and did better. That summer they did everything together. They got summer jobs at the same hamburger heaven, they went to movies together after work, although Vincent never paid for Jane. They still occasionally dressed up in old clothes and pretended to be a weird couple, but it no longer felt careless and filled with absurd invention. It was beginning to occur to them that they might conceivably end up looking like that.

In her first year at university Jane stopped going out with other boys: she needed a part-time job to help pay her way, and that and the schoolwork and Vincent took up all her time. She thought she might be in love with Vincent. She thought that maybe they should make love, to find out. She had never done such a thing, entirely; she had been too afraid of the untrustworthiness of men, of the gravity of love, too afraid of consequences. She thought, however, that she might trust Vincent.

But things didn't go that way. They held hands, but they didn't hug; they hugged, but they didn't pet; they kissed, but they didn't neck. Vincent liked looking at her, but he liked it so much he would never close his eyes. She would close hers and then open them, and there would be Vincent, his own eyes shining in the light from the streetlamp or the moon, peering at her inquisitively as if waiting to see what odd female thing she would do next, for his delighted amusement. Making love with Vincent did not seem altogether possible.

(Later, after she had flung herself into the current of opinion that had swollen to a river by the late sixties, she no longer said "making love"; she said "having sex." But it amounted to the same thing. You had sex, and love got made out of it whether you liked it or not. You woke up in a bed or more likely on a mattress, with an arm around you, and found yourself wondering what it might be like to keep on doing it. At that point Jane would start looking at her watch. She had no intention of being left in any lurches. She would do the leaving herself. And she did.)

Jane and Vincent wandered off to different cities. They wrote each other postcards. Jane did this and that. She ran a co-op food store in Vancouver, did the financial stuff for a diminutive theater in Montreal, acted as managing editor for a small publisher, ran the publicity for a dance company. She had a head for details and for adding up small sums—having to scrape her way through university had been instructive—and such jobs were often available if you didn't demand much money for doing them. Jane could see no reason to tie herself down, to make any sort of soul-stunting commitment, to anything or anyone. It was the early seventies; the old heavy women's world of girdles and precautions and consequences had been swept away. There were a lot of windows opening, a lot of doors: you could look in, then you could go in, then you could come out again.

She lived with several men, but in each of the apartments there were always cardboard boxes, belonging to her, that she never got around to unpacking; just as well, because it was that much easier to move out. When she got past thirty she decided it might be nice to have a child, sometime, later. She tried to figure out a way of doing this without becoming a mother. Her own mother had moved to Florida, and sent rambling, grumbling letters, to which Jane did not often reply.

Jane moved back to Toronto, and found it ten times more interesting than when she'd left it. Vincent was already there. He'd come back from Europe, where he'd been studying film; he'd opened a design studio. He and Jane met for lunch, and it was the same: the same air of conspiracy between them, the same sense of their own potential for outrageousness. They might still have been sitting in Jane's garden, beside the cosmos flowers, drinking forbidden gin and making fun.

Jane found herself moving in Vincent's circles, or were they orbits? Vincent knew a great many people, people of all kinds; some were artists and some wanted to be, and some wanted to know the ones who were. Some had money to begin with, some made money; they all spent it. There was a lot more talk about money, these days, or among these people. Few of them knew how to manage it, and Jane found herself helping them out. She developed a small business among them, handling their money. She would gather it in, put it away safely for them, tell them what they could spend, dole out an allowance. She would note with interest the things they bought, filing their receipted bills: what furniture, what clothing, which *objets*. They were delighted with their money, enchanted with it. It was like milk and cookies for them, after school. Watching them play with their money, Jane felt responsible and indulgent, and a little matronly. She stored her own money carefully away, and eventually bought a townhouse with it.

All this time she was with Vincent, more or less. They'd tried being lovers but had not made a success of it. Vincent had gone along with this scheme because Jane had wanted it, but he was elusive, he would not make declarations. What worked with other men did not work with him: appeals to his protective instincts, pretenses at jealousy, requests to remove stuck lids from jars. Sex with him was more like a musical workout. He couldn't take it seriously, and accused her of being too solemn about it.

She thought he might be gay, but was afraid to ask him; she dreaded feeling irrelevant to him, excluded. It took them months to get back to normal.

He was older now, they both were. He had thinning temples and a widow's peak, and his bright inquisitive eyes had receded even further into his head. What went on between them continued to look like a courtship, but was not one. He was always bringing her things: a new, peculiar food to eat, a new grotesquerie to see, a new piece of gossip, which he would present to her with a sense of occasion, like a flower. She in her turn appreciated him. It was like a yogic exercise, appreciating Vincent; it was like appreciating an anchovy, or a stone. He was not everyone's taste.

There's a black-and-white print on the television, then another: the nineteenth century's version of itself, in etchings. Sir John Franklin, older and fatter than Jane had supposed; the *Terror* and the *Erebus*, locked fast in the crush of the ice. In the high Arctic, a hundred and fifty years ago, it's the dead of winter. There is no sun at all, no moon; only the rustling northern lights, like electronic music, and the hard little stars.

What did they do for love, on such a ship, at such a time? Furtive solitary gropings, confused and mournful dreams, the sublimation of novels. The usual, among those who have become solitary.

Down in the hold, surrounded by the creaking of the wooden hull and the stale odors of men far too long enclosed, John Torrington lies dying. He must have known it; you can see it on his face. He turns towards Jane his tea-colored look of puzzled reproach.

Who held his hand, who read to him, who brought him water? Who, if anyone, loved him? And what did they tell him about whatever it was that was killing him? Consumption, brain fever, Original Sin. All those Victorian reasons, which meant nothing and were the wrong ones. But they must have been comforting. If you are dying, you want to know why.

. . .

In the eighties, things started to slide. Toronto was not so much
fun anymore. There were too many people, too many poor people. You could see them begging on the streets, which were
clogged with fumes and cars. The cheap artists' studios were
torn down or converted to coy and upscale office space; the artists
had migrated elsewhere. Whole streets were torn up or knocked
down. The air was full of windblown grit.

People were dying. They were dying too early. One of Jane's
clients, a man who owned an antique store, died almost overnight of bone cancer. Another, a woman who was an entertainment lawyer, was trying on a dress in a boutique and had a heart
attack. She fell over and they called the ambulance, and she
was dead on arrival. A theatrical producer died of AIDS, and a
photographer; the lover of the photographer shot himself, either
out of grief or because he knew he was next. A friend of a friend
died of emphysema, another of viral pneumonia, another of
hepatitis picked up on a tropical vacation, another of spinal
meningitis. It was as if they had been weakened by some mysterious agent, a thing like a colorless gas, scentless and invisible, so
that any germ that happened along could invade their bodies,
take them over.

Jane began to notice news items of the kind she'd once
skimmed over. Maple groves dying of acid rain, hormones in the
beef, mercury in the fish, pesticides in the vegetables, poison
sprayed on the fruit, God knows what in the drinking water. She
subscribed to a bottled spring-water service and felt better for a
few weeks, then read in the paper that it wouldn't do her much
good, because whatever it was had been seeping into everything.
Each time you took a breath, you breathed some of it in. She
thought about moving out of the city, then read about toxic
dumps, radioactive waste, concealed here and there in the
countryside and masked by the lush, deceitful green of waving
trees.

. . .

Vincent has been dead for less than a year. He was not put into the permafrost or frozen in ice. He went into the Necropolis, the only Toronto cemetery of whose general ambience he approved; he got flower bulbs planted on top of him, by Jane and others. Mostly by Jane. Right now John Torrington, recently thawed after a hundred and fifty years, probably looks better than Vincent.

A week before Vincent's forty-third birthday, Jane went to see him in the hospital. He was in for tests. Like fun he was. He was in for the unspeakable, the unknown. He was in for a mutated virus that didn't even have a name yet. It was creeping up his spine, and when it reached his brain it would kill him. It was not, as they said, responding to treatment. He was in for the duration.

It was white in his room, wintry. He lay packed in ice, for the pain. A white sheet wrapped him, his white thin feet poked out the bottom of it. They were so pale and cold. Jane took one look at him, laid out on ice like a salmon, and began to cry.

"Oh Vincent," she said. "What will I do without you?" This sounded awful. It sounded like Jane and Vincent making fun, of obsolete books, obsolete movies, their obsolete mothers. It also sounded selfish: here she was, worrying about herself and her future, when Vincent was the one who was sick. But it was true. There would be a lot less to do, altogether, without Vincent.

Vincent gazed up at her; the shadows under his eyes were cavernous. "Lighten up," he said, not very loudly, because he could not speak very loudly now. By this time she was sitting down, leaning forward; she was holding one of his hands. It was thin as the claw of a bird. "Who says I'm going to die?" He spent a moment considering this, revised it. "You're right," he said. "They got me. It was the Pod People from outer space. They said, 'All I want is your poddy.' "

Jane cried more. It was worse because he was trying to be funny. "But what *is* it?" she said. "Have they found out yet?"

Vincent smiled his ancient, jaunty smile, his smile of detachment, of amusement. There were his beautiful teeth, juvenile as ever. "Who knows?" he said. "It must have been something I ate."

Jane sat with the tears running down her face. She felt desolate: left behind, stranded. Their mothers had finally caught up to them and been proven right. There were consequences after all; but they were the consequences to things you didn't even know you'd done.

The scientists are back on the screen. They are excited, their earnest mouths are twitching, you could almost call them joyful. They know why John Torrington died; they know, at last, why the Franklin Expedition went so terribly wrong. They've snipped off pieces of John Torrington, a fingernail, a lock of hair, they've run them through machines and come out with the answers.

There is a shot of an old tin can, pulled open to show the seam. It looks like a bomb casing. A finger points: it was the tin cans that did it, a new invention back then, a new technology, the ultimate defense against starvation and scurvy. The Franklin Expedition was excellently provisioned with tin cans, stuffed full of meat and soup and soldered together with lead. The whole expedition got lead-poisoning. Nobody knew it. Nobody could taste it. It invaded their bones, their lungs, their brains, weakening them and confusing their thinking, so that at the end those that had not yet died in the ships set out in an idiotic trek across the stony, icy ground, pulling a lifeboat laden down with toothbrushes, soap, handkerchiefs, and slippers, useless pieces of junk. When they were found ten years later, they were skeletons in tattered coats, lying where they'd collapsed. They'd been heading back towards the ships. It was what they'd been eating that had killed them.

Jane switches off the television and goes into her kitchen—all white, done over the year before last, the outmoded butcher-block counters from the seventies torn out and carted away—to make herself some hot milk and rum. Then she decides against it; she won't sleep anyway. Everything in here looks ownerless. Her toaster oven, so perfect for solo dining, her microwave for the vegetables, her espresso maker—they're sitting around waiting for her departure, for this evening or forever, in order to assume their final, real appearances of purposeless objects adrift in the physical world. They might as well be pieces of an exploded spaceship orbiting the moon.

She thinks about Vincent's apartment, so carefully arranged, filled with the beautiful or deliberately ugly possessions he once loved. She thinks about his closet, with its quirky particular outfits, empty now of his arms and legs. It has all been broken up now, sold, given away.

Increasingly the sidewalk that runs past her house is cluttered with plastic drinking cups, crumpled soft-drink cans, used take-out plates. She picks them up, clears them away, but they appear again overnight, like a trail left by an army on the march or by the fleeing residents of a city under bombardment, discarding the objects that were once thought essential but are now too heavy to carry.

WEIGHT

I am gaining weight. I'm not getting bigger, only heavier. This doesn't show up on the scales: technically, I'm the same. My clothes still fit, so it isn't size, what they tell you about fat taking up more space than muscle. The heaviness I feel is in the energy I burn up getting myself around: along the sidewalk, up the stairs, through the day. It's the pressure on my feet. It's a density of the cells, as if I've been drinking heavy metals. Nothing you can measure, although there are the usual nubbins of flesh that must be firmed, roped in, worked off. *Worked*. It's all getting to be too much work.

Some days, I think I'm not going to make it. I will have a hot flash, a car crash. I will have a heart attack. I will jump out the window.

This is what I'm thinking as I look at the man. He's a rich man, that goes without saying: if he weren't rich, neither of us would be here. He has excess money, and I'm trying to get some of it out of him. Not for myself; I'm doing nicely, thank you. For what we used to call charity and now call good causes. To be precise, a shelter for battered women. Molly's Place, it's called. It's named after a lawyer who was murdered by her husband, with a claw hammer. He was the kind of man who was good with tools. He had a workbench in the cellar. The lathe, the vise, the buzz saw, the works.

I wonder if this other man, sitting so cautiously across the tablecloth from me, has a workbench in the cellar too. He doesn't have the hands for it. No calluses or little nicks. I don't tell him about the claw hammer, or about the arms and legs hidden here and there around the province, in culverts, in wooded glades, like Easter eggs or the clues in some grotesque treasure hunt. I know how easily frightened such men can be by such possibilities. Real blood, the kind that cries out to you from the ground.

We've been through the ordering, which involved the rueful production of the reading glasses, by both of us, for the scanning of the ornate menu. We have at least one thing in common: our eyes are going. Now I smile at him and twiddle the stem of my wineglass, and lie judiciously. This isn't even my thing, I tell him. I got sucked into it because I have a hard time saying no. I'm doing it for a friend. This is true enough: Molly was a friend.

He smiles and relaxes. *Good*, he's thinking. I am not one of those earnest women, the kind who lecture and scold and open their own car doors. He's right, it's not my style. But he could have figured that out from my shoes: women like that do not wear shoes like this. I am not, in a word, *strident*, and his instinct in asking me to lunch has been justified.

This man has a name, of course. His name is Charles. He's already said "Call me Charles." Who knows what further delights await me? "Chuck" may lie ahead, or "Charlie." *Charlie is my darling. Chuck, you big hunk.* I think I'll stick with Charles.

The appetizers arrive, leek soup for him, a salad for me, endive with apples and walnuts, veiled with a light dressing, as the menu puts it. *Veiled.* So much for brides. The waiter is another out-of-work actor, but his grace and charm are lost on Charles, who does not reply when ordered to enjoy his meal.

"Cheers," says Charles, lifting his glass. He's already said this once, when the wine appeared. Heavy going. What are the odds I can get through this lunch without any mention of the bottom line?

Charles is about to tell a joke. The symptoms are all there: the slight reddening, the twitch of the jaw muscle, the crinkling around the eyes.

"What's brown and white and looks good on a lawyer?"

I've heard it. "I'll bite. What?"

"A pit bull."

"Oh, that's terrible. Oh, you are awful."

Charles allows his mouth a small semicircular smile. Then, apologetically: "I didn't mean woman lawyers, of course."

"I don't practice anymore. I'm in business, remember?" But maybe he meant Molly.

Would Molly have found this joke funny? Probably. Certainly, at first. When we were in law school, working our little butts off because we knew we had to be twice as good as the men to end up less than the same, we used to go out for coffee breaks and kill ourselves laughing, making up silly meanings for the things we got called by the guys. Or women in general got called: but we knew they meant us.

"*Strident.* A brand of medicated toothpick used in the treatment of gum disease."

"Okay! *Shrill.* As in the Greater Shrill. A sharp-beaked shorebird native to the coasts of . . ."

"California? Yes. *Hysteria?*"

"A sickly scented flowering vine that climbs all over Southern mansions. *Pushy?*"

"Pushy. That's a hard one. Rude word pertaining to female anatomy, uttered by drunk while making a pass?"

"Too obvious. How about a large, soft velvet cushion . . ."

"Pink or mauve . . ."

"Used for reclining on the floor, while . . ."

"While watching afternoon soaps," I finished, not satisfied. There should be something better for *pushy*.

Molly was pushy. Or you could call it determined. She had to be, she was so short. She was like a scrappy little urchin, big eyes, bangs over the forehead, tough little chin she'd stick out when she got mad. She was not from a good home. She'd made it on brains. Neither was I, so did I; but it affected us differently. I, for instance, was tidy and had a dirt phobia. Molly had a cat named Catty, a stray, of course. They lived in cheerful squalor. Or not squalor: disorder. I couldn't have stood it myself, but I liked it in her. She made the messes I wouldn't allow myself to make. Chaos by proxy.

Molly and I had big ideas, then. We were going to change things. We were going to break the code, circumvent the old boys' network, show that women could do it, whatever it might be. We were going to take on the system, get better divorce settlements, root for equal pay. We wanted justice and fair play. We thought that was what the law was for.

We were brave but we had it backwards. We didn't know you had to begin with the judges.

But Molly didn't hate men. With men, Molly was a toad-kisser. She thought any toad could be turned into a prince if he was only kissed enough, by her. I was different. I knew a toad was a toad and would remain so. The thing was to find the most congenial among the toads and learn to appreciate their finer points. You had to develop an eye for warts.

I called this compromise. Molly called it cynicism.

Across the table, Charles is having another glass of wine. I think he's deciding that I am a good sport. So necessary in a woman with whom you're considering what used to be called an illicit affair; because that's what this lunch is really about. It's a mutual interview, for positions vacant. I could have made my charity plea in Charles's office and been turned down shortly and sweetly. We could have kept it formal.

Charles is good-looking, in the way such men are, although if you saw him on a street corner, lacking a shave and with his hand out, you might not think so. Such men always seem the same age. They were longing to be this age when they were twenty-five, and so they imitated it; and after they pass this age, they will try to imitate it again. The weightiness of authority is what they want, and enough youth left to enjoy it. It's the age called *prime*, like beef. They all have that beefy thing about them. A meaty firmness. They all play something: they begin with squash, progress through tennis, end with golf. It keeps them in trim. Two hundred pounds of hot steak. I should know.

All of it swathed in expensive, dark blue suiting, with a thin stripe. A conservative tie down the front, maroon with a little design. This one has horses.

"Are you fond of horses, Charles?"

"What?"

"Your tie."

"Oh. No. Not particularly. Gift from my wife."

I'm putting off any renewed mention of Molly's Place until dessert—never make the heavy pitch till then, says business etiquette, let the guy suck up a little protein first—although if my guess is right and Charles too is concerned with his weight, we'll both skip dessert and settle for double espresso. Meanwhile I listen to Charles, as I dole out the leading questions. The ground rules are being quietly set forth: two mentions of the wife already, one of the son at college, one of the teenage daughter. Stable family is the message. It goes with the horse tie.

It's the wife who interests me most, of course. If men like Charles did not have wives, they would have to invent them. So useful for fending off the other women, when they get too close. If I were a man, that's what I'd do: invent a wife, put one together from bits and pieces—a ring from a pawnshop, a photo or two snuck out of someone else's album, a three-minute sentimental drone about the kids. You could fake phone calls to yourself;

you could send postcards to yourself, from Bermuda, or better, Tortuga. But men like Charles are not thorough in their deceptions. Their killer instincts are directed elsewhere. They get snarled up in their own lies or give themselves away by shifty eye movements. At heart, they are too sincere.

I, on the other hand, have a devious mind and little sense of guilt. My guilt is about other things.

I already suspect what his wife will look like: overtanned, overexercised, with alert leathery eyes and too many tendons in her neck. I see these wives, packs of them, or pairs or teams, loping around in their tennis whites, over at the club. Smug, but jumpy. They know this is a polygamous country in all but name. I make them nervous.

But they should be grateful to me for helping them out. Who else has the time and expertise to smooth the egos of men like Charles, listen to their jokes, lie to them about their sexual prowess? The tending of such men is a fading art, like scrimshaw or the making of woolen rose mantelpiece decorations. The wives are too busy for it, and the younger women don't know how. I know how. I learned in the old school, which was not the same as the one that gave out the ties.

Sometimes, when I have amassed yet another ugly wristwatch or brooch (they never give rings; if I want one of those, I buy it myself), when I've been left stranded on a weekend in favor of the kids and the Georgian Bay cottage, I think about what I could tell and I feel powerful. I think about dropping an acerbic, vengeful little note through the mailbox of the wife in question, citing moles strategically placed, nicknames, the perverse habits of the family dog. Proofs of knowledge.

But then, I would lose power. Knowledge is power only as long as you keep your mouth shut.

Here's one for you, Molly: *menopause.* A pause while you reconsider men.

At long last, here come the entrées, with a flashing of teeth and a winsome glance from the waiter. Veal scallopini for Charles, who has evidently not seen those sordid pictures of calves being bleached in the dark, seafood *en brochette* for me. I think: Now he'll say "Cheers" again, and then he'll make some comment about seafood being good for the sex drive. He's had enough wine for that, by now. Next he'll ask me why I'm not married.

"Cheers," says Charles. "Any oysters in there?"

"No," I say. "Not a one."

"Too bad. Good for what ails you."

Speak for yourself, I think. He gives a meditative chew or two. "How is it that you never got married—an attractive woman like you?"

I shrug my shoulder pads. What should I tell him? The dead fiancé story, lifted from the great-aunt of a friend? No. Too World War I. Should I say, "I was too choosy"? That might scare him: if I'm hard to please, how will he manage to please me?

I don't really know why. Maybe I was waiting for the big romance. Maybe I wanted True Love, with the armpits airbrushed out and no bitter aftertaste. Maybe I wanted to keep my options open. In those days, I felt that anything could happen.

"I was married once," I say, sadly, regretfully. I hope to convey that I did the right thing but it didn't work out. Some jerk let me down, in a way too horrible to go into. Charles is free to think he could have done better.

There's something final about saying you were married once. It's like saying you were dead once. It shuts them up.

It's funny that Molly was the one who got married. You'd think it would have been me. I was the one who wanted the two children, the two-car garage, the antique dining table with the rose bowl in the center. Well, at least I've got the table. Other women's husbands sit at it, and I feed them omelets, while they surreptitiously consult their watches. But if they even hint at divorcing the wife, I heave them out the door so fast they can't remember where they left their boxer shorts. I've never wanted to make the commitment. Or I've never wanted to take the risk. It amounts to the same thing.

There was a time when my married friends envied me my singleness, or said they did. I was having fun, ran the line, and they were not. Recently, though, they've revised this view. They tell me I ought to travel, since I have the freedom for it. They give me brochures with palm trees on them. What they have in mind is a sunshine cruise, a shipboard romance, an adventure. I can think of nothing worse: stuck on an overheated boat with a lot of wrinkly women, all bent on adventure too. So I stuff the brochures in behind the toaster oven, so convenient for solo dinners, where one of these days they will no doubt burst into flame.

I get enough adventure, right around here. It's wearing me out.

Twenty years ago, I was just out of law school; in another twenty, I'll be retired, and it will be the twenty-first century, for whoever's counting. Once a month I wake in the night, slippery with terror. I'm afraid, not because there's someone in the room, in the dark, in the bed, but because there isn't. I'm afraid of the emptiness, which lies beside me like a corpse.

I think: What will become of me? I will be alone. Who will visit me in the old-age home? I think of the next man as an aging horse must think of a jump. Will I lose my nerve? Can I still pull it off? Should I get married? Do I have the choice?

In the daytime, I am fine. I lead a rich full life. There is, of course, my career. I shine away at it like an antique brass. I add on to it like a stamp collection. It props me up: a career like an underwired brassiere. Some days I hate it.

"Dessert?" says Charles.

"Will you?"

Charles pats his midriff. "Trying to cut down," he says.

"Let's just have a double espresso," I say. I make it sound like a delicious conspiracy.

Double espresso. A diabolical torture devised by the Spanish Inquisition, involving a sack of tacks, a silver bootjack, and two three-hundred-pound priests.

. . .

Molly, I let you down. I burned out early. I couldn't take the pressure. I wanted security. Maybe I decided that the fastest way to improve the lot of women was to improve my own.

Molly kept on. She lost that baby-fat roundness; she developed a raw edge to her voice and took to chain-smoking. Her hair got dull and her skin looked abraded, and she paid no attention. She began to lecture me about my lack of seriousness, and also about my wardrobe, for which I overspent in her opinion. She began to use words like *patriarchy*. I began to find her strident.

"Molly," I said. "Why don't you give it up? You're slamming your head against a big brick wall." I felt like a traitor saying it. But I'd have felt like a traitor if I hadn't said it, because Molly was knocking herself out, and for peanuts. The kind of women she represented never had any money.

"We're making progress," she'd say. Her face was getting that ropy look, like a missionary's. "We're accomplishing something."

"Who is this *we?*" I'd say. "I don't see a lot of people helping you out."

"Oh, they do," she said vaguely. "Some of them do. They do what they can, in their own way. It's sort of like the widow's mite, you know?"

"What widow?" I said. I knew but I was exasperated. She was trying to make me feel guilty. "Quit trying for sainthood, Molly. Enough is enough."

That was before she married Curtis.

"Now," says Charles. "Cards on the table, eh?"

"Right," I say. "Well, I've explained the basic position to you already. In your office."

"Yes," he says. "As I told you, the company has already allocated its charitable donations budget for this year."

"But you could make an exception," I say. "You could draw on next year's budget."

"We could, if—well, the bottom line is that we like to think we're getting something back for what we put in. Nothing blatant, just what you might call good associations. With hearts and kidneys, for instance, there's no problem at all."

"What's wrong with battered women?"

"Well, there would be our company logo, and then right beside it these battered women. The public might get the wrong idea."

"You mean they might think the company was doing the battering itself?"

"In a word, yes," says Charles.

It's like any negotiation. Always agree, then come at them from a different angle. "You have a point," I say.

Battered women. I can see it in lights, like a roadside fast-food joint. *Get some fresh.* Sort of like onion rings and deep-fried chicken. A terrible pun. Would Molly have laughed? Yes. No. Yes.

Battered. Covered in slime, then dipped into hell. Not so inappropriate, after all.

Molly was thirty when she married Curtis. He wasn't the first man she'd lived with. I've often wondered why she did it. Why him? Possibly she just got tired.

Still, it was a strange choice. He was so dependent. He could hardly let her out of his sight. Was that the appeal? Probably not. Molly was a fixer. She thought she could fix things that were broken. Sometimes she could. Though Curtis was too broken even for her. He was so broken he thought the normal state of the world was broken. Maybe that's why he tried to break Molly: to make her normal. When he couln't do it one way, he did it another.

He was plausible enough, at first. He was a lawyer, he had the proper suits. I could say I knew right away that he wasn't totally glued together, but it wouldn't be true. I didn't know. I didn't like him a lot, but I didn't know.

For a while after the wedding I didn't see that much of Molly.

She was always busy doing something or other with Curtis, and then there were the children. A boy and a girl, just what I'd always expected, for myself. Sometimes, it seemed that Molly was leading the life I might have led, if it hadn't been for caution and a certain fastidiousness. When it comes to the crunch, I have a dislike of other people's bathtub rings. That's the virtue in married men: someone else does the maintenance.

"Is everything all right?" asks the waiter, for the fourth time. Charles doesn't answer. Perhaps he doesn't hear. He's the sort of man for whom waiters are a kind of warmblooded tea trolley.

"Wonderful," I say.

"Why don't these battered women just get a good lawyer?" says Charles. He's genuinely baffled. No use telling him they can't afford it. For him, that's not a concept.

"Charles," I say. "Some of these guys *are* good lawyers."

"Nobody I know," says Charles.

"You'd be surprised," I say. "Of course, we take personal donations too."

"What?" says Charles, who has not followed me.

"Not just corporate ones. Bill Henry over at ConFrax gave two thousand dollars." Bill Henry had to. I know all about his useful right-buttock birthmark, the one shaped like a rabbit. I know his snore pattern.

"Ah," says Charles, caught unawares. But he will not be hooked without a struggle. "You know I like to put my money where it's doing some real good. These women, you get them out, but I've been told they just go right back and get battered again."

I've heard it before. They're addicted. They can't get enough of having their eyes punched in. "Give it to the Heart Foundation," I say, "and those ungrateful triple by-passes will just croak anyway, sooner or later. It's like they're asking for it."

"Touché," says Charles. Oh, good. He knows some French. Not a complete oaf, unlike some. "How about I take you out for dinner on, say"—he consults his little book, the one they all carry around in the breast pocket—"Wednesday? Then you can convince me."

"Charles," I say, "that's not fair. I would adore to have dinner with you but not as the price of your donation. Give first, and then we can have dinner with a clear conscience."

Charles likes the idea of a clear conscience. He grins and reaches for his checkbook. He is not going to look cheaper than Bill Henry. Not at this stage of the game.

Molly came to see me at my office. She didn't phone first. It was right after I'd left my last high-class flunky company position and set up on my own. I had my own flunkies now and I was wrestling with the coffee problem. If you're a woman, women don't like bringing you coffee. Neither do men.

"Molly, what's wrong?" I said. "Do you want coffee?"

"I'm so wired already I couldn't stand it," she said. She looked it. There were half-circles under her eyes the size of lemon wedges.

"It's Curtis," she said. "Could I sleep over at your place tonight? If I have to?"

"What's he done?" I said.

"Nothing," she said. "Not yet. It isn't what he's done, it's how he is. He's heading straight for the edge."

"In what way?"

"A while ago he started saying I was having affairs at work. He thought I was having an affair with Maurice, across the hall."

"Maurice!" I said. We'd both gone to law school with Maurice. "But Maurice is gay!"

"We aren't talking rational here. Then he started saying I was going to leave him."

"And were you?"

"I wasn't. But now, I don't know. Now I think I am. He's driving me to it."

"He's paranoid," I said.

"*Paranoid*," said Molly. "A wide-angle camera for taking

snapshots of maniacs." She put her head down on her arms and laughed and laughed.

"Come over tonight," I said. "Don't even think about it. Just do it."

"I don't want to rush it," said Molly. "Maybe things will work out. Maybe I can talk him into getting some help. He's been under a lot of strain. I have to think about the kids. He's a good father."

Victim, they said in the papers. Molly was no victim. She wasn't helpless, she wasn't hopeless. She was full of hope. It was hope that killed her.

I called her the next evening. I thought she would've come over, but she hadn't. She hadn't phoned either.

Curtis answered. He said Molly had gone on a trip.

I asked him when she'd be back. He said he had no idea. Then, he started to cry. "She's left me," he said.

Good for her, I thought. She's done it, after all.

It was a week later that the arms and legs started turning up.

He killed her in her sleep, I'll give him that much credit. She never knew. Or so he said, after he got around to remembering. He claimed amnesia, at first.

Dismemberment. The act of conscious forgetting.

I try not to think of Molly like that. I try to remember her whole.

Charles is walking me to the door, past white tablecloth after white tablecloth, each one held in place by at least four pin-striped elbows. It's like the *Titanic* just before the iceberg: power and influence disporting themselves, not a care in the world. What do they know about the serfs down in steerage? Piss all, and pass the port.

I smile to the right, I smile to the left. There are some familiar faces here, some familiar birthmarks. Charles takes my elbow, in a proprietary though discreet way. A light touch, a heavy hand.

I no longer think that anything can happen. I no longer want to think that way. *Happen* is what you wait for, not what you do; and *anything* is a large category. I am unlikely to get murdered by this man, for instance; I am unlikely to get married to him either. Right now, I don't even know whether I'll go so far as dinner on Wednesday. It occurs to me that I don't really have to, not if I don't want to. Some options at least remain open. Just thinking about it makes my feet hurt less.

Today is Friday. Tomorrow morning I'll go power-walking in the cemetery, for the inner and outer thighs. It's one of the few places you can do it in this city without getting run over. It isn't the cemetery Molly's buried in, whatever of her they could put together. But that doesn't matter. I'll pick out a tombstone where I can do my leg stretches, and I'll pretend it's hers.

Molly, I'll say. We don't see eye to eye on some things and you wouldn't approve of my methods, but I do what I can. The bottom line is that cash is cash, and it puts food on the table.

Bottom line, she will answer. What you hit when you get as far down as you're going. After that you stay there. Or else you go up.

I will bend, I will touch the ground, or as close to it as I can get without rupture. I will lay a wreath of invisible money on her grave.

WILDERNESS
TIPS

P rue has folded two red ban-
danna handkerchiefs into triangles and tied them together at
one set of corners. The second set of corners is tied behind
her back, the third around her neck. She's wrapped another
bandanna, a blue one, around her head and made a little reef
knot at the front. Now she's strutting the length of the dock, in
her improvised halter top and her wide-legged white shorts, her
sunglasses with the white plastic frames, her platform sandals.

"It's the forties look," she says to George, hand on her hip,
doing a pirouette. "Rosie the Riveter. From the war. Remember
her?"

George, whose name is not really George, does not remember. He spent the forties rooting through garbage heaps and
begging, and doing other things unsuitable for a child. He has
a dim memory of some film star posed on a calendar tattering
on a latrine wall. Maybe this is the one Prue means. He remem-

bers for an instant his intense resentment of the bright, ignorant smile, the well-fed body. A couple of buddies had helped him take her apart with the rusty blade from a kitchen knife they'd found somewhere in the rubble. He does not consider telling any of this to Prue.

George is sitting in a green-and-white striped canvas deck chair, reading *The Financial Post* and drinking Scotch. The ashtray beside him overflows with butts: many women have tried to cure him of smoking; many have failed. He looks up at Prue from behind his paper and smiles his foxy smile. This is a smile he does with the cigarette held right in the center of his mouth: on either side of it his lips curl back, revealing teeth. He has long canines, miraculously still his.

"You weren't born then," he says. This isn't true, but he never misses the chance to bestow a compliment when there's one just lying around. What does it cost? Not a cent, which is something the men in this country have never figured out. Prue's tanned midriff is on a level with his face; it's still firm, still flexible and lithe. At that age his mother had gone soft—loose-fleshed and velvety, like an aging plum. These days they eat a lot of vegetables, they work out, they last longer.

Prue lowers the sunglasses to the end of her nose and looks at him over the plastic rims. "George, you are totally shameless," she says. "You always were." She gives him an innocent smile, a mischievous smile, a smile with a twist of real evil in it. It's a smile that wavers like a gasoline slick on water, shining, changing tone.

This smile of Prue's was the first interesting thing George stumbled over when he hit Toronto, back in the late fifties. It was at a party thrown by a real-estate developer with Eastern European connections. He'd been invited because refugees from Hungary were considered noteworthy back then, right after the uprising. At that time he was young, thin as a snake, with a dangerous-looking scar over one eye and a few bizarre stories. A collectible. Prue had been there in an off-the-shoulder black dress. She'd raised her glass to him, looked over the rim, hoisted the smile like a flag.

The smile is still an invitation, but it's not something George will follow up on—not here, not now. Later, in the city, perhaps. But this lake, this peninsula, Wacousta Lodge itself, are his refuge, his monastery, his sacred ground. Here he will perform no violations.

"Why is it you cannot bear to accept a gift?" says George. Smoke blows into his eyes; he squints. "If I were younger, I would kneel. I would kiss both your hands. Believe me."

Prue, who has known him to do these things back in more impetuous times, turns on her heel. "It's lunchtime," she says. "That's what I came to tell you." She has heard refusal.

George watches her white shorts and her still shapely thighs (with, however, their faint stippling of dimpled fat) going wink, wink, wink through the clear sunlight, past the boathouse, along the stone path, up the hill to the house. From up there a bell is ringing: the lunch bell. For once in her life, Prue is telling the truth.

George takes one more look at the paper. Quebec is talking Separatism; there are Mohawks behind the barricades near Montreal, and people are throwing stones at them; word is the country is falling apart. George is not worried: he's been in countries that were falling apart before. There can be opportunities. As for the fuss people here make about language, he doesn't understand it. What's a second language, or a third, or a fourth? George himself speaks five, if you count Russian, which he would prefer not to. As for the stone-throwing, it's typical. Not bombs, not bullets: just stones. Even the uproar here is muted.

He scratches his belly under the loose shirt he wears; he's been gaining a little too much around the middle. Then he stubs out his cigarette, downs the heel of his Scotch, and hauls himself out of his deck chair. Carefully, he folds the chair and places it inside the boathouse: a wind could come up, the chair could be sent sailing into the lake. He treats the possessions and rituals of Wacousta Lodge with a tenderness, a reverence, that would baffle those who know him only in the city. Despite what some would call his unorthodox business practices, he is in some ways a conservative man; he loves traditions. They are thin on the ground in this country, but he knows one when he sees one, and does it homage. The deck chairs here are like the escutcheons elsewhere.

As he walks up the hill, more slowly than he used to, he hears the sound of wood being split behind the kitchen wing. He hears a truck on the highway that runs along the side of the lake; he hears wind in the white pines. He hears a loon. He remembers the first time he heard one, and hugs himself. He has done well.

Wacousta Lodge is a large, oblong, one-story structure with board-and-batten walls stained a dark reddish brown. It was built in the first years of the century by the family's great-grandfather, who made a bundle on the railways. He included a maid's room and a cook's room at the back, although no maid or cook had ever been induced to stay in them, not to George's knowledge, certainly not in recent years. The great-grandfather's craggy, walrus-whiskered face, frowning above the constriction of a stiff collar, hangs oval-framed in the washroom, which is equipped only with a sink and a ewer. George can remember a zinc bathtub, but it's been retired. Baths take place in the lake. For the rest, there's an outhouse, placed discreetly behind a clump of spruce.

What a lot of naked and semi-naked bodies the old man must have seen over the years, thinks George, lathering his hands, and how he must have disapproved of them. At least the old boy isn't condemned to the outhouse: that would be too much for him. George makes a small, superstitious, oddly Japanese bow towards the great-grandfather as he goes out the door. He always does this. The presence of this scowling ancestral totem is one of the reasons he behaves himself, more or less, up here.

The table for lunch is set on the wide, screened-in veranda at the front of the house, overlooking the lake. Prue is not sitting at it, but her two sisters are: dry-faced Pamela, the eldest, and soft Portia, the youngest of the three and George's own wife. There is also Roland, the brother, large, rounded, and balding. George, who is not all that fond of men on purely social occasions because there are few ways he can manipulate them, gives Roland a polite nod and turns the full force of his vulpine smile upon the two women. Pamela, who distrusts him, sits up straight and pretends not to notice. Portia smiles at him, a wistful, vague smile, as if he were a cloud. Roland ignores him, though not on purpose, because Roland has the inner life of a tree, or possibly of a stump. George can never tell what Roland is thinking, or even if he is thinking at all.

"Isn't the weather marvelous?" George says to Pamela. He has learned over the years that the weather is the proper opening topic here for any conversation at all. Pamela is too well brought up to refuse an answer to a direct question.

"If you like postcards," she says. "At least it's not snowing." Pamela has recently been appointed a Dean of Women, a title George has not yet figured out completely. The Oxford dictionary has informed him that a dean might be the head of ten monks in a monastery, or "as tr. med. L. *decanus*, applied to the *teoðing-ealdor*, the headman of a *tenmannetale*." Much of what Pamela says sounds more or less like this: incomprehensible, though it might turn out to have a meaning if studied.

George would like to go to bed with Pamela, not because she is beautiful—she is much too rectilinear and slab-shaped for his tastes, she has no bottom at all, and her hair is the color of dried grass—but because he has never done it. Also, he wants to know what she would say. His interest in her is anthropological. Or perhaps geological: she would have to be scaled, like a glacier.

"Did you have a nice read?" says Portia. "I hope you didn't get sunburned. Is there any news?"

"If you can call it news," says Pamela. "That paper's a week old. Why is 'news' plural? Why don't we say 'olds'?"

"George likes old stuff," says Prue, coming in with a platter of food. She's put on a man's white shirt over her kerchief arrangement but hasn't done it up. "Lucky for us ladies, eh? Gobble up, everyone. It's yummy cheese-and-chutney sandwiches and yummy sardines. George? Beer or acid rain?"

George drinks a beer, and eats and smiles, eats and smiles, while the family talks around him—all but Roland, who absorbs his nutriments in silence, gazing out at the lake through the trees, his eyes immobile. George sometimes thinks Roland can change color slightly to blend in with his backgrounds; unlike George himself, who is doomed to stand out.

Pamela is complaining again about the stuffed birds. There are three of them, kept under glass bells in the living room: a duck, a loon, a grouse. These were the bright ideas of the grandfather, meant to go with the generally lodge-like décor: the mangy bearskin rug, complete with claws and head; the miniature birchbark canoe on the mantelpiece; the snowshoes, cracked and drying, crossed above the fireplace; the Hudson's Bay blanket nailed to the wall and beset by moths. Pamela is sure the stuffed birds will get moths too.

"They're probably a sea of maggots, inside," she says, and George tries to picture what a sea of maggots would look like. It's her metaphoric leaps, her tangled verbal stringworks, that confuse him.

"They're hermetically sealed," says Prue. "You know: nothing goes in, nothing comes out. Like nuns."

"Don't be revolting," says Pamela. "We should check them for frass."

"Who, the nuns?" says Prue.

"What is frass?" says George.

"Maggot excrement," says Pamela, not looking at him. "We could have them freeze-dried."

"Would it work?" says Prue.

Prue, who in the city is the first with trends—the first white kitchen, the first set of giant shoulder pads, the first leather pants suit have been hers over the years—is here as resistant to change as the rest of them. She wants everything on this peninsula to stay exactly the way it always has been. And it does, though with a gradual decline into shabbiness. George doesn't mind the shabbiness, however. Wacousta Lodge is a little slice of the past, an alien past. He feels privileged.

A motorboat goes by, one of the plastic-hulled, high-speed kind, far too close. Even Roland flinches. The wake jostles the dock.

"I hate those," says Portia, who hasn't shown much interest in the stuffed-bird question. "Another sandwich, dear?"

"It was so lovely and quiet here during the war," says Pamela. "You should have been here, George." She says this accusingly, as if it's his fault he wasn't. "Hardly any motorboats, because of the gas rationing. More canoes. Of course, the road wasn't built then, there was only the train. I wonder why we say 'train of thought' but never 'car of thought'?"

"And rowboats," says Prue. "I think all those motorboat people should be taken out and shot. At least the ones who go too fast." Prue herself drives like a maniac, but only on land.

George, who has seen many people taken out and shot, though not for driving motorboats, smiles, and helps himself to a sardine. He once shot three men himself, though only two of them were strictly necessary. The third was a precaution. He still feels uneasy about that, about the possibly harmless one with his too-innocent informer's eyes, his shirtfront dappled with blood. But there would be little point in mentioning that, at lunch or at any other time. George has no desire to be startling.

It was Prue who brought him north, brought him here, during their affair, the first one. (How many affairs have there been? Can they be separated, or are they really one long affair, with interruptions, like a string of sausages? The interruptions were Prue's marriages, which never lasted long, possibly because she was monogamous during them. He would know when a marriage was nearing its end: the phone at his office would ring and it would be Prue, saying, "George. I can't do it. I've been so good, but I just can't go on. He comes into the bathroom when I'm flossing my teeth. I long to be in an elevator with you, stuck between floors. Tell me something *filthy*. I hate love, don't you?")

. . .

His first time here he was led in chains, trailed in Prue's wake, like a barbarian in a Roman triumph. A definite capture, also a deliberate outrage. He was supposed to alarm Prue's family, and he did, though not on purpose. His English was not good, his hair was too glossy, his shoes too pointed, his clothes too sharply pressed. He wore dark glasses, kissed hands. The mother was alive then, though not the father; so there were four women ranged against him, with no help at all from the impenetrable Roland.

"Mother, this is George," said Prue, on the dock where they were all sitting in their ancestral deck chairs, the daughters in bathing suits with shirts over them, the mother in striped pastels. "It's not his real name, but it's easier to pronounce. He's come up here to see wild animals."

George leaned over to kiss the mother's sun-freckled hand, and his dark glasses fell off into the lake. The mother made cooing sounds of distress, Prue laughed at him, Roland ignored him, Pamela turned away in irritation. But Portia—lovely, small-boned Portia, with her velvet eyes—took off her shirt without a word and dove into the lake. She retrieved his dark glasses for him, smiling diffidently, handing them up to him out of the water, her wet hair dripping down over her small breasts like a water nymph's on an Art Nouveau fountain, and he knew then that she was the one he would marry. A woman of courtesy and tact and few words, who would be kind to him, who would cover up for him; who would pick up the things he had dropped.

In the afternoon, Prue took him for a paddle in one of the leaking canvas-covered canoes from the boathouse. He sat in the front, jabbing ineptly at the water with his paddle, thinking about how he would get Portia to marry him. Prue landed them on a rocky point, led him up among the trees. She wanted him to make his usual rakish, violent, outlandish brand of love to her on the reindeer moss and pine needles; she wanted to break some family taboo. Sacrilege was what she had in mind: that was as clear to him as if he'd read it. But George already had his plan of attack worked out, so he put her off. He didn't want to desecrate Wacousta Lodge: he wanted to marry it.

That evening at dinner he neglected all three of the daughters in favor of the mother: the mother was the guardian; the mother was the key. Despite his limping vocabulary he could be devastatingly charming, as Prue had announced to everyone while they ate their chicken-noodle soup.

"Wacousta Lodge," he said to the mother, bending his scar and his glinting marauder's eyes towards her in the light from the kerosene lamp. "That is so romantic. It is the name of an Indian tribe?"

Prue laughed. "It's named after some stupid book," she said. "Great-grandfather liked it because it was written by a general."

"A major," said Pamela severely. "In the nineteenth century. Major Richardson."

"Ah?" said George, adding this item to his already growing cache of local traditions. So there were books here, and houses named after them! Most people were touchy on the subject of their books; it would be as well to show some interest. Anyway, he *was* interested. But when he asked about the subject of this book it turned out that none of the women had read it.

"I've read it," said Roland, unexpectedly.

"Ah?" said George.

"It's about war."

"It's on the bookshelf in the living room," the mother said indifferently. "After dinner you can have a look, if you're all that fascinated."

It was the mother (Prue explained) who had been guilty of the daughters' alliterative names. She was a whimsical woman, though not sadistic; it was simply an age when parents did that—named their children to match, as if they'd come out of an alphabet book. The bear, the bumblebee, the bunny. Mary and Marjorie Murchison. David and Darlene Daly. Nobody did that anymore. Of course, the mother hadn't stopped at the names themselves but had converted them into nicknames: Pam, Prue, Porsh. Prue's is the only nickname that has stuck. Pamela is now too dignified for hers, and Portia says it's already bad enough, being confused with a car, and why can't she be just an initial?

Roland had been left out of the set, at the insistence of the father. It was Prue's opinion that he had always resented it. "How can you tell?" George asked her, running his tongue around her navel as she lay in her half-slip on the Chinese carpet in his office, smoking a cigarette and surrounded by sheets of paper that had been knocked off the desk during the initial skirmish. She'd made sure the door was unlocked: she liked to run the risk of intrusion, preferably by George's secretary, whom she suspected of being the competition. Which secretary, and when was that? The spilled papers were part of a take-over plan—the Adams group. This is how George keeps track of the various episodes with Prue: by remembering what other skulduggery he was up to at the time. He'd made his money quickly, and then he'd made more. It had been much easier than he'd thought; it had been like spearing fish by lamplight. These people were lax and trusting, and easily embarrassed by a hint of their own intolerance or lack of hospitality to strangers. They weren't ready for him. He'd been as happy as a missionary among the Hawaiians. A hint of opposition and he'd thicken his accent and refer darkly to Communist atrocities. Seize the moral high ground, then grab what you can get.

After that first dinner, they'd all gone into the living room, carrying their cups of coffee. There were kerosene lamps in there, too—old ones, with globe shades. Prue took George flagrantly by the hand and led him over to the bookcase, which was topped with a collection of clam shells and pieces of driftwood from the girls' childhoods. "Here it is," she said. "Read it and weep." She went to refill his coffee. George opened the book, an old edition that had, as he'd hoped, a frontispiece of an angry-looking warrior with tomahawk and paint. Then he scanned the shelves. *From Sea to Sea. Wild Animals I Have Known. The Collected Poems of Robert Service. Our Empire Story. Wilderness Tips.*

"Wilderness Tips" puzzled him. "Wilderness" he knew, but

"tips"? He was not immediately sure whether this word was a verb or a noun. There were asparagus tips, as he knew from menus, and when he was getting into the canoe that afternoon in his slippery leather-soled city shoes Prue had said, "Be careful, it tips." Perhaps it was another sort of tip, as in the "Handy Tips for Happy Homemakers" columns in the women's magazines he had taken to reading in order to improve his English—the vocabularies were fairly simple and there were pictures, which was a big help.

When he opened the book he saw he'd guessed right. *Wilderness Tips* was dated 1905. There was a photo of the author in a plaid wool jacket and a felt hat, smoking a pipe and paddling a canoe, against a backdrop that was more or less what you could see out the window: water, islands, rocks, trees. The book itself told how to do useful things, like snaring small animals and eating them—something George himself had done, though not in forests—or lighting a fire in a rainstorm. These instructions were interspersed with lyrical passages about the joys of independence and the open air, and descriptions of fish-catching and sunsets. George took the book over to a chair near one of the globed lamps; he wanted to read about skinning knives, but Prue came back with his coffee, and Portia offered him a chocolate, and he did not want to run the risk of displeasing either of them, not at this early stage. That could come later.

Now George again walks into the living room, again carrying a cup of coffee. By this time he's read all of the books in the great-grandfather's collection. He's the only one who has.

Prue follows him in. The women take it in turns to clear and do the dishes, and it isn't her turn. Roland's job is the wood-splitting. There was an attempt once to press George into service with a tea towel, but he jovially broke three wineglasses, exclaiming over his own clumsiness, and since then he has been left in peace.

"You want more coffee?" Prue says. She stands close to him, proffering the open shirt, the two bandannas. George isn't sure he wants to start anything again, but he sets his coffee down on the top of the bookcase and puts his hand on her hip. He wants to check out his options, make sure he's still welcome. Prue sighs—a long sigh of desire or exasperation, or both.

"Oh, George," she says. "What should I do with you?"

"Whatever you like," says George, moving his mouth close to her ear. "I am merely a lump of clay in your hands." Her earlobe holds a tiny silver earring in the form of a shell. He represses an impulse to nibble.

"Curious George," she says, using one of her old nicknames for him. "You used to have the eyes of a young goat. Lecher eyes."

And now I'm an old goat, thinks George. He can't resist, he wants to be young again; he runs his hand up under her shirt.

"Later," Prue says triumphantly. She steps back from him and aims her wavering smile, and George upsets his cup of coffee with his elbow.

"*Fene egye meg*," he says, and Prue laughs. She knows the meaning of these swear-words, and worse ones, too.

"Clumsy bugger," she says. "I'll get a sponge."

George lights a cigarette and awaits her return. But it is Pamela who appears, frowning, in the doorway, with a deteriorating scrub cloth and a metal bowl. Trust Prue to have found some other urgent thing to do. She is probably in the outhouse, leafing through a magazine and plotting, deciding when and where she will next entice him.

"So, George, you've made a mess," says Pamela, as if he were a puppy. If she had a rolled-up newspaper, thinks George, she'd give me a swat on the nose.

"It's true, I'm an oaf," says George amiably. "But you've always known that."

Pamela gets down on her knees and begins to wipe. "If the plural of 'loaf' is 'loaves,' what's the plural of 'oaf'?" she says. "Why isn't it 'oaves'?" George realizes that a good deal of what she says is directed not to him or to any other listener but simply to herself. Is that because she thinks no one can hear her? He finds the sight of her down on her knees suggestive—stirring, even. He catches a whiff of her: soap flakes, a tinge of something sweet. Hand lotion? She has a graceful neck and throat. He wonders if she's ever had a lover, and, if so, what he was like. An insensitive man, lacking in skill. An oaf.

"George, you smoke like a furnace," she says, without turning around. "You really should stop, or it'll kill you."

George considers the ambiguity of the phrase. "Smoking like a furnace." He sees himself as a dragon, fumes and red flames pouring out of his ravenous maw. Is this really her version of him? "That would make you happy," he says, deciding on impulse to try a frontal attack. "You'd love to see me six feet underground. You've never liked me."

Pamela stops wiping and looks at him over her shoulder. Then she stands up and wrings the dirty cloth out into the bowl. "That's juvenile," she says calmly, "and unworthy of you. You need more exercise. This afternoon I'll take you canoeing."

"You know I'm hopeless at that," says George truthfully. "I always crash into rocks. I never see them."

"Geology is destiny," says Pamela, as if to herself. She scowls at the stuffed loon in its glass bell. She is thinking. "Yes," she says at last. "This lake is full of hidden rocks. It can be dangerous. But I'll take care of you."

Is she flirting with him? Can a crag flirt? George can hardly believe it, but he smiles at her, holding the cigarette in the center of his mouth, showing his canines, and for the first time in their lives Pamela smiles back at him. Her mouth is quite different when the corners turn up; it's as if he were seeing her upside down. He's surprised by the loveliness of her smile. It's not a knowing smile, like Prue's, or saintly, like Portia's. It's the smile of an imp, of a mischievous child, mixed in with something he'd never expected to find in her. A generosity, a carelessness, a largesse. She has something she wishes to give him. What could it be?

After lunch and a pause for digestion, Roland goes back to his chopping, beside the woodshed out behind the kitchen. He's splitting birch—a dying tree he cut down a year ago. The beavers had made a start on it, but changed their minds. White birch don't live long anyway. He'd used the chain saw, slicing the trunk neatly into lengths, the blade going through the wood like a knife through butter, the noise blotting out all other noises—the wind and waves, the whining of the trucks from the highway across the lake. He dislikes machine noises, but they're easier to tolerate when you're making them yourself, when you can control them. Like gunshot.

Not that Roland shoots. He used to: he used to go out for a deer in season, but now it's unsafe, there are too many other men doing it—Italians and who knows what—who'll shoot at anything moving. In any case, he's lost the taste for the end result, the antlered carcasses strapped to the fronts of cars like grotesque hood ornaments, the splendid, murdered heads peering dull-eyed from the tops of mini-vans. He can see the point of venison, of killing to eat, but to have a cut-off head on your wall? What does it prove, except that a deer can't pull a trigger?

He never talks about these feelings. He knows they would be held against him at his place of work, which he hates. His job is managing money for other people. He knows he is not a success, not by his great-grandfather's standards. The old man sneers at him every morning from that rosewood frame in the washroom, while he is shaving. They both know the same thing: if Roland were a success he'd be out pillaging, not counting the beans. He'd have some gray, inoffensive, discontented man counting the beans for him. A regiment of them. A regiment of men like himself.

He lifts a chunk of birch, stands it on end on the chopping block, swings the axe. A clean split, but he's out of practice. Tomorrow he will have blisters. In a while he'll stop, stoop and pile, stoop and pile.There's already enough wood, but he likes doing this. It's one of the few things he does like. He feels alive only up here.

Yesterday, he drove up from the center of the city, past the warehouses and factories and shining glass towers, which have gone up, it seems, overnight; past the subdivisions he could swear weren't there last year, last month. Acres of treelessness, of new townhouses with little pointed roofs—like tents, like an invasion. The tents of the Goths and the Vandals. The tents of the Huns and the Magyars. The tents of George.

Down comes his axe on the head of George, which splits in two. If Roland had known George would be here this weekend, he wouldn't have come. Damn Prue and her silly bandannas and her open shirt, her middle-aged breasts offered like hot, freckled muffins along with the sardines and cheese, George sliding his oily eyes all over her, with Portia pretending not to notice. Damn George and his shady deals and his pay-offs to town councillors; damn George and his millions, and his spurious, excessive charm. George should stay in the city where he belongs. He's hard to take even there, but at least Roland can keep out of his way. Here at Wacousta Lodge he's intolerable, strutting around as if he owned the place. Not yet. Probably he'll wait for them all to croak, and then turn it into a lucrative retirement home for the rich Japanese. He'll sell them Nature, at a huge margin. That's the kind of thing George would do.

Roland knew the man was a lizard the first time he saw him. Why did Portia marry him? She could have married somebody decent, leaving George to Prue, who'd dredged him up from God knows where and was flaunting him around like a prize fish. Prue deserved him; Portia didn't. But why did Prue give him up without a struggle? That wasn't like her. It's as if there had been some negotiation, some invisible deal between them. Portia got George, but what did she trade for him? What did she have to give up?

Portia has always been his favorite sister. She was the youngest, the baby. Prue, who was the next youngest, used to tease her savagely, though Portia was remarkably slow to cry. Instead, she would just look, as if she couldn't quite figure out what Prue was doing to her or why. Then she would go off by herself. Or else Roland would come to her defense and there would be a fight, and Roland would be accused of picking on his sister and be told he shouldn't behave that way because he was a boy. He doesn't remember what part Pamela used to take in all this.

Pamela was older than the rest of them and had her own agenda, which did not appear to include anyone else at all. Pamela read at the dinner table and went off by herself in the canoe. Pamela was allowed.

In the city they were in different schools or different grades; the house was large and they had their own pathways through it, their own lairs. It was only here that the territories overlapped. Wacousta Lodge, which looks so peaceful, is for Roland the repository of the family wars.

How old had he been—nine? ten?—the time he almost killed Prue? It was the summer he wanted to be an Indian, because of *Wilderness Tips*. He used to sneak that book off the shelf and take it outside, behind the woodshed, and turn and re-turn the pages. *Wilderness Tips* told you how to survive by yourself in the woods—a thing he longed to do. How to build shelters, make clothing from skins, find edible plants. There were diagrams too, and pen-and-ink drawings—of animal tracks, of leaves and seeds. Descriptions of different kinds of animal droppings. He remembers the first time he found some bear scat, fresh and reeking, and purple with blueberries. It scared the hell out of him.

There was a lot about the Indians, about how noble they were, how brave, faithful, clean, reverent, hospitable, and honorable. (Even these words sound outmoded now, archaic. When was the last time Roland heard anyone praised for being *honorable*?) They attacked only in self-defense, to keep their land from being stolen. They walked differently too. There was a diagram, on page 208, of footprints, an Indian's and a white man's: the white wore hobnailed boots, and his toes pointed outward; the Indian wore moccasins, and his feet went straight ahead. Roland has been conscious of his feet ever since. He still turns his toes in slightly, to counteract what he feels must be a genetically programmed waddle.

That summer he ran around with a tea towel tucked into the front of his bathing suit for a loincloth and decorated his face with charcoal from the fireplace, alternating with red paint swiped from Prue's paintbox. He lurked outside windows, listening in. Trying to make smoke signals, he set fire to a small patch of undergrowth down near the boathouse, but put it out before he was caught. He lashed an oblong stone to a stick handle with a leather lace borrowed from one of his father's boots; his father was alive then. He snuck up on Prue, who was reading comic books on the dock, dangling her legs in the water.

He had his stone axe. He could have brained her. She was not Prue, of course: she was Custer, she was treachery, she was the enemy. He went as far as raising the axe, watching the convincing silhouette his shadow made on the dock. The stone fell off, onto his bare foot. He shouted with pain. Prue turned around, saw him there, guessed in an instant what he was doing, and laughed herself silly. That was when he'd almost killed her. The other thing, the stone axe, had just been a game.

The whole thing had just been a game, but it wounded him to let go of it. He'd wanted so badly to believe in that kind of Indian, the kind in the book. He'd needed them to exist.

Driving up yesterday, he'd passed a group of actual Indians, three of them, at a blueberry stand. They were wearing jeans and T-shirts and running shoes, the same as everybody else. One of them had a transistor radio. A neat maroon mini-van was parked beside the stand. So what did he expect from them, feathers? All that was gone, lost, ruined, years and years before he was born.

He knows this is nonsense. He's a bean counter, after all; he deals in the hard currency of reality. How can you lose something that was never yours in the first place? (But you can, because *Wilderness Tips* was his once, and he's lost it. He opened the book today, before lunch, after forty years. There was the innocent, fusty vocabulary that had once inspired him: Manhood with a capital M, courage, honor. The Spirit of the Wild. It was naive, pompous, ridiculous. It was dust.)

Roland chops with his axe. The sound goes out through the trees, across the small inlet to the left of him, bounces off a high ridge of rock, making a faint echo. It's an old sound, a sound left over.

. . .

Portia lies on her bed, listening to the sound of Roland chopping wood, having her nap. She has her nap the way she always has, without sleeping. The nap was enforced on her once, by her mother. Now she just does it. When she was little she used to lie here—tucked safely away from Prue—in her parents' room, in her parents' double bed, which is now hers and George's. She would think about all kinds of things; she would see faces and animal shapes in the knots of the pine ceiling and make up stories about them.

Now the only stories she ever makes up are about George. They are probably even more unrealistic than the stories he makes up about himself, but she has no way of really knowing. There are those who lie by instinct and those who don't, and the ones who don't are at the mercy of the ones who do.

Prue, for instance, is a blithe liar. She always has been; she enjoys it. When they were children she'd say, "Look, there's a big snot coming out of your nose," and Portia would run to the washroom mirror. Nothing was there, but Prue's saying it made it somehow true, and Portia would scrub and scrub, trying to wash away invisible dirt, while Prue doubled over with laughter. "Don't believe her," Pamela would say. "Don't be such a sucker." (One of her chief words then—she used it for lollipops, for fish, for mouths.) But sometimes the things Prue said were true, so how could you ever know?

George is the same way. He gazes into her eyes and lies with such tenderness, such heartfelt feeling, such implicit sadness at her want of faith in him, that she can't question him. To question him would turn her cynical and hard. She would rather be kissed; she would rather be cherished. She would rather believe.

She knew about George and Prue at the beginning, of course. It was Prue who brought him up here first. But after a while George swore to her that the thing with Prue hadn't been serious, and, anyway, it was over; and Prue herself seemed not to care. She'd already had George, she implied; he was used, like a dress.

If Portia wanted him next it was nothing to her. "Help yourself," she said. "God knows there's enough of George to go around."

Portia wanted to do things the way Prue did; she wanted to get her hands dirty. Something intense, followed by careless dismissal. But she was too young; she didn't have the knack. She'd come up out of the lake and handed George's dark glasses to him, and he'd looked at her in the wrong way: with reverence, not with passion—a clear gaze with no smut in it. After dinner that evening he'd said, with meticulous politeness, "Everything here is so new to me. I like you to be my guide, to your wonderful country."

"Me?" Portia said. "I don't know. What about Prue?" She was already feeling guilty.

"Prue does not understand obligations," he said (which was true enough, she didn't, and this insight of George's was impressive). "You understand them, however. I am the guest; you are the host."

"Hostess," said Pamela, who had not seemed to be listening. "A 'host' is male, like 'mine host' in an inn, or else it's the wafer you eat at Communion. Or the caterpillar that all the parasites lay their eggs on."

"You have a very intellectual sister, I think," said George, smiling, as if this quality in Pamela were a curiosity, or perhaps a deformity. Pamela shot him a look of pure resentment, and ever since that time she has not made any effort with him. He might as well be a bump on a log as far as she's concerned.

But Portia doesn't mind Pamela's indifference; rather, she cherishes it. Once she wanted to be more like Prue, but now it's Pamela. Pamela, considered so eccentric and odd and plain in the fifties, now seems to be the only one of them who got it right. Freedom isn't having a lot of men, not if you think you have to. Pamela does what she wants, nothing more and nothing less.

It's a good thing there's one woman in the universe who can take George or leave him alone. Portia wishes she herself could be so cool. Even after thirty-two years, she's still caught in the breathlessness, the airlessness of love. It's no different from the first night, when he'd bent to kiss her (down by the boathouse, after an evening paddle) and she'd stood there like a deer in the glare of headlights, paralyzed, while something huge and unstoppable bore down on her, waiting for the scream of brakes, the shock of collision. But it wasn't that kind of kiss: it wasn't sex George wanted out of her. He'd wanted the other thing—the wifely white cotton blouses, the bassinets. He's sad they never had children.

He was such a beautiful man then. There were a lot of beautiful men, but the others seemed blank, unwritten on, compared to him. He's the only one she's ever wanted. She can't have him, though, because nobody can. George has himself, and he won't let go.

This is what drives Prue on: she wants to get hold of him finally, open him up, wring some sort of concession out of him. He's the only person in her life she's never been able to bully or ignore or deceive or reduce. Portia can always tell when Prue's back on the attack: there are telltale signs; there are phone calls with no voice attached; there are flights of sincere, melancholy lying from George—a dead giveaway. He knows she knows; he treasures her for saying nothing; she allows herself to be treasured.

There's nothing going on now, though. Not at the moment, not up here, not at Wacousta Lodge. Prue wouldn't dare, and neither would George. He knows where she draws the line; he knows the price of her silence.

Portia looks at her watch: her nap is over. As usual, it has not been restful. She gets up, goes into the washroom, splashes her face. She applies cream lightly, massaging it in around her fallen eyes. The question at this age is what kind of dog you will shortly resemble. She will be a beagle, Prue a terrier. Pamela will be an Afghan, or something equally unearthly.

Her great-grandfather watches her in the mirror, disapproving of her as he always has, although he was dead long before she was born. "I did the best I could," she tells him. "I married a man like you. A robber king." She will never admit to him or to anyone else that this might possibly have been a mistake. (Why does her father never figure in her inner life? Because he wasn't there, not even as a picture. He was at the office. Even in the summers—especially in the summers—he was an absence.)

Outside the window, Roland has stopped chopping and is sitting on the chopping block, his arms on his knees, his big hands dangling, staring off into the trees. He is her favorite; he was the one who always came to her defense. That stopped when she married George. Faced with Prue, Roland had been effective, but George baffled him. No wonder. It's Portia's love that protects George, walls him around. Portia's stupid love.

Where is George? Portia wanders the house, looking for him. Usually at this time of day he'd be in the living room, extended on the couch, dozing; but he isn't there. She looks around the empty room. Everything is as usual: the snowshoes on the wall, the birchbark canoe she always longed to play with but couldn't because it was a souvenir, the rug made out of a bearskin, dull-haired and shedding. That bear was a friend once, it even had a name, but she's forgotten it. On the bookcase there's an empty coffee cup. That's a slip, an oversight; it shouldn't be there. She has the first stirrings of the feeling she gets when she knows George is with Prue, a numbness that begins at the base of the spine. But no, Prue is in the hammock on the screened veranda, reading a magazine. There can't be two of her.

"Where's George?" Portia asks, knowing she shouldn't.

"How the hell should I know?" says Prue. Her tone is peevish, as if she's wondering the same thing. "What's the matter—he slipped his leash? Funny, there's no bimbo secretaries up here." In the sunlight she has a disorderly look: her too-orange lipstick is threading into the tiny wrinkles around her mouth; her bangs are brazen; things are going askew.

"There's no need to be nasty," says Portia. This is what their mother used to say to Prue, over the body of some dismembered doll, some razed sandbox village, a bottle of purloined nail polish hurled against the wall; and Prue never had an answer then. But now their mother isn't here to say it.

"There *is*," says Prue with vehemence. "There is a need."

Ordinarily, Portia would just walk away, pretending she hadn't heard. Now she says, "Why?"

"Because you always had the best of everything," says Prue.

Portia is astounded. Surely she is the mute one, the shadow; hasn't she always played wallflower to Prue's frantic dancer? "What?" she says. "What did I always have?"

"You've always been too good for words," says Prue with rancor. "Why do you stay with him, anyway? Is it the money?"

"He didn't have a bean when I married him," says Portia mildly. She's wondering whether or not she hates Prue. She isn't sure what real hatred would feel like. Anyway, Prue is losing that taut, mischievous body she's done such damage with, and, now that's going, what will she have left? In the way of weapons, that is.

"When *he* married *you*, you mean," says Prue. "When Mother married you off. You just stood there and let the two of them do it, like the little suck you were."

Portia wonders if this is true. She wishes she could go back a few decades, grow up again. The first time, she missed something; she missed a stage, or some vital information other people seemed to have. This time she would make different choices. She would be less obedient; she would not ask for permission. She would not say "I do" but "I am."

"Why didn't you ever fight back?" says Prue. She sounds genuinely aggrieved.

Portia can see down the path to the lake, to the dock. There's a canvas deck chair down there with nobody in it. George's newspaper, tucked underneath, is fluttering: there's a wind coming up. George must have forgotten to put his chair away. It's unlike him.

"Just a minute," she says to Prue, as if they're going to take a short break in this conversation they've been having in different ways for fifty years now. She goes out the screen door and down the path. Where has George got to? Probably the outhouse. But his canvas chair is rippling like a sail.

She stoops to fold up the chair, and hears. There's someone

in the boathouse; there's a scuffling, a breathing. A porcupine, eating salt off the oar handles? Not in broad daylight. No, there's a voice. The water glitters, the small waves slap against the dock. It can't be Prue; Prue is up on the veranda. It sounds like her mother, like her mother opening birthday presents—that soft crescendo of surprise and almost pained wonder. Oh. Oh. *Oh*. Of course, you can't tell what age a person is, in the dark.

Portia folds the chair, props it gently against the wall of the boathouse. She goes up the path, carrying the paper. No sense in having it blow all over the lake. No sense in having the clear waves dirtied with stale news, with soggy human grief. Desire and greed and terrible disappointments, even in the financial pages. Though you had to read between the lines.

She doesn't want to go into the house. She skirts around behind the kitchen, avoiding the woodshed where she can hear the *chock, chock* of Roland piling wood, goes back along the path that leads to the small, sandy bay where they all swam as children, before they were old enough to dive in off the dock. She lies down on the ground there and goes to sleep. When she wakes up there are pine needles sticking to her cheek and she has a headache. The sun is low in the sky; the wind has fallen; there are no more waves. A dead flat calm. She takes off her clothes, not bothering even to listen for motorboats. They go so fast anyway she'd just be a blur.

She wades into the lake, slipping into the water as if between the layers of a mirror: the glass layer, the silver layer. She meets the doubles of her own legs, her own arms, going down. She floats with only her head above water. She is herself at fifteen, herself at twelve, herself at nine, at six. On the shore, attached to their familiar reflections, are the same rock, the same white stump that have always been there. The cold hush of the lake is like a long breathing-out of relief. It's safe to be this age, to know that the stump is her stump, the rock is hers, that nothing will ever change.

There's a bell, ringing faintly from the distant house. The dinner bell. It's Pamela's turn to cook. What will they have? A strange concoction. Pamela has her own ideas about food.

The bell rings again, and Portia knows that something bad is about to happen. She could avoid it; she could swim out further, let go, and sink.

She looks at the shore, at the water line, where the lake ends. It's no longer horizontal: it seems to be on a slant, as if there'd been a slippage in the bedrock; as if the trees, the granite outcrops, Wacousta Lodge, the peninsula, the whole mainland were sliding gradually down, submerging. She thinks of a boat—a huge boat, a passenger liner—tilting, descending, with the lights still on, the music still playing, the people talking on and on, still not aware of the disaster that has already overcome them. She sees herself running naked through the ballroom—an absurd, disturbing figure with dripping hair and flailing arms, screaming at them, "Don't you see? It's coming apart, everything's coming apart, you're sinking. You're finished, you're over, you're dead!"

She would be invisible, of course. No one would hear her. And nothing has happened, really, that hasn't happened before.

HACK
WEDNESDAY

Marcia has been dreaming about babies. She dreams there is a new one, hers, milky-smelling and sweet-faced and shining with light, lying in her arms, bundled in a green knitted blanket. It even has a name, something strange that she doesn't catch. She is suffused with love, and with longing for it, but then she thinks, Now I will have to take care of it. This wakes her up with a jolt.

Downstairs the news is on. Something extra has happened, she can tell by the announcer's tone of voice, by the heightened energy. A disaster of some kind; that always peps them up. She isn't sure she's ready for it, at least not so early. Not before coffee. She considers the window: a whitish light is coming through it; maybe it's snowing. In any case, it's time to get up again.

Time is going faster and faster; the days of the week whisk by like panties. The panties she's thinking about are the kind she had when she was a little girl, in pastels, with "Monday,"

"Tuesday," "Wednesday" embroidered on them. Ever since then the days of the week have had colors for her: Monday is blue, Tuesday is cream, Wednesday is lilac. You counted your way through each week by panty, fresh on each day, then dirtied and thrown into the bin. Marcia's mother used to tell her that she should always wear clean panties in case a bus ran over her, because other people might see them as her corpse was being toted off to the morgue. It wasn't Marcia's potential death that loomed uppermost in her mind, it was the state of her panties.

Marcia's mother never actually said this. But it was the kind of thing she ought to have said, because the other mothers really did say it, and it has been a useful story for Marcia. It embodies the supposed Anglo-Canadian prudery, inhibition, and obsession with public opinion, and as such has mythic force. She uses it on foreigners, or on those lately arrived.

Marcia eases herself out of bed and finds the slippers, made from dyed-pink sheepskin, which were given to her last Christmas by her twenty-year-old daughter, out of concern for her aging feet. (Her son, at a loss as usual, gave her chocolates.) She struggles into her dressing gown, which has surely become smaller than it used to be, then gropes through the panty drawer. No embroidery in here, no old-fashioned nylon, even. Romance has given way to comfort, as in much else. She is thankful to God she doesn't live in the age of corsets.

Fully dressed except for the bright pink sheepskin slippers, which she keeps on because of the coldness of the kitchen floor, Marcia makes her way down the stairs and along the hallway. Walking in the slippers, which are slightly too big and flop around, she waddles slightly. Once she was light on her feet, a waif. Now she casts a shadow.

Eric is sitting at the kitchen table having his morning rage. His once red hair, now the color of bleached-out sand, is standing straight up on his head like a bird's crest, and he's run his hands through it in exasperation. There's marmalade in it again, off his toast.

"Ass-licking suck," he says. Marcia knows that this is not directed at her: the morning paper is spread all over the table.

They canceled—Eric canceled—their subscription to this paper five months ago, in a fit of fury over its editorial policies and its failure to use recycled newsprint, although it's the paper Marcia writes her column for. But he can't resist the temptation: every so often he ducks out before Marcia is up and buys one from the corner box. The adrenalin gets him going, now that he's no longer allowed coffee.

Marcia turns down the radio, then kisses the bristly back of his neck. "What is it today?" she says. "The benefits of Free Trade?"

There's a tearing sound, like fingernails on a blackboard. Outside the glass kitchen door, the cat has dug its claws into the screen and is sliding slowly down it. This is its demand to be let in. It has never bothered to learn meowing.

"One of these days I'm going to kill that beast," says Eric. It's Marcia's belief that Eric would never do such a thing, because he is tender-hearted to a fault. Eric's view of himself is more savage.

"You poor baby!" says Marcia, scooping up the cat, which is overweight. It's on a diet, but mooches in secret from the neighbors. Marcia sympathizes.

"I just let the damn thing out. In, out, in, out. It can't make up its mind," says Eric.

"It's confused," says Marcia. The cat has wriggled free of her. She measures coffee into the little espresso machine. If she were truly loyal to Eric she would give up coffee, too, to spare him the torture of watching her drink it. But then she would be asleep all the time.

"It's picking up on the national mood," says Eric. "Yesterday it shat in the bathtub."

"At least it didn't use the rug," says Marcia. She peels an envelope of moist cat kibble. The cat rubs up against her legs.

"It would have if it had thought about it," says Eric. "Some groveling hymn to George Bush." He's back on the editorial page.

"What's he done now?" says Marcia, helping herself to Cheerios. Eric won't eat them because they're American. Ever since the Free Trade deal with the States went through he has refused to purchase anything from south of the border. They've been having a lot of root vegetables this winter: carrots, potatoes, beets. Eric says the pioneers did it, and, anyway, frozen orange juice is overrated. At lunches out, Marcia furtively eats avocados and hopes Eric won't smell them on her breath.

"This is the Panama invasion," says Eric, distinguishing it from a multitude of other invasions. "You know how many they're up to this century? Down there? Forty-two."

"That's a lot," says Marcia, in her mollifying voice.

"They don't think of it as invading," says Eric. "They think of it as agriculture. Sort of like spraying for bugs."

"Were you cold out there? Did you freeze your paws?" says Marcia, picking up the cat again, which has turned up its nose at the kibble. It gives a piglike grunt. She's missing the children. Tomorrow they will be home for the holidays, they and their laundry. The children are hers, not hers and Eric's, though even they don't seem to notice this anymore. Their real father has become a figment, somewhere in Florida. For Christmas he sends them oranges, which is about all Marcia ever hears of him.

"It's a drug thing," says Eric. "They're going to arrest Noriega, and presto, ten thousand poverty-stricken junkies will be cured."

"He hasn't behaved well," says Marcia.

"That's not the point," says Eric.

Marcia sighs. "I suppose this means you'll be picketing the American Consulate again," she says.

"Me and a few assorted loonies, and five superannuated Trots," says Eric. "Same old bunch."

"Dress up warm," says Marcia. "There's a wind-chill factor."

"I'll wear my earmuffs," says Eric: this is his one concession to subzero weather. "Trots are a nuisance."

"The Mounties think that *you're* one," says Marcia.

"Oh, yeah, I forgot—and two Mounties disguised as bag ladies. Or else those jerks from Ca-Sissies. They might as well wear clown suits, they're so obvious."

Ca-Sissies is Eric's name for csis, which really means Canadian Security Intelligence Service. Ca-Sissies taps his phone, or so Eric believes. He teases them: he'll phone up one of his pals and say words like "sabotage" and "bomb," just to activate the tapes. Eric says he's doing Ca-Sissies a favor: he's making them feel important. Marcia says it would interfere with her ever having an affair, because they might listen in and then blackmail her.

Eric is not worried. "You have good taste," he says. "There's no one in this city worth having an affair with."

Marcia knows that lack of worth has never stopped anyone in this regard. The reason she doesn't have affairs, or hasn't had any lately, is simple laziness. Too much energy is required; also, she no longer has the body for it, for the initial revelations and displays. She would not have an affair without doing something about her thighs, and buying appropriate underwear. In addition, she would not risk losing Eric. Eric can still surprise her, in many ways. She knows the general format of the schemes he's likely to come up with, but not the details. Surprise is worth a lot.

"Love is blind," says Marcia. "Well, I'm off to the temple of free speech." She's glad he's going to picket. It means he's not too old for it, after all. She kisses him again, on the top of his rumpled, sticky head. "See you for dinner. What're we having?"

Eric thinks for a moment. "Turnips," he says.

"Oh good," says Marcia. "We haven't had those for a while."

Marcia puts on her cardigan and her heavy black wool winter coat—not fur, Eric is against fur these days, although Marcia has pointed out that fur is the native way of life and is also biodegradable. She barely gets away with the sheepskin slippers: luckily, their vibrant color makes them look fake. She adds her boots, her scarf, her lined gloves, and her white wool hat. Thus padded, she takes a breath, clenches all her flesh together, and heads through the door, into the winter. The cat shoots out between her legs and immediately thinks better of it. Marcia lets it back in.

This is the coldest December in a hundred years. At night it hits thirty below; car tires are square in the morning, frostbite cases crowd the hospitals. Eric says it's the greenhouse effect. Marcia is puzzled by this: she thought the greenhouse effect was supposed to make it warmer, not colder. "Freak weather," Eric says tersely.

There's ice all over the steps; there has been for days. Marcia has suggested that the mailman may slip on it and sue them, but Eric refuses to use salt: he's in pursuit of some new product that Canadian Tire never seems to have in stock. Marcia holds on to the railing and takes tiny steps downward and wonders if she's getting osteoporosis. She could fall; she could shatter like a dropped plate, like an egg. These are the sorts of possibilities that never occur to Eric. Only large catastrophes concern him.

The sidewalk has been chiseled free of ice, or at least a sort of trail has been made in it, suitable for single file. Marcia makes her way along this, towards the subway station. When she comes out onto Bloor Street it's less treacherous underfoot, but gustier. She breaks into a slow, lumbering trot and reaches the Bathurst station wheezing.

Three of the city's homeless are staked out inside the door. All are young men; two of them are Native Indians, one isn't. The one that isn't puts the twist on Marcia for some change. He says he just wants to eat, which seems to Marcia a modest enough wish: she knows a lot of people who want a good deal more. He is pallid and stubble-faced, and he doesn't meet her eyes. To him she's just a sort of broken pay phone, the kind you can shake to make extra quarters come out.

The two Indians watch without much expression. They look fed up. They've had it with this city, they've had it with suicide as an option, they've had it with the twentieth century. Or so Marcia supposes. She doesn't blame them: the twentieth century has not been a raving success.

At the newsstand she buys a chocolate bar and a *True Woman* magazine, the first Canadian-made but bad for you, the second an outright Yankeeland betrayal. But she's entitled: she gets enough virtuous eating and reality principle in the rest of her life, so for half an hour she'll play hooky and wreck her blood sugar and read escapist trash. She squashes onto the train with the other wool-swaddled passengers and is adroit enough to get a seat, where she thumbs through the holiday fashions and the diet of the month, licking chocolate from her fingers. Then she settles into a piece entitled, with misplaced assurance, "What Men Really Think." It's all about sex, of course. Marcia has news for them: the sum total of what men really think is quite a lot bigger than that.

She changes trains, gets off at Union, slogs up the stairs to street level. There's an escalator, but looking at all those slender bodies has made her worried. Eric thinks she has nice thighs; but then Eric leads a sheltered life.

There are underground mazes downtown, underground shopping malls, underground tunnels that can get you from one building to another. You could spend the whole winter underground, without ever going outside. But Marcia feels a moral obligation to deal with winter instead of merely avoiding it. Also, she has a lot of difficulty locating herself on the "You Are Here" diagrams placed at intervals to help out those lacking in orientation skills. She prefers to be aboveground, where there are street signs.

Just recently she got thoroughly lost down there; the only good thing that happened was that she discovered a store called The Tacki Shoppe, which sold pink flamingo eggs and joke books about sex in middle age, and bottles of sugar pills labeled Screwital. It also sold small pieces of the Berlin Wall, each in its own little box, with a certificate of authenticity included. They cost $12.95. She bought a piece to put in Eric's stocking: they still keep up the habit of jokes in their stockings, from when the children were younger. She is not sure Eric will find this gift funny; more likely, he will make some remark about the trivialization of history. But the children will be interested. The truth is that Marcia secretly wants this piece of the Wall for herself. It's a souvenir for her, not of a place—she has never been to Berlin—but of a time. *This is from the Christmas the Wall came tumbling down*, she will say in later years; to her grandchildren, she hopes. Then she will try to remember what year it was.

More and more, she is squirreling away bits of time—a photo here, a letter there; she wishes she had saved more of the children's baby clothes, more of their toys. Last month, when Eric took an old shirt that dated from their first year together and cut it up for dishcloths, she saved the buttons. No doubt, after the Berlin Wall fragment has been fingered and exclaimed over on Christmas morning, it will end up in this magpie cache of hers.

The wind is worse here, funneling between the glassy high-rise office buildings. After a block of walking into it, bent over and holding her ears, Marcia takes a taxi.

The paper Marcia writes for is housed in a bland, square, glass-walled, windowless building, put up at some time in the seventies, when airlessness was all the rage. Despite its uninformative exterior, Marcia finds this building sinister, but that may be because she knows what goes on inside it.

The paper is called, somewhat grandiosely, *The World*. It is a national institution of sorts, and, like many other national institutions these days, it is falling apart. Eric says that *The World* has aided the national disintegration in other areas, such as Free Trade, so why should it be exempt itself? Marcia says that, even so, it is a shame. *The World* stood for something once, or so she likes to believe. It had integrity, or at least more integrity than it does now. You could trust it to have principles, to attempt fairness. Now the best you can say of it is that it has a fine tradition behind it, and has seen better days.

Better in some ways, worse in others. For instance, by cutting its staff and tailoring itself for the business community, it is now making more money. It has recently been placed under new management, which includes the editor, a man called Ian Emmiry. Ian Emmiry was promoted suddenly, over the heads of his elders and seniors, while the unsuspecting former editor was on vacation. This event was staged like a military coup in one of the hotter, seedier nations. It was almost like having a chauffeur promoted to general as the result of some hidden affiliation or pay-off, and has been resented as much.

The journalists who have been there a long time refer to Ian Emmiry as Ian the Terrible, but not in front of the incoming bunch: Ian the Terrible has his spies. There are fewer and fewer of the older journalists and more and more of the newer ones, hand-picked by Ian for their ability to nod. A slow transformation is going on, a slow purge. Even the comic strips at the back have been gutted: for instance, "Rex Morgan, M.D.," with its wooden-faced doctor and its impossibly cheerful and sexless nurse, is no longer to be found. Marcia misses it. It was such a soothing way to start the day, because nothing in it ever changed. It was an antidote to news.

Marcia wanders through the newsroom in search of a free computer. There are no more typewriters, no more clatter, not much of the casual hanging around, the loitering and chit-chat that Marcia links with the old sound of the news being pounded out, drilled out as if from rock. Everything is computers now: Ian the Terrible has seen to that. He is big on systems. The journalists, the new breed, are crouched in front of their comput-ers at their open-plan desks, cooking up the news; they look like pieceworkers in a garment factory.

Marcia does not have her own desk here, because she's not on staff: she's a columnist on contract. So, as Ian said (placing a well-kept hand on her shoulder, his eyes like little zinc nails), she might as well work at home. He would like her to have a computer there, where she would be safely quarantined; he would like her to beam in her columns by modem. Barring that, he would like her to drop her copy off and have it keyboarded into the system by someone else. He suspects her of seditious tendencies. But Marcia has assured him, smiling, that Eric will not allow a computer in the house—he's such a Luddite, but what can you do!—and that she would never expect anyone else to deal with her messy copy. Who could read her handwritten alterations? she has said, diffidently. No, she really has to type the column into the system herself, she tells Ian. She does not say "keyboard," and Ian notices this hold-out. Maybe he grits his teeth. It's hard to tell: he has the kind of teeth that appear to be permanently gritted.

Marcia could have a computer at home if she liked. Also, she could bring in clean copy. But she wants to come down here. She wants to see what's going on. She wants the gossip.

Marcia's column appears in the section of the paper that still calls itself "Lifestyles," although surely it will have to think up some new heading soon. "Lifestyles" was the eighties; the nineties are coming, and already steps are being taken to differentiate the decades. Summings-up clutter the papers, radio and television are droning earnestly on about what the eighties meant and what the nineties will mean. People are already talking about a seventies revival, which puzzles Marcia. What is there to revive? The seventies were the sixties until they became the eighties. There were no seventies, really. Or maybe she missed out on them, because that was when the children were small.

Her column, which is read by some men as well as by many women, is about issues. Social issues, problems that may come up: caring for the aged at home, breast-feeding in public, bulimia in the workplace. She interviews people, she writes from the particular to the general; she believes, in what she considers to be an old-fashioned, romantic way, that life is something that happens to individuals, despite the current emphasis on statistics and trends. Lately things have taken a grimmer turn in Marcia's column: there's been more about such things as malnutrition in kindergartens, wife-beating, overcrowding in prisons, child abuse. How to behave if you have a friend with AIDS. Homeless people who ask for hand-outs at the entrances to subway stations.

Ian does not like this new slant of Marcia's; he doesn't like her bad news. Businessmen don't want to read about this stuff, about people who can't work the system. Or so Ian says. She's heard this through the grapevine. He has called her style "hysterical." He thinks she's too soppy. Probably she is too soppy. Her days at *The World* are probably numbered.

As she opens a new file on the computer, Ian himself appears. He has on a new suit, a gray one. He looks laminated.

"We got some mail on that column of yours," he says. "The one about free needles for junkies."

"Oh," says Marcia. "Hate mail?"

"Most of it," says Ian. He's pleased by this. "A lot of people don't think taxpayers' money should be spent on drugs."

"It's not *drugs*," says Marcia irritably, "it's public health." Even to herself she sounds like a child talking back. In Ian's mind another little black mark has just gone on her chart. Up yours, she thinks, smiling brightly. One of these days she'll say something like that out loud, and then there will be trouble.

Marcia wonders what will happen if she gets fired. Something else may turn up for her; then again, she's getting older, and it may not. She might have to freelance again, or, worse, ghost-write. Usually it's politicians who want the stories of their lives graven in stone for the benefit of future ages, or at least these are the ones who are willing to pay. She did that sort of thing when she was younger and more desperate, before she got the column, but she isn't sure she has the stamina for it anymore. She's bitten her tongue enough for one lifetime. She isn't sure she still has the knack of lying.

Luckily, she and Eric have the mortgage on their house almost paid off, and the children are within a few years of finishing university. Eric makes some money on his own, of course. He writes engorged and thunderous books of popular history, about things like the fur trade and the War of 1812, in which he denounces almost everybody. His former colleagues, the academic historians, cross the street to avoid him, partly because they may remember the faculty meetings and conferences at which he also denounced everybody, before he resigned, but partly because they disapprove of him. He does not partake of their measured vocabularies. His books sell well, much better than theirs, and they find that annoying.

But, even with the royalties from Eric's books, there will not be enough money. Also, Eric is slowing down. It has come to him lately that these books have not changed the course of history, and he is running out of steam. Even his denunciations, even his pranks, are rooted in a growing despair. His despair is not focused on any one thing; it's general, like the increasingly bad city air. He doesn't say much about it, but Marcia knows it's there. Every day she fights against it, and breathes it in.

Sometimes he talks about moving—to some other country, somewhere with more self-respect, or somewhere warmer. Or just somewhere else. But where? And how could they afford it?

Marcia will have to bestir herself. She will have to cut corners. She will have to beg—in some way, somehow. She will have to compromise.

Marcia has almost finished typing her column into the computer when her friend Gus drifts by. He says hello to attract her attention, raises his hand in a glass-lifting motion, signals her with a finger: one o'clock. It's an invitation to lunch, and Marcia nods. This charade goes with their shared, only half-humorous pretense that the walls have ears and that it's dangerous for them to be seen too openly together.

The restaurant, their usual, is a Spanish one, well above Bloor Street and far enough away from *The World* so that they don't expect to run into anyone from there. They arrive at it separately, Marcia first; Gus makes an entrance for her with his coat collar turned up, pausing in the doorway to do a furtive skulk. "I don't think I was followed," he says.

"Ian has his methods," says Marcia. "Maybe he's a Mountie in disguise. Or CIA, I wouldn't put it past him. Or maybe he's subverted the staff here. He used to be a waiter." This is untrue, but it's part of an ongoing series of theirs: the former jobs of Ian. (Washroom attendant. Numismatist. Gerbil breeder.)

"No!" says Gus. "So that's where he got his unctuous charm! Well, that's where I got mine. I did six months of it—in Soho, no less—back when I was a beardless youth. Never be rude to a waiter, darling. They'll spit on your steak in the kitchen."

Marcia orders a sangria, and settles her widening bottom thankfully into her chair. Here she can eat imported food without feeling like a traitor. She intends to order blood oranges if she can get them. Those, and garlic soup. If Eric cross-examines her later, her conscience will be clear.

Gus is Marcia's latest buddy, and mole, at the paper. Her latest and her last: the others have all been fired or have left. Gus himself is not one of the old guard. He was imported only a few months ago to edit the Entertainment section, in one more of Ian the Terrible's attempts to shore up the credibility of his eroding paper. Even Ian knows there's something wrong, but he's failed to make the connections: he's failed to realize that even businessmen have other interests, and also standards. They've figured out that you can no longer read *The World* to find out what's going on, only to find out what's going on inside Ian's head.

He made a mistake with Gus, though. Gus has his own ideas.

Gus is tall and barrel-shaped and has dark, curly hair. He might be in his mid-thirties, or even younger. He has square, white, even teeth, the same size all the way along, like Mr. Punch. This gives him a formidable grin. He is English and Jewish, both at once. To Marcia he seems more English; still, she isn't sure whether his full name is Augustus or Gustav or something else entirely. Possibly he is also gay: it's hard for her to tell with literate Englishmen. Some days they all seem gay to her, other days they all seem not gay. Flirtation is no clue, because Englishmen of this class will flirt with anything. She's noticed this before. They will flirt with dogs if nothing else is handy. What they want is a reaction: they want their charm to have an effect, to be reflected back to them.

Gus flirts with Marcia, lightly and effortlessly, almost as if it were piano practice; or that's what Marcia thinks. She has no intention of taking him seriously and making a fool of herself. Anyway, he's too young. It's only in magazines like *True Woman* that younger men take a severe erotic interest in older women without making invidious comparisons involving body parts. Marcia prefers her dignity, or she intends to prefer it if offered the choice.

Today Gus's flirtation takes the form of an exaggerated interest in Eric, whom he has never met. He wants to know all about Eric. He's found out that Eric's nickname at the paper is Eric the Red, and asks Marcia with false innocence if this has anything to do with Vikings. Marcia finds herself explaining that it's just the way *The World* people think: they think anyone who doesn't agree with them is a communist. Eric is not a communist; instead he's a sort of Tory, but not the kind they have in England. Not even the kind they have now in Canada: Eric thinks the Canadian Tory government is made up mostly of used-car salesmen on the make. He is outraged by the Prime Minister's two hundred new suits, not because there are two hundred of them but because they were ordered in Hong Kong. He thinks the taxpayers' money should go to local tailors.

Gus quirks an eyebrow, and Marcia realizes that this conversation is becoming too complicated. As a sort of joke, she says that Gus will never be able to understand Eric unless he studies the War of 1812. That is a war Gus clearly does not remember. He gets out of it by saying that he used to think "interesting Canadian" was an oxymoron, but that Eric is obviously an exception; and Marcia sees that what he is in search of is eccentricity, and that he has made the mistake of deciding that this is where Eric fits in. She is annoyed, and smiles and orders another drink to keep from showing it. Eric is not so eccentric. About a lot of things he's even right. This doesn't always make him less maddening, but Marcia does not like having him patronized.

Now Gus turns the full force of his attention onto Marcia herself. How does she manage monogamy? he wants to know. Monogamy is something Marcia and Eric have a reputation for, as others have a reputation for heavy drinking. Monogamy, Gus implies, is a curious anthropological artifact, or else a sort of heroic feat. "How do you do it?" he asks.

No, Marcia thinks, he is not gay. "I wasn't always monogamous," she wants to say. She did not get from one marriage to another along a tidy route. She got there by bad judgments, escapades, misery; Eric himself began as a tumultuous and improbable scuffle. But if she confesses to any of this Gus will only become nosy, or—worse—skeptical, and beg her to tell all. Then, when she does, he'll assume the polite, beady-eyed expression the English get when they think you're too quaint for words, or else boring as hell.

So Marcia avoids the subject, and entertains Gus in other ways. She trots out for him the story of the panties embroidered with the days of the week, and her mother's warnings about being run over by a bus. From there she goes on to construct for him the Canada of old; she describes the dark and dingy Toronto beer parlors with their evil-smelling Men Only sections, she describes the Sunday blue laws. Marcia isn't sure why she wants to make her country out as such a dour and Gothic place. Possibly she wants war stories, like other people. Possibly she wants to appear brave or stalwart, to have endured the rigors of citizenship in such a country. She is suspicious of her own motives.

She tells on, however. She describes Mackenzie King, the longest-ruling Canadian Prime Minister, deciding state policy with the help of his dead mother, who, he was convinced, was inhabiting his pet terrier. Gus thinks she's making this up, but no, she assures him, it's entirely true. There are documents.

This brings them to the end of the garlic soup. When the deep-fried calamari arrive, Gus takes his turn. What he has to offer is gossip about *The World*. "Ian the Terrible is trying to organize us into pods," he says. He looks delighted: he has something to add to the list of local absurdities he is compiling, for when he returns to England. He doesn't know yet that he will return, but Marcia knows. Canada will never be a real place for him.

"Pods?" says Marcia.

"As in killer whales," says Gus. "Three writers to a pod, with a pod leader. He thinks it will promote team spirit."

"He might as well write the whole paper all by himself," says Marcia, trying not to sound bitter. She thinks the pod idea is extremely stupid, but at the same time she is feeling left out, because she herself has not been included in a pod. She will miss out on something, some of the fun.

"He's working on it," says Gus. "He's cut back on the Letters

to the Editor to make space for a new column, written by guess
who?"

"No," says Marcia with dismay. "Called what?"

" 'My Opinionzzzz,' " says Gus, grinning his alarming grin.
"No. I lie. 'The Snorey of My Life,' by Ian Emmiry."

"You're cruel," Marcia murmurs, trying to disguise her approval.

"Well, he deserves it. The man should be hanged for the
willful infliction of grievous terminal boredom. He wants the
Entertainment section to put on a bun-fest called The Critical
Forum. He thinks we should all come in on free overtime to
listen to some moldy old university professor rabbit on about
how to keep from going stale. This is not a fabrication."

"My God," says Marcia. "What'll you do?"

"I'm egging him on," says Gus. "I smile, and smile, and am
a villain."

"They won't stand for it," says Marcia.

"That's the general idea," says Gus, grinning from ear to
ear. He's mobile. He does not have a mortgage, or children, or
monogamy.

Marcia has downed her second drink too quickly. Now she
has lost the thread. Instead of listening, she is staring at Gus,
imagining what it would in fact be like to have an affair with
him. Too many witticisms, she thinks. Also, he would tell.

She looks at him, shining as he is with naughty pleasure, and
all of a sudden she sees what he would have been like as a small
boy. A ten-year-old. With that grin, he would have been the class
joker. Nobody would have got the better of him, not even the
bullies. He'd have known everyone's weak place, where to get
the knife in. How to protect himself.

She often thinks this way about men, especially after a drink
or two. She can just look at a face and see in past the surface, to
that other—child's—face which is still there. She has seen Eric
in this way, stocky and freckled and defiant, outraged by schoolyard lapses from honor. She has even seen Ian the Terrible, a
stolid, plodding boy who must have known others thought of
him as dull; she has seen him studying hard, hoping in vain for

a best friend, storing up his revenges. It has helped her to forgive him, somewhat.

Marcia returns to the conversation. She seems to have missed several paragraphs: now Gus has switched focus and is talking about Noriega. "He's hiding out in the jungle," he says. "He's thumbing his nose at them. They'll never get him—he'll be off to Cuba or somewhere—and then it'll just be back to the old graft and squalor, with a brand-new CIA flunky." He lifts his glass, signals for a refill. He's drinking white wine. "A year from now it'll all be fish-wrap."

Marcia thinks about Noriega, crouching in some tropical thicket or camped out in the hills. She remembers the newspaper photos of him, the round, ravaged, frozen-looking face, the face of a dogged scapegoat. When he was a child it would have been much the same. He would have had those blanked-out eyes very early; they would have been inflicted on him. This is what makes her a soppy columnist, she thinks—she does not believe that children are born evil. She is always too ready to explain.

Marcia goes to the washroom to deal with her overload of san-grias, and to redo her face. It is far later than she has thought. In the mirror she is shiny-eyed, with flushed cheeks; her hair flies out in disheveled tendrils. From the side—she can just see, rolling her eyes—she has the makings of a double chin. Her first husband used to tell her she looked like a Modigliani; now she resembles a painting from a different age. A plump bacchante of the eighteenth century. She even looks a little dangerous. She realizes with some alarm that Gus is not out of the question, because she herself is not. Not yet.

Marcia force-marches herself up the stairs of the Bathurst sta-tion. For a moment she pictures what these squeaky-clean tiled tunnels would be like overgrown with moss or festooned with giant ferns; or underwater, when the greenhouse effect really gets going. She notices she is no longer thinking in terms of *if*—only of *when*. She must watch this tendency to give up, she must get herself under control.

By now it's after five; the three homeless men are gone. Maybe they will be there tomorrow; maybe she will talk with them and write a column about life on the street or the plight of Native people in the city. If she does, it will change little, either for them or for her. They will get a panel discussion, she will get hate mail. She used to think she had some kind of power.

It's dark and cold, the wind whistles past her; in the store-fronts the Christmas decorations twinkle falsely. Mostly these are bells and tinsel; the angels and Madonnas and the babes in mangers have been downplayed as being not sufficiently univer-sal. Or maybe they just don't sell things. They don't move the goods.

Marcia hurries north, not dawdling to look. Her bladder is bursting; it doesn't function the way it did; she shouldn't have had that last cup of coffee; she will disgrace herself on the street, like a child in a soggy-bottomed snowsuit, caught out on the way home from school.

When she reaches the house she finds the front steps thoughtfully strewn with kitty litter. Eric has been at work. This becomes more apparent when she rushes to the bathroom, only to find that the toilet paper has been removed. It's been replaced with a stack of newsprint oblongs, which she finds—once she is gratefully sitting and at last able to read—to consist of this morning's *World* business section, neatly scissored.

Eric is in the kitchen, humming to himself as he mashes the turnips. He did away with paper towels some time ago. He wears a white chef's apron, on which to wipe his hands. Earlier dinners have left their tracks; already from tonight's there are several cheerful smears of orange turnip.

The radio news is on: there is more fighting in Panama, there are more dead bodies, there is more rubble, and more homeless children wandering around in it; there are more platitudes. Con-spiracy theories are blooming like roses. President Noriega is nowhere to be found, although much is being made of the voo-doo paraphernalia and the porn videos that are said to litter his former headquarters. Marcia, having ghost-written the lives of other politicians, does not find any of these details remarkable. Certainly not the porn. As for the voodoo, if that's what it would take to win, most of them would use it like a shot.

"Eric," she says. "That cut-up newspaper in the bathroom is going too far."

Eric gives her a stubborn look; stubborn, and also pleased. "If they won't recycle at one end, they'll have to be recycled at the other," he says.

"That stuff will clog the toilet," says Marcia. An appeal based on poisonous inks absorbed through the nether skin, she knows, will not move him one jot.

"The pioneers did it," says Eric. "There was always a mail-order catalogue, on farms. There was never toilet paper."

"That was different," says Marcia patiently. "They had out-houses. You just like the thought of wiping your bum on all those company presidents."

Eric looks sly; he looks caught out. "Anything new in the tar pits?" he says, changing the subject.

"Nope," Marcia says. "More of the same. Actually it's sort of like the Kremlin down there. The Kremlin in the fifties," she amends, in view of recent ideological renovations. "Ian the Terrible is making them work in pods."

"As in whales?" says Eric.

"As in peas," says Marcia. She sits down at the kitchen table, rests her elbows on it. She will not push him on the toilet-paper issue. She'll let him enjoy himself for a few days, or until the first overflow. Then she will simply change things back.

Along with the turnips they're having baked potatoes, and also meat loaf. Eric still allows meat; he doesn't even apologize for it. He says men need it for their red corpuscles; they need it more than women do. Marcia could say something about that, but does not wish to mention such blood-consuming bodily func-tions as menstruation and childbirth at the dinner table, so she refrains. She also says nothing about having lunch with Gus: she knows that Eric considers Gus—sight unseen, judged only by his feature pieces, which are mostly about Hollywood films—to be trivial and supercilious, and would think worse of her for eating deep-fried calamari with him, especially while Eric himself has been selflessly picketing the U.S. Consulate.

She will not ask Eric about this expedition, not yet. She can tell from his industriousness with the turnips that it has not gone well. Maybe nobody else showed up. There is a candle on the table, there are wineglasses. An attempt at salvaging what is left of the day.

The meat loaf smells wonderful. Marcia says so, and Eric turns off the radio and lights the candle and pours the wine, and gives her a single, beatific smile. It's a smile of acknowledgment, and also of forgiveness—forgiveness for what, Marcia could hardly say. For being as old as she is, for knowing too much. These are their mutual crimes.

Marcia smiles, too, and eats and drinks, and is happy, and outside the kitchen window the wind blows and the world shifts and crumbles and rearranges itself, and time goes on.

What happens to this day? It goes where other days have gone, and will go. Even as she sits here at the kitchen table, eating her applesauce, which is (according to the *Ontario Wintertime Cookbook*) identical to the applesauce the pioneers ate, Marcia knows that the day itself is seeping away from her, that it will go and will continue to go, and will never come back. Tomorrow the children will arrive, one from the east, one from the west, where they attend their respective universities, being educated in distance. The ice on their winter boots will melt and puddle inside the front door, leaving salt stains on the tiles, and there will be heavy footsteps on the cellar stairs as they descend to do their laundry. There will be rummagings in the refrigerator, crashes as things are dropped; there will be bustle and excitement, real and feigned. The daughter will attempt to organize Marcia's wardrobe and correct her posture, the son will be gallant and awkward and patronizing; both will avoid being hugged too closely, or too long.

The old decorations will be dragged out and the tree will be put up, not without an argument about whether or not a plastic one would be more virtuous. A star will go on top. On Christmas Eve they will all drink some of Eric's killer eggnog and peel the oranges sent by Marcia's first husband. They will play carols on the radio and open one present each, and the children will be restless because they will think they are too old for this, and Eric will take wasteful Polaroids that will never make their way into the albums they always mean to keep up to date, and Noriega will seek asylum at the Vatican Embassy in Panama City. Marcia will learn about this from the news, and from the pages of the contraband *World* that Eric will smuggle into the house and shred later for emergency kitty litter—having used up the real thing on the front steps—and the cat will reject it, choosing instead one of Marcia's invitingly soft pink sheepskin slippers.

Then Christmas Day will come. It will be a Monday, yet another Monday, pastel blue, and they will eat a turkey and some more root vegetables and a mince pie that Marcia will have finally got around to making, while Noriega sleeps unmothered in a room in a house ringed with soldiers, dreaming of how he got there or of how he will get out, or dreaming of killing he has done or would like to do, or dreaming of nothing, his round face pocked and bleak as an asteroid. The piece of the Berlin Wall that Marcia has given Eric in his stocking will get lost under the chesterfield. The cat will hide.

Marcia will get a little drunk on the eggnog, and later, after the dishes are done, she will cry silently to herself, shut into the bathroom and hugging in her festive arms the grumbling cat, which she will have dragged out from under a bed for this purpose. She will cry because the children are no longer children, or because she herself is not a child anymore, or because there are children who have never been children, or because she can't have a child anymore, ever again. Her body has gone past too quickly for her; she has not made herself ready.

It's all this talk of babies, at Christmas. It's all this hope. She gets distracted by it, and has trouble paying attention to the real news.

ABOUT THE AUTHOR

Margaret Atwood was born in Ottawa and grew up in northern Ontario, Quebec, and Toronto. She has lived in many other cities, including Boston, Vancouver, Montreal, and London, and has traveled extensively.

The author of more than twenty books, including poetry, fiction, and nonfiction, Ms. Atwood is perhaps best known for her seven novels, *The Edible Woman*, *Surfacing*, *Lady Oracle*, *Life Before Man*, *Bodily Harm*, *The Handmaid's Tale*, and *Cat's Eye*, and for her two previous collections of short fiction, *Dancing Girls* and *Bluebeard's Egg*. Her work has been published in more than twenty countries.

Margaret Atwood lives in Toronto with novelist Graeme Gibson and their daughter Jess.